Praise for *House of the Winds*

"Yun's first novel is a warm and vivid reminiscence of the relationship between a girl and her mother . . . Eloquently written in a language that is both metaphorical and poetic."
—*Library Journal*

"This is a novel full of beautiful and vivid descriptions: the shape of fruit, the play of light, the sensuous qualities of water, warmth, touch." —*Booklist*

"The story blends and weaves its colors like a needle creating an embroidery . . . It is richly written and starkly written, a charming and terrifying read." —*Korean Quarterly*

"A beautifully told story of a young girl growing up in a Korea emerging from the devastation of occupation and civil war. Intertwining memory, myths, dreams and imagination, the young narrator captures a world in which the old and the new, the innocent and the cunning, the East and the West, all clash and embrace. . . . Each chapter is like a panel of a delicately painted screen, depicting a small—and exotic, to Western eyes—world unto itself. But ultimately, Yun unfolds the screen to reveal a much larger—and unexpectedly familiar—vista."
—Rebecca Stowe

"Through the haunting and evocative prose of Mia Yun's fine novel we see, feel and know a Korea which until now, depite our participation in its modern-day civil war, has yet remained hidden from us. She beautifully melds Korea's enduring strength, achievements, and above all, its tragic past within an almost contemporary setting. She is especially concerned that in the telling of her country's history, an all-important group has been left out. She writes: 'Korea seemed . . . a bloodied Eden full of the voiceless souls of women . . . ' Mia Yun is one Korean woman who will be heard." —Barney Rossett

House of the Winds

Mia Yun

PENGUIN BOOKS

PENGUIN BOOKS
Published by the Penguin Group
Penguin Putnam Inc., 375 Hudson Street,
New York, New York 10014, U.S.A.
Penguin Books Ltd, 27 Wrights Lane, London W8 5TZ, England
Penguin Books Australia Ltd, Ringwood, Victoria, Australia
Penguin Books Canada Ltd, 10 Alcorn Avenue,
Toronto, Ontario, Canada M4V 3B2
Penguin Books (N.Z.) Ltd, 182–190 Wairau Road,
Auckland 10, New Zealand

Penguin Books Ltd, Registered Offices:
Harmondsworth, Middlesex, England

First published in the United States of America by InterLink Books,
an imprint of Interlink Publishing Group, Inc. 1998
Published in Penguin Books 2000

1 3 5 7 9 10 8 6 4 2

PUBLISHER'S NOTE
This is a work of fiction. Names, characters, places, and incidents are
either the product of the author's imagination or are used fictitiously,
and any resemblance to actual persons, living or dead, business
establishments, events, or locales is entirely coincidental.

THE LIBRARY OF CONGRESS HAS CATALOGED
THE HARDCOVER EDITION AS FOLLOWS:
Yun, Mia, 1956–
House of the winds/Mia Yun.
p.   cm. —(Emerging voices. New international fiction)
ISBN 1-56656-305-4 (hc.)
ISBN 0 14 02.9194 6 (pbk.)
I. Title.   II. Series.
1998   98–
—dc21

Printed in the United States of America
Set in Palatino

FOR MOTHERS AND DAUGHTERS

"... it is only with the heart that one can see rightly; what is essential is invisible to the eye."

Antoine de Saint-Exupéry
The Little Prince

CONTENTS

CHAPTER 1

HOUSE OF THE WINDS

*P*reserve your memories. Once you start unraveling them, there is no stopping. They become living things. Out of your control. With the careless way your mind works, you add one new detail after another, imagined or freshly remembered. You see the same simple afternoon light that long ago shone on your mother's hand and give it a ghostly soul. Here and there, you stumble onto secrets although they were not secrets at the time. You were a child. You saw but didn't understand. Your visions were narrow. You understood a pear to be an apple.

It is enough that you were once your mother's child who sucked out the last drop of milk from her breasts, already depleted by your sister and brother before you. Don't question why you were your mother's child, not any other woman's. Why your father was who and what he was. It matters little if he was a shameful swindler or a notorious womanizer. It *matters only to the ancestors who remember everything clearly even in their graves.*

When mother died, I buried my memories with her. But dreams came. There is no controlling dreams. Night after night, I plowed through dreams. Dreams became memories. Memories became dreams. They fed on my fear and grew powerful and dark, breathing and heaving inside me. I was like a frightened young girl carrying a secret life inside her body. I took a swath of long cloth and tightened it around my swollen belly so that the thing inside would die, asphyxiated. But night after night, memories burst upon the scenes in my dreams. The dreams shifted inside me each night, a full moon waning and a crescent expanding back to a full circle.

One night, they became so full and living inside me, they broke loose uncontrollably, as the water breaks in the uterus ready to give birth. I let go and memories gushed out, to my surprise, as songs and poetry, unleashing little truths hidden so far from me. The pear that I once took for an apple. I am glad mother didn't try to explain then what I saw was an apple not a pear. She said, Here, everything's in front of you and it is up to you how you see and remember. She trusted my eyes.

I was standing with mother in the middle of the sunny cabbage patch behind our little house in Seoul. I had just been bathed and dressed in a white ruffled dress, starched and ironed as stiffly as cardboard. Over the spring cabbages in white bloom, a butterfly came fluttering its wings, transparent pieces of white silk in the sunlight. Mother pointed at the white butterfly and said that it was the soul of a little girl in an afternoon nap. Whenever a child takes a nap, his or her soul flies off for an outing as a butterfly.

The next day, the white butterfly returned. Mother said the butterfly was the lost soul of a girl who never came back from her afternoon nap. While the butterfly was out fluttering over our cabbage patch, the child's mother put make-up on the child's face. When the butterfly flew back to slip into the girl's body, it couldn't recognize the child's face any longer. The butterfly saw the red lips and dark eyebrows and pink rouged cheeks and thought it had come to the wrong child. It circled around the child for a while before it flapped its wings and flew away forever. The child's mother cried and wailed in vain. Afterwards, the white butterfly forever hovered on a spring day over our cabbage patch.

This story of the butterfly stayed with me the whole spring. I became a child who was afraid of taking an afternoon nap. While all the children napped away afternoons, their souls out to flower beds, I would think of the white butterfly, the lost soul of the unfortunate child, forever lingering over the cabbage patch.

When the summer rolled in, the white cabbage flowers were long gone. So was the white butterfly. All around us, the summer burst with colors and perfume. In our flower bed bloomed marvels-of-Peru, rose mosses, yellow ox eyes, cockscombs, touch-me-nots and roses. The steaming brown soil in the flower bed choked the air and earthworms turned constantly beneath the rotting balsam roots.

It was the most beautiful hue of blue. Almost lavender. The color of morning glories that opened up every morning outside the window. We called them "trumpet flowers." All summer, their vines twisted up and up the rusting wrought iron grill toward the rain gutter.

Mother's favorite, though, was the moonflower. Moonflowers bloomed at the end of a long, heat-hushed afternoon, when dusk came softly and swiftly, steadily dripping persimmon red and azalea pink over the tiled rooftops. They were as big as Korean bronze gongs and lush as white satin. But later, when the sky turned into a huge dark blue dome, they became pale, blue-tinged porcelain. It was the loneliest flower in the world. Floating alone into the night mist.

It was always then, when moonflowers stretched their petals out widest, that the muffled sounds of dusk — children running and shouting, doors opening and closing — were replaced by the noisy chirping of crickets and long-horned grasshoppers.

Brother and I often stretched out on the veranda floor like two starfish and picked out Scorpion and Orion and the Big Dipper from the night sky, densely pricked with chipped pieces of diamond. If we fixed our eyes on the sky long enough, we felt as though it were churning. It became a huge spinning silver disk on the top of an acrobat's bamboo pole. One of the stories mother told us that summer was about a farmer who suffered from a constant fear that the sky might collapse on him. How did the story go? Just like all the stories mother told us, it began with "Once upon a time when the tigers smoked pipes, there lived..." and went from there.

Often in dreams, the stories were reincarnated. I became a part of the animated epics. I was the dweller of the huts and caves. I was the lonely roamer who crossed mountains and woods, rivers and sea and flew to heaven. I was a man, a woman, a boy, a girl, a child, a hare, a bird and a heavenly creature. It was through special luck, it seemed, that I had been returned to wake up in my own bed every morning. I would have hated mother to become the sad, wailing woman who lost her child.

It was that summer, through the blue rain of an evening, that mother rushed through the baby-blue gate of ours, its paint flaking off here and there. She must have been coming from the market. She was holding a red, meshed nylon bag through which pushed summer vegetables: cucumbers, scallions and purple eggplants. I still see her standing under the eaves, shaking off the rain from her wet hair, glistening black henna. And hear her voice that echoed through the blue rainy evening. Her voice was that of a laughing cuckoo's — if a cuckoo could laugh. I realize now how young she was. How vibrant her voice was. How softly and luminously her skin glowed. But what I saw then with my child eyes was not her youth but her white summer blouse running with red colors from the embroidered flowers on her chest. The flowers she embroidered with deep red, mango-red and azalea-pink threads. It looked as though she was bleeding from her heart and for the first time my heart felt for her. I do not know from where this sudden sadness sprouted.

◆   ◆   ◆

In my brother's first grade Korean textbook I inherited and learned to read, there were pictures of family — grandparents, parents and children and a dog named Badduki. Mother cut out the pictures for me and they were my toys. I kept them in a tin cookie can mother let me have. It was red colored with silver flowers painted on the cover. An uncle of ours had brought it from America when he returned (with airs about him, mother said) after his study. Although the cookies were long gone, it still smelled of sweet sugar and butter. Each time I opened it, I inhaled deeply. It was that sweet buttery smell of the cookie can that I would long associate with America. Not the stories I heard about American soldiers during the Korean War, or the American missionary who had converted my devout Buddhist grandmother to a Christian or my grandmother's uncle who returned with a Ph.D. from Columbia University to become a famous politician after Korea became independent. Later, another uncle returned from America bringing us children electric pencil sharpeners and pink and blue plastic hair pins. But they didn't have the same magic of the butter cookie can. I also learned that not everything American was benign and magical and beautiful. The first time mother tried her American electric iron that spring, the current transformer box on the electric pole outside the house blew up with a loud explosion, sending off red and blue fiery sparks and causing a blackout along the entire stretch of the street. We spent the night in the dimness of the candlelight. The American electric iron was so powerful, it even brought about a coup. For we were roused out of sleep in the middle of that night by the crackling noise of firing guns. In the pitch dark of the room, we crowded around mother. But the noise soon died down and we slipped back into sleep. It wasn't till morning when mother learned there had been a military coup overnight. We didn't know what was a coup d'état. All morning, the radio played spirit-lifting military music. Mother's voice was all hope and expectations. So it was a good thing — this coup. And I still had my tin cookie can that smelled buttery-sweet.

One sun-bursting afternoon that summer, while mother washed clothes by the water pump, I took the tin cookie can out to the veranda floor. As I set up a household with my paper dolls, the blue gate of ours was flung open and brother rushed in. In a buzz-cut and shorts and canvas shoes. His arms were flailing. He must have ordered me to hurry out after him. I hastily abandoned my paper dolls and the tin cookie can and followed brother out of the blue gate of our house.

I scooted after him to the end of our street, past the same wooden gates of other houses, painted in gray, green and brown, past the sun-bleached brick walls tangled with vines and stood where the street forked away in four different directions. There brother stopped in front of the yellow stucco clinic which was cut in half by a sharp, slanting shadow. He then pointed at the blood-stained wall and my heart leaped with the strangest fascination. It was there, behind the clinic, on a restless hot July night, a doctor's beautiful wife was murdered by her jilted lover. We stood there for what seemed like forever, time frozen and still, staring at the stain where the shade of a tall tree fell like a spider web.

As the summer progressed, the stains on the wall grew fainter and darker as the murder story itself. On dead summer afternoons, bored children still marched there to look at the blood stains on the wall and talk boastfully of things they didn't understand. Then the rainy season came and went and with that, the memory of the murder. The children now passed the clinic only on their way to the stream to frolic away afternoons. But till this day, the murder and the strange fascination I felt have remained with me.

I didn't understand then what it meant, a woman being murdered by a man. It was something a child should not know and should not understand. Women whispered when they talked about it, holding children at bay with their careful eyes. Years later when I began to steal stories of passion from pulpy women's magazines and pored through *Jane Eyre, Madame Bovary, Wuthering Heights* and *Of Human Bondage*, I remembered the murder again and I understood.

I resurrected the doctor's beautiful wife; I gave her long black hair and dark eyes that were enticing to men and a little sad ordinarily. And a mouth of a rose petal and a neck of an elongated stem I'd seen in Modigliani paintings. The summer dress she had on that night was a sleeveless pastel pink, made of muslin. Her white sandals on her feet had little bows on top, encircled with pink plastic rings.

I imagined the night of murder when she stood behind the yellow stucco clinic with her lover. The night must have been stifling and quiet except for the sound of a far away dog. The air thick with the smell of moss and dirt and acacia bloom. She stood with her back on the stucco wall. Her hands felt its cool rough surface. The dim light on the electric pole lamp sputtered and filtered the night mist and shone on the lover's dark summer face. She must have seen his eyes, dark as onyx and of a million storms. Reckless with passion.

First, it sounded like a dreamy murmur of the far away sea, her lover's voice. But soon, it became a rolling wave, rushing to the shore, gathering speed. A chill gripped her. There was a desperate urgency in her lover's voice demanding and cajoling and pleading with her to run away with him. No. No. She murmured and turned her eyes away. She then felt her lover's hands grip her arms. They were hot, so hot, they seemed to sear her skin. Marking her.

It was only for the briefest second that she glimpsed a flash of light in her lover's hand. A sharp blade. She turned to flee. There was a struggle. A crisscrossing of shadows on the wall. A minute or two later, she staggered around the yellow stucco clinic, leaving a trail of blood behind her. And fell on the spot where the thick brown moss erased the yellow paint from the wall.

I wonder what these women who lived on the quiet streets behind the shady gardens thought of the murder of the doctor's wife that summer. What did mother think? Did it become a symbol, a dilemma or even a lesson? Or just something to gossip about? A welcome distraction from their small lives. Or a warning? Bridle unfulfilled passions and longings. Life had to be contained.

At home behind the blue gate of ours, it was as if the murder, like the coup, had never happened. Every morning, it was still to the sun-soaked world we woke up. Mother still cooked and cleaned and washed. Early each afternoon, like clockwork, mother was out by the water pump. In the sunlight, she looked as effervescent as a spring swallow. Then the water pump burped. Soap bubbles blossomed in the steel basin over the laundry pile. And there sprang the sudden guttural noise of the pumped-out water hitting the bottom of the tin bucket.

While mother scrubbed and rinsed the clothes, brother and I took ladybugs and, squatting around a little stainless basin full of water, tried to float them over the blue sky and fluffy bits of white clouds. The ladybugs always seemed to fly away just as mother took the rung-out sheets to the clothes line. There, on the river-wide white folds of spread sheets, the ladybugs flitted. Black polka dots against orange.

In late afternoon when the sun tilted and the sunlight pulled out of the veranda, leaving it cool and dark as a cave, mother ironed starched sheets and embroidered pillow covers turning them out as stiff as new cardboard. We sprawled on the floor with books and sucked on the candy mother made with brown sugar melt and cinnamon powder. The spicy, sugary taste of cinnamon candy on our tongues, the chu-chu sound of hissing steam and mother's melodic, two-tone voice and the clean smell of flour starch... They were our afternoon songs and manna.

I believed then mother was perfectly happy behind the blue gate. She had us children. We children made her happy. Mother needed nothing else — I believed — but her children and her house with the blue gate. (I remember the gate had started to rot black where the paint had flaked off.) For us children, home was a round balloon, a big bubble filled with warm and gentle wind that warded off sharp edges from the outside world. We might dash off to the world outside where we learned to fight and compete with other children but we returned home, rushing and flinging open the gate, always assured that we would be healed and comforted in our house of the winds. That the strange dust that rained on us outside would evaporate without a trace. That mother would be always waiting for us so that we could, at any time, come and ask her for the moon and the stars.

We also knew that mother would never hesitate to put her last coins in our anxiously held-out palms when the boy in tattered shorts and flip-flops came around in the middle of a hot, quiet afternoon hollering, "Ice cake, here! Ice cake!" Wasn't it a happy sing-song, the voice of mother telling us not to run as we raced outside to catch the boy before he turned around the corner? He carried a marvelous aluminum box slung around his shoulder. We knew exactly how the boy would slide open a shiny panel of the aluminum box and how icy white fog would float out to reveal a neat stack of red bean ice cake on wooden sticks inside. That they would be hard as stone.

No, we never suspected that worry lurked behind mother's face that lit up like a brilliant sunflower when we returned licking the fast melting ice, slobbering all over our shirts. I so firmly believed that we children made her happy. I also believed the story she told me: that while we children slept she took out her magic wand hidden inside the closet and hit it a couple of times with a secret command only she knew. That was how she got hold of rice, noodles, vegetables and dresses that fed us and clothed us. Brother often wondered aloud why mother didn't simply get lots of money with the magic wand. With that money, she could buy us anything. Yes, why didn't she, I wondered too. Mother knew how much I longed for a pair of red enamel shoes that shined like... Like nothing else! Nothing else shined like red enamel shoes. Apparently, mother couldn't command the magic wand for money. According to her, the magic wand could only be used sparingly, no greed was granted. For a long time, we believed the magic wand story and begged her to let us see the magic wand. But mother could command the wand only when no one was around.

♦ ♦ ♦

Toward the end of our street where it seemed to lose its track, there rose a small hill in the shape of an up-turned rice bowl. The entire street must have looked like that before they leveled it and built those identical little "people's houses" with tiled roofs, encircling gardens, small wooden gates and gray brick walls. Up on the hill, in the middle of the pumpkin field, lived the push-faced woman people referred to as the Pumpkin Wife and who first planted an idea of father in my head.

Every day in the late afternoon, we saw her in black cotton dungarees and short, not-so-white, white *jeogori*, carrying her pumpkin-filled basket on top of her head to the marketplace. Whenever she raised her arms to steady her basket, beneath her threadbare undershirt, her two old, elongated breasts yo-yoed up and down. For the whole world to see. She was a country woman who knew no shame.

Every afternoon when we children played on the street, the Pumpkin Wife would come rattling down from her pumpkin field, hide herself behind her gate and peep out, her eyeballs rolling between the knotted beams. She must have been a vulture in her previous life. Fast she would yank me up from the street corner and march me up to her house. There she always planted me in front of her on the long and narrow veranda floor. "Sit still," she said and undid my braids which mother had carefully plaited into two symmetrical strands earlier. I knew soon she would pluck that sticky-looking green bottle sitting on the raw pine shelf. It held gooey yellow oil inside and it came from the castor-oil plants that flourished around her pumpkin field. I also knew that she would pour it on her cracked palm and rub it all over my hair, humming like a jolly bird. Where did she get that well-greased, fine-toothed bamboo comb of hers? It seemed to appear out of nowhere. She wielded it like a sword when she combed down my hair, parting it this way and that, frequently jabbing me at the sides with her elbows. Miserable and fidgety I would sit in front of the Pumpkin Wife while she braided my hair back, pulling each strand like a horse tail she was riding.

Then she would cackle for no reason as if she picked up a cue from the air and would start asking me questions in that conspiring tone of hers. "Do you know where your father is? Does he send letters? When was the last time he was home? What's the story about your father?"

I always gingerly shook my head to the questions the Pumpkin Wife released like beans from a sack. Her questions were a puzzlement. I really knew none of the sort of things the Pumpkin Wife was dying to know about my father. I had no memory of him. He was a man in fairy tale stories and palm-sized snapshots, some already fading. Without smells or sounds. "What a tight-lipped child you are!" The Pumpkin Wife would exclaim in frustration and pull my hair even harder and tighter.

When finally she tied the last braid with a rubber band, after what seemed like an eternal torture, the Pumpkin Wife always brought out a little cracked hand mirror and held it up to my nose seeking a smile from my lips. "Good? Good! You look as pretty as Choon-hyang on a spring day waiting for her lover!" she would declare. Then impatiently pulling me by the wrist, she would rattle down again to take me home.

I can still hear the Pumpkin Wife's raspy voice calling out to mother as she pushed our gate, "Are you in, Young Wife? Here's your baby girl." Mother used to look out and wince at the sight of me tottering after the Pumpkin Wife, looking like a monstrous child with so many horns sticking out and up. Mother could see how tortured I was; the Pumpkin Wife had pulled my hair away so tightly from my skull, my eyes slanted up and away like a samurai's. In the meantime, the Pumpkin Wife would inch in and sit astride the edge of the floor, laughing; a signal that she was ready to gossip away the rest of the afternoon.

"You know that woman with fat cheeks. The one who plucks her eyebrows like two crescent moons," she said one of those afternoons. "I hear her husband fools around a lot. Who would guess it from the way he looks! So thin like a nail! A rusty nail, at that. Where does he get the strength I wonder." The Pumpkin Wife chortled, flashing her gold teeth with the rest of her rotting ones.

"I wish you wouldn't talk about such things in front of a child," mother chided the Pumpkin Wife, extracting me from her hand.

"Believe me, Young Wife. A girl is never too young to learn about such things. Girls should learn what it's all about. We grew up knowing not a thing about men and got married. You should have seen me, trembling like a rat on my wedding night." She inched toward mother and slapped me on my shoulder and laughed. "Anyway, the moon-faced woman finds out each and every time he fools around because her husband is the type who talks all his secrets in his sleep. I say he needn't go to church for a confession. I hear in the Catholic Church, you have to confess your sins in a little curtained box. Do you know anything about Catholics? When you make a confession, someone from the church listens to you behind a curtain. He's said to represent God or Jesus. Who could believe such a scheme, Ha!" The Pumpkin Wife laughed raucously. "Anyway, talk about the cheeky woman's hubby fooling around! Where's your baby girl's father? I don't see any man going in or out except your little son. There must be a story behind it, am I wrong?" The Pumpkin Wife could jabber on and on. It was this kind of talk from the Pumpkin Wife that jabbed a little puncture into the bubble mother blew up so round and perfect, that made the winds leak and mother weary and me, a child with a question.

"No. No story behind it," mother answered wearily, refusing to satisfy the Pumpkin Wife's curiosity.

"Are you sure he's not running a separate household with a mistress? Someone told me your husband is very good looking. Men are all the same. You have to keep a close watch on them all the time. I myself once caught my husband with a woman. I knew something was up. He'd come home, change into a clean shirt and go out again. I followed him one day and caught him with a woman in a tea house. He was so surprised, he started shaking. I dragged him all the way home. After that, he didn't dare set his eyes on another woman," the Pumpkin Wife said boastfully. "Anyway, a young woman like you without a man around, that's tough. Let me tell you. What goes on at night between you and your hubby, that's what keeps a woman going during the day despite all the troubles. Doesn't it make sense?" The Pumpkin Wife chortled again, her eyes narrowed in secretive pleasure. Mother blushed.

"Oh, by the way," the Pumpkin Wife slapped her thigh and changed her subject belatedly, her voice an octave lower, putting her and mother on a common ground. "You tell me otherwise, but is there a single woman in Korea who hasn't got a story behind her? I tell you, Young Wife, there's nothing like mine. I lost my son during the war. For a mother to lose a child! My heart has been torn open and bled a million times." She started sniveling and wiped her eyes with the back of her hand. "*Aiigo! Aiigo*, my lousy lot!" Suddenly she was crying, her sniveling full blown into a funereal mourning. She hit the floor with the palm of her hand

and wailed as if she had just lost her son again for the hundredth time. Mother with her soft heart brushed aside her irritation and comforted the fickle and emotional Pumpkin Wife. It wasn't until she had her cries heard and tear ducts drained, the Pumpkin Wife ambled out through the gate that afternoon for the tenth and twentieth time, mumbling a *chang*, a lamenting monologue. "I wish to live only five hundred years and why all these troubles!" she sang, half laughing and half crying.

After the Pumpkin Wife was gone, the evening settled uneasily at home. Across the dinner table, we children argued. Mother saw that the Pumpkin Wife had now planted a word in my mouth: father. Her baby girl wondering out loud why she had no father or if she had a father why he was not around like other children's fathers. Mother heard her son talking to his sister derisively. "Of course we have a father. How did we come out if we had no father?" Mother smirked when I answered, "We didn't need a father to come out." I pleaded with mother to confirm it. Hadn't she told me, I asked, children were gifts from a mountain spirit to lonely mothers. Like the Virgin Mary, a mother received a child from the mountain spirit, the benevolent old man with a three-*ja* long snow-white beard. And each child came heralded by a birth dream.

Mother had told me all her birth dreams she had for us three children. For sister, her first child, mother dreamed of an owl with a jade beak perching on a white tree and for brother, of a boy tumbling down a huge golden hoop on a rolling hill of green grass. For me, her third and last child, she received a gift of three perfect soft persimmons from a tiger she met on a lonely country road.

I insisted I knew all about how children came into this world. And we were also the lucky ones, the children with lost souls — the white butterflies over our cabbage patch — who came back to life. Brother laughed and laughed, calling me a silly and a dim head. He knew how a child was made; between a father and a mother at night. He also said with great authority that all the children that were made at night were girls. A mother who wanted a boy had to go to a marketplace and buy a penis for her child. If I had wanted to be a boy, it was too late, he said, as the penis had to be bought right away. I wondered if it was true. During the Korean War when mother lived in Pusan, a southern port city, our sister used to beg mother to take her to the famous fish market called *Jagalchi Shijang*, Pebble Beach Market, and buy her a penis. She called it "a pepper." I didn't know why she wanted to go to a fish market for a penis. No wonder though that sister wanted a penis even in the midst of war. A child with a penis in Korea was spoiled and revered like a god.

We went on arguing, making up nonsense in our rattled brains and getting nowhere. Rice flew out of our babbling mouths and chopsticks sailed from our hands. When finally we pleaded with mother to take a side and clear up the matter, she told us to be quiet and finish our meal. When we grew up to be old enough to know, she said, we would know.

On the way to the market, across a small, arched stone bridge over the canal, there was a beauty parlor. That was where mother went when she wanted her straight hair to swell up like a tall, round hat. One afternoon, mother took me to the same beauty parlor and asked a plump beautician for a cut and a perm. I was scooped up and propped on a pink-colored chair in front of a long panel of mirrors. Inside the mirror, the beauty parlor sat in replica. There, in the mirror, mother sat smiling as the eager beautician chopped my hair short all over, rolled each strand up in a tiny pink roll and sprayed foul smelling liquid all over. The foul smell followed me all the way when I went home wearing a pink plastic shower cap over my head. Later, mother took me back to have the rolls removed. I was propped on a pink chair again. Beside me, three women also sat in chairs in the mirror wearing white gowns. Mother again smiled in the mirror as little tight curls popped out from the rolls. The women in chairs laughed and cheered. "Looks like she's growing fried noodles on her head!" "A grown up woman shrunk in size!" But unfazed and rather triumphant, mother happily paraded me back home. The Pumpkin Wife had no more excuses to barge in through the gate in the afternoons.

The next day, the Pumpkin Wife raced down to the street from the pumpkin field. When she saw me running around, wearing curls on my head, "like so many cotton balls," her mouth gaped. Soon she was rattling back up to her pumpkin field. Smiling, she returned with a bamboo basket full of fresh pumpkin leaves. She yanked me up nonetheless and marched me in front of her to our house.

"Are you in, Young Wife? I brought some pumpkin leaves for you. Steam them up over rice this evening. Your children will love them."

Mother swallowed her defeat and politely offered the Pumpkin Wife a glass of cooled barley tea. Yes, politely, as the Pumpkin Wife was an elder. An elder was to be respected even when she wasn't deserving.

"Don't bother, Young Wife. I'll be going soon," she said as she planted her bony behind firmly on the cool floor of ours. "What beautiful flowers you've got! When we lived under the Japanese, we kept planting flowers too. That was the only thing certain in our miserable existence. Flowers flowered every spring, no matter what. What solace the flowers were!" The Pumpkin Wife had a way of starting a talk and it always did the trick.

The Pumpkin Wife continued rattling down her pumpkin field to our house, always carrying something in her bamboo basket — some more pumpkin leaves or sunflower seeds or a sponge cucumber. The Pumpkin Wife never stopped trying to pry out the story behind the absence of my father. Mother still went on frustrating the Pumpkin Wife. They were two women in a tug of war.

Then one afternoon, the Pumpkin Wife entered with her face sallow and legs wobbling and won over mother's heart. She slouched down on the floor and watched in silence mother in the flower bed pulling out balsams infested with earthworms. Her long silence made mother wonder. The Pumpkin Wife had never before needed encouragement to talk. She always talked and talked, chortled and chortled and wailed and bellowed all by herself.

After a while, the Pumpkin Wife broke her silence and blurted out impatiently, "Young Wife, you must have a restless soul! Leave those worms alone and come and talk with me." She pulled down the towel from her head and blew her nose into it. "How time flies! It's hard to believe but it's been ten long years since I left my home in the North. And I wait and wait hoping some day to go back home. It doesn't look like the day will come soon, does it? In the meantime, my body is withering and my feet are rotting. I'm afraid I'll die without ever seeing my family and home again. It's not too much to ask, is it? I want to go back home to die. I want to be buried at the foot of the little hill that stands behind the house I used to live in. That's all. But I am stuck here with my crumbling body. Dying of homesickness! On a quiet afternoon like this, my mind keeps wandering back home. The river, the hill and the village, I remember everything as if seeing a picture in front of me.

"I know what you think, Young Wife. You think this old woman is full in the stomach and has nothing to do but complain. Maybe you're right. Sometimes it feels like I've lived a thousand years. I was born in 1901. In Kaesung, famous for the top-quality ginseng. My father was a ginseng merchant when I was growing up. He roamed the whole country selling ginseng. That was before those Japanese savages came. Under the damn Japs, life was long on hardship and short on joy. But life goes on and I married and had children. Never had enough to eat in those days, especially in the spring. Every year after harvest, the Japs came and took all the rice away, leaving just enough to survive winter. Then even winter barley would run out. We were all starving by springtime. Nothing left to eat. We all climbed the hills with a basket and went around looking for roots and tree barks. Lucky you were to go to bed at night without feeling hungry. My intestines were so shrunk those years, afterwards even when we had enough, I could never eat more than a small bowl of rice at a time.

"Thirty-six years of that. By the time the Japs lost the war, my family had been all broken up. Japs were after my in-laws and they had to flee to Manchuria. They suspected them of harboring a young man involved in the independence movement. All they did was to see to it that he safely made it across the Yalu River. Soon after, they had to wade across the same river, hunted down by the Japs. They had to sneak out of the village in the middle of the night. Like thieves. Old story. All my stories are old stories.

"After the Japanese surrendered, I thought we would finally live in peace. Who knew? What a curse! A war would break out and in the confusion of the damn war, I would lose my son and daughter. I'm a mother without children. What does that make me? A cripple. The worst kind of cripple."

When she talked about her past, the Pumpkin Wife turned from an incorrigible gossiper and an unwelcome intruder to an eloquent poet. She pulled out stories from her sad life as if fine threads from silkworms. It mattered little that she often changed her story about her son she had lost during the war. One afternoon she would insist that her son, a communist soldier, died thousands of deaths at the hands of the Southern army; then the next afternoon, her son mysteriously became a war prisoner, a cripple who lost a leg to gangrene. One moment, she said her son had gone back to North Korea when they exchanged prisoners and the next, her son was alive somewhere in the South. But it was all the same, she had lost her son to the war.

"For a while, it looked like the Americans were going to make it, too. If they had, I would have my son with me. Would be enjoying my old life with my grandson on my lap. Wouldn't be here lamenting my sad lot to you, Young Wife," she pined, stealing a look at mother.

"If you are wondering whether I'm a commie, you're wrong, Young Wife. I may have lived under commies in the North but when the Americans came and liberated us, I ran out in my bare feet to welcome them. My son fighting for commies and I, welcoming the Yankee liberators. Such a story only in our land. Didn't the Americans push all the way up to the Yalu River? I'm certain they would have made it if it hadn't been winter. The soft Americans knew no such bitter cold as in the mountains. Then the Chinese commies came through the mountains like ants, a sea of ants, flying banners, clanging gongs and banging drums. I heard how they made all sorts of loud noises to confuse the Americans. The Chinese. And there were more than a million of them! Americans killed the Chinese like flies but more kept coming and coming. Didn't they call it "The Sea of Men Strategy" or something? Just like the sea can't be drained.

"It was during the January 4th retreat when me and my useless hubby hurriedly joined thousands of people and followed the Americans to the South. We thought we would return soon. Otherwise we wouldn't have left, I swear on my ancestors' name. We were leaving behind a daughter with her little girl, not to mention a son fighting for the North Korean army. What went into my head? This old bag wanted to live so much. I left home just like I was going out to the field to return in the evening. My biggest regret is that we didn't even get to say good-bye to the children. There was no way to see my son, him fighting in the war who-knows-where. But my daughter! She was married and lived with her husband's family in another village. The commies were coming down fast. We had no time to go over and say goodbye. Later, that was what killed me. That I didn't even say goodbye. That I left my daughter to wonder and worry about us forever. But how could I have imagined that we would never see them again. The war's over now but the country is cut in half.

"It was bitter cold when we followed the Americans south. The damn January wind! It was as ferocious as the wrath of a woman scorned. It slashed your bare skin open. Then snow started and it was even worse. Behind the wet snow drift, everything just disappeared. You could barely see the road ahead. And I was wearing nothing but a padded *jeogori* and thin dungarees underneath *chima*. I was constantly shaking like aspen leaves. We must have walked hundreds of *li* like that. Shivering and slipping. You see, we had thin rubber shoes on and they were no good for the snow-frozen roads. Still, it was worse for the people with little children. Some abandoned them on the road. It was terrible to see those children crying for their mothers in the cold but there was nothing I could do but go on. Tell me what parents would abandon their own child like that unless they themselves were dying? Some abandoned one child to save the rest. They abandoned a girl to save a boy. The war made people do unheard-of things. Mind you, Young Wife, no line between good people and bad people in such circumstances.

"One day, too hungry and cold and tired to continue, we wandered off the road. It was getting dark and the temperature was dipping fast. Lucky we were because not too long after, we came to an abandoned farm house. In the kitchen, we found some frozen rice. Right away, my hubby gathered some kindling wood and built a fire. I cooked all the rice in the big steel pot. It was enough to feed ten young men with healthy appetites. We crouched in the cold room and stuffed ourselves with rice and *kimchi* we had found inside a jar buried in the back of the house. It was the most delicious meal I had ever had. The simple hot rice and *kimchi*. They just melted in my mouth. We ate and ate until we were stuffed to the nose. Soon, we couldn't keep our eyes open. I couldn't tell how long we had been sleeping. A noise woke me up. It seemed to come from the kitchen. Scared out of my wits, I shook my hubby. He was so dead to the world, he wouldn't have known it had somebody picked him up and carried him away. I shook him again and finally he peeled his eyes open. He was mad that I woke him up. He rolled around wanting to go back to sleep. Just then, a jangling noise broke out in the kitchen. That got his attention. He sprang up. Together, we crawled to the door that connected the kitchen. With my wet finger, I rubbed out a hole on the rice paper and peeped in. It was pitch dark but after a while, I could make out a hunched figure. I told my hubby to hurry and light the wick. Holding the light, we pushed open the door. Guess who we found! A young man in a tattered North Korean army uniform. He was hunched over on the mud floor holding a fist full of half-frozen rice. We had startled him. He turned his head and looked up at us. His eyes were shiny with fear but soon all the lights went out of his eyes and they were like two black pieces of cold coal. He was at the end of his rope. He didn't bother to run! He stayed crouched on the floor. His whole body was trembling and shaking.

"The moment I saw him, it was our son I thought of. How he could easily have been our own son. Dying of cold and hunger. I assured him and invited him into the room. He seemed so relieved. He stood up and that's when we noticed his feet. His shoes were falling apart and they were held together by filthy rags. I tell you they were no winter shoes. I bet he had been wearing the same shoes since the war started in the summer. No wonder he had such bad frostbite. His feet were swollen humongous and he could barely walk without dragging his feet. I made him sit in the warmest spot in the room and filled a bowl high with rice and gave it to him with a bowl of *kimchi*. How he devoured the rice. Didn't even bother to chew it. Just swallowed it down the throat. Faster than a crab hides its eyes! And then he had another bowl and yet another. I had never seen anyone put away so much rice so quick. Do you know what happened? Not long after, he developed a terrible stomach cramp. His tummy started to bulge. And before we knew what was happening, he was holding his stomach and rolling on the floor in pain! His face was puffy and red. His eyeballs were popping out of their sockets. He was wheezing. He was like a cart wheel stuck in mud, struggling to pull out. Then he just dropped dead. Right in front of our eyes! Can you imagine the shock! Apparently, this happened a lot during the war. Starving people would gorge on food and drop dead. We waited till the first light of the dawn and started digging the ground to bury him. But the ground was frozen hard as a rock. So what did we do? We just left him dead in the house and continued on our way. You could say our good deed killed a man.

"We managed to reach the south alive but I ended up losing several toes from frostbite. Here, let me show you!" The Pumpkin Wife took off her cotton sock and pushed her scarred foot out to the middle of the floor. Mother took a quick glance and turned her eyes away. The Pumpkin Wife giggled happily for the revulsion she caused and the sympathy she had finally won.

The stories the Pumpkin Wife told mesmerized me. I would sit on mother's lap and soak them up deliciously. The sadder, the better. Sad stories were often the most beautiful stories. In Korean folk tales, beautiful birds cried instead of singing. Green frogs cried at river bends when it rained worrying about mother frogs' graves being washed away. Korean musical instruments, *gayagums* and *geomungos*, all strutted out the most beautiful music in haunting, sad melodies. The bell that reached farthest with the most subtle reverberation in Korea, echoed a child's cry for his mother. Everything cried and cried beautifully in Korea. People saw the best in sad things and sadness spurred them on to the future. Sadness was an inspiration.

The summer gradually thinned into autumn as the Pumpkin Wife babbled and laughed and choked on her tears, cleansing the rinds of her sadness, her stories always endless and abundant, every moment of her past life catastrophic.

CHAPTER 2

HOUSE OF THE WOMEN

*M*other took dreams seriously. When another mundane day folded into a weary night, she closed her eyes and let herself gladly be carried away into the land of dreams. There, she shed her proper behavior and became as free as a soaring lark. In her Technicolor dreams, possibilities were limitless.

Once she told us how in one of her dreams she had set fire to the house of her childhood and watched the searing flames swallow up the beautiful old wooden house. However shameful it was, it was nonetheless a sign of good luck. The next day, an unexpected guest came bringing her a gift: light blue silk with white polka-dots for her hanbok. This made her a firm believer in dreams.

Besides being an arsonist, she also turned into a thief, a murderess, an adulteress and a carnivorous animal. In one memorable dream, she turned *into an eagle. All night she flew high over deep glacial ravines and meandering rivers. She was the sole purveyor of that breathtaking view. And the wonderful sensation of flying! She then understood what "free as an eagle" exactly meant. In dreams, her shame was easily overtaken by her amazement and gleefulness. She loved that leap of fate or whatever one calls it.*

Each morning when she woke up, it was the dreams she first remembered. She interpreted those dreams of hers. Dreams of fire, pigs, clear running water and stepping into feces were exceptionally good omens. A simple and sure bet for a winning lottery ticket.

When mother was growing up, she was surrounded by women who also took dreams seriously and tinkered with their luck. Her mother, a devout Presbyterian, was particularly superstitious about them. Mother had learned from her how to interpret her own dreams. But when her dreams turned bizarre, leaving her at a loss, she made her imagination fly and managed to make some sense out of them one way or another. Mother had never heard of Jung or Freud. But I think they would have learned something from her dream analysis.

That summer when the Pumpkin Wife constantly ambled in and out of our blue gate house, mother kept dreaming of losing her children. She dreamed of us straying far by ourselves in the city streets and mazes of winding alleys never to return home. She dreamed of her children with street ghosts in their feet venturing out to unknown corners and falling prey to a stranger clamoring for the sacrifice of children or to lepers craving children's organs as a cure for their disease. These scenarios that she herself had concocted to warn us children had come back to haunt her in her own dreams.

Mother used to wake up with these repeating dreams and beg us children not to go far away each time we rushed to play outside. It was a summer of anxiety for her. She would remind us of the story of a lazy man who left his home to avoid his nagging wife and was turned into a cow to plow the fields for the rest of his life. An example of what could happen to someone who left home. Mother often rushed outside the gate and made sure that we children were safe. The whole summer, we were not allowed to stray from the single familiar street where our house stood shouldering the walls of neighbors. She was assured by the noise of children shrieking and laughing as they played hopscotch and jack stones, carelessly erasing the neat rib traces of a Zen temple ground left by bush-clover brooms each morning.

One August night, mother's dream turned particularly bizarre. She dreamed of a man wearing a woman's mask. The mask had a hideous face of an old woman with dark moles all over. As she watched, the man with the mask jerked this way and that way, whirling arms as in a Korean mask dance. She saw how each time he jerked, those movable jaws on the mask cracked, changing expressions on the mask. One moment, the face was crying with the saddest contortions of facial muscles and the next, it was laughing hilariously. Mother was appalled by that ugly face and tried to turn away. But as often happened in dreams, she couldn't move. She had no choice but to watch as the man in the mask continued to dance and narrate the story of a woman in joy, grief, suffering and torture.

When it was over, the man took off the mask and secured it on mother's face despite her protests. Mother felt taken over by that ugly woman's soul in the mask right away. Her jaws moved uncontrollably and her masked face turned from an expression of exultation to that of horror. Encouraged by mother's performance, the man then placed three threads into her hands. She looked at them quizzically when at the end of the threads her three children appeared connected like puppets. Her children looked helplessly at her, their limbs stiffly hanging down. She carefully pulled the threads and immediately her children came alive, moving at her command. Mother thought it was so funny. She laughed and her children laughed. How marvelous, mother thought! By pulling the threads in different ways, she made her children dance and play. They looked like

Kkoktukkaksi *dolls in a traditional marionette play.*

Then suddenly out of nowhere, the Pumpkin Wife appeared cackling as usual, her elongated breasts bouncing up and down under her short jeogori. Mother immediately became suspicious of the Pumpkin Wife as she had that mischievous twinkle in her eyes. Mother knew the Pumpkin Wife was up to no good. She was about to pull the threads toward her to protect her children when the Pumpkin Wife pulled out a dagger from underneath her dungarees and severed the threads. Her children instantly crumbled to the ground. Deflated dolls. Mother screamed in horror. Her children were dead. The Pumpkin Wife roared with laughter and kneeled to the ground and blew her rotten breath into the children's nostrils. One by one, mother's children came back to life. But they were no longer under her control as the threads connecting them to her had been snapped. Her children ran away in three different directions, like wild ponies in a Western movie. She pleaded with her children not to run away from her but they didn't listen. Mother said, "Please, my children, you haven't learned the story of your mother. Let me tell you the story of your mother!" She thought surely if her children had known her history, they would remain with her. But they disappeared into the dark background. Mother cried in her despair until she woke herself up with her own sobbing.

It was a beautiful morning, hot with the gold-dust of sunlight. We children squatted inside bath jars by the water pump, splashing the water after the paper boats to keep them in sail. Mother was distracted. It was the vivid and morbid dream of the night before. The Pumpkin Wife severing the threads in her hand. She mindlessly lathered soap on a towel and carelessly scrubbed our sunwarmed backs. When mother's hand reached the ticklish spot under the arm, brother giggled, squirmed and whimpered, making the soap bubbles fly. Up and away they went, floating in cottony clumps and blooming rainbow colors in the sunlight.

Suddenly, mother was in a hurry. She fished out our paper boats and rushed us through the bath. She wrapped us in towels and chased us back inside, goose-bumped and blue-lipped. She had decided the dream of the Pumpkin Wife was a warning to be heeded. For a dream is like a fish bone lodged in the throat. Something that just can't be ignored.

We stepped into the room where across the oil-papered floor, a wide swath of sunlight pooled like a river of yellow oil. Brother turned, lifted his water-wrinkled finger and pointed to the top of the paulownia tree chest. There, mother had laid out her stiff muslin *hanbok* and clean outfits of ours. In a neat, folded stack. All starched and ironed crisp.

The blue gate closed with a soft hiccup behind us and we walked out to the street. We proudly passed our envious friends staring at us from behind an electric pole where we often played hide and seek, and crossed the street with mother. In the distance, the air was faded orange and the sky over the canal was one seamless blue sheet, a breeze-swelled silk scarf, a twelve-sectioned river-blue *chima* unfurling from the clothesline. Mother's crisp muslin *hanbok* swished and swished like the rubbed wings of dragon flies. Breezes passed by, tickling our noses with the smell of mother's Coty-powdered skin and of the moth balls inside her paulownia tree chest.

We hopped and skipped up the lazily climbing sidewalk parallel to the canal. Down the sloping bank, the canal lay in shallow scummy green water after the rainy season. Pebble-bedded and weeded. Often accompanying mother to and from the market place, we crossed the canal, over a small, arched stone bridge. But as if she had finally captured a perfect moment, mother told us how she had crawled across the very same canal when the Korean War broke out.

She was carrying our sister, mother's only child then, strapped on her back. As she slid down the bank, bombs exploded around her in deafening booms, shaking the ground and leaving huge craters in it. Her feet slipped and she tumbled to the bottom, spattered by a rain of mud. Mother heard her baby daughter shriek but there was no time to stop and check. She immediately went down on her hands and knees and started crawling across the dry canal. It was embedded with broken pebbles and infested with sharp-bladed weeds. They cut, scraped and jabbed her knees and arms. The air grew thick with the smell of smoke and powder. And bullets sailed by and over her, making high-pitched "ping," "ping," "ping" sounds. Her heart pounded. Beads of sweat rolled down and stung her eyes. Her ears rang. She could hardly breathe or see. Too scared to look up or to stop, she closed her eyes tight and clenched her jaws and just kept crawling toward the other side of the canal.

Mother didn't know how she had made it. It had felt like forever, like a passage of three autumns, to crawl across the pebble-embedded canal. When mother finally crawled back up the bank, she could barely walk. Her legs wobbled like a drunken man's. And it was only then, when she had finally crawled up the bank, mother remembered her baby daughter, strapped on her back. She wasn't moving at all. She lay there on her back as still as a sack of stones and as quiet as a mouse. Mother felt her heart plunge to the pit of her stomach. Fearing the worst, mother hastily pulled her child around.

"She wasn't breathing!" mother said. Her face was the color of an eggplant. In panic, she shook and shook her child. Her child was dead with a bullet lodged in her head. Then suddenly, the compact little child stirred in her arms. Her little mouth opened and sucked in the air, drawing a deep breath. Then she burst into the loudest cry a child had ever made.

"Your sister could have been easily killed by one of those flying bullets," mother declared breathlessly, her voice rising in pitch. "After surviving that traumatic experience and the war, your sister became such a headstrong child."

"It was Sunday morning, on June 25th when the war broke out. Your father didn't know it when he left home that morning. He didn't come home that night, the night after and the night after that. In the meantime, the communists were pushing closer and closer to Seoul. So after a sleepless night, I decided to go to your grand-mother's house. It took me hours to walk to her house that day. When I went out that morning, some of the buildings were already flying red communist flags and outside hospitals I passed, there were hundreds of men lying around, maimed and bleeding. That same day, the communists from the north took Seoul.

"We spent a night at grandmother's house and the next day headed south. Somewhere along the way down to Pusan, your sister and I got separated from your grandmother. There were millions of refugees on the road. There was little hope to find your grandmother. So for the rest of the way, it was just me with your sister. She was only one year old and couldn't walk. So I had to carry her on my back all the way. When she got hungry and tired, she cried and cried!

"Now, it seems so long ago when all that happened. I never imagined one day I would be walking the same street with you children," mother said. She seemed to say, here was your mother who had a history in the very city you children live in, in the city that had known many kings and queens, a foreigner's long occupation and a war before you came along.

Seized by a sudden apprehension, mother's steps hastened. The memory of the war always brought back the same anxiety to her. The fear of another war and the fear of losing her children. Mother squeezed our hands tighter and hurried toward the big boulevard where cars were swirling in the yellow dusty film of the sun. We asked mother expectantly where we were going.

"To your grandmother's," mother replied carelessly. In our disappointment, we instantly pictured grandmother's mean, many-folded face of a lioness and heard her, a matriarch of her faithless children and grandchildren, saying in her savoring diction, "Ask, and it shall be given you; seek, and you shall find; knock, and it shall be opened unto you." And felt like running away. Never ask grandmother what she meant by that. Ask who? Seek where? Knock on which door? Grandmother would look back at you disdainfully for asking such silly questions. Instead of answering you, she would immediately quote you Chapter Eleven, Hebrews, mystifying you further: "Now faith is the substance of things hoped for, the evidence of things not seen." Grandmother, in her tireless campaign for God and His only begotten son Jesus, always bombarded us with a rosary of oblique words, puzzling promises and whimpering nagging. She could turn her back in a snapping second on the teachings of love and forgiveness and become vindictive and bitter.

We walked up the sidewalk of the boulevard, an arched spine of a dancer, and quickly erased grandmother's voice. How effortlessly we became a part of the constantly moving throng! Of men and women coming and going with their light strolling steps as if toward nowhere. Of men in their fedora hats and wide trousers and women in pastel blue and pink and white dresses. And up on the Mia-ri hill ahead of us, we could see streams of parasols creeping up, bobbing up and down above women's heads, like a beautiful floating mosaic. The sun was hot. The air was thick and sulfurous. Noises boomed.

All of a sudden, mother froze and pointed up at the huge

billboard outside a movie theater. There, her favorite actress was crying in the arms of her favorite actor. Mother had already seen the movie several times at a discount rate during the slow afternoon hours when she could have the dark and dank theater almost all to herself. She had told us the story to the last detail: a sad love story of a man and a woman separated during the Korean War. Mother could so vividly describe the tearful scene, the fateful moment when the old lovers meet again after the war, in a pine grove, each married to someone else. Without much difficulty mother saw herself in the place of the beautiful and tragic heroine. How gladly mother would have switched her place with the heroine's at the snap of a finger! That vicarious pleasure of living the life of passion, tragedy and love was so great, mother got goose bumps all over her when she talked about it.

Flanking mother, we stood under the hot sun for a long second, looking up at the billboard, at the two lovers larger than life. How dizzily heroic they seemed, their final embrace for everybody to see. We might not have understood the full scope of adult love, but we instantly understood the tragedy of it. We children had been born akin to the tragedy that had flowed for thousands of years in the veins of the Korean soul. Each second as we stood breathing in the sulphurous air poisoned by bus fumes, the lovers' tragedy grew more tantalizing. The embracing arms of the actor tighter, the tear drops of the actress bigger. Reluctantly we moved on, incomprehensibly affected by the story of tragic love.

At the foot of the hill, a streetcar idled in the sun like a toy made of wood and chrome. Brother kicked his feet and raced down the hill ahead of us. The seams at the heels of his well-worn black cloth shoes were ready to burst; a little sign of hard times. Mother's voice telling him not to run quickly dissolved in the noise of the traffic. Brother stopped and turned and grinned. Trapped in the sun's blinding spot, his crew cut hair was peach fuzz at the ends. Mother smiled and clucked her tongue.

The streetcar finally jerked forward clinking and clanking, squawking and jangling, sending up that infectious sound of ding-donging bells into the fuzzy summer air and negotiating its way as slow as an earthworm. We climbed up the hard wooden seat, pressed our noses to the window and watched the city lurch by outside, sliding and slipping backward. Soon, we left the city of tragic love behind and entered the city of curious bustle and purpose. Stilled scenes of life flitted by, fleeting frame by frame. Tiled buildings crowded with dangling signs, hatted vendors pulling carts, lanes that narrowed away, dark-skinned women tending piles of bleeding strawberries and blushing peaches, a long marathon of stone walls of a palace, its ancient roof lines, swirling outward and soaring upward and old men clad in traditional white with top-knots and long beards fanning in the shade of tall poplar trees. The city with a million faces. Constantly flowing. It was not a giant hand that swallowed up children as mother had often warned us. Where lepers with mangled hands lurked in corners to claim children's organs. It was a palette of many colors. Of shifting forms and still silhouettes, of shade and light and of old and new. Wonderful and chaotic all at once. And most of all, it was neutral to God! Even indifferent to God! Nobody pushing God's messages. Telling you to ask, seek, and knock. And if we were lucky, I thought, we might even forget our way to grandmother's and end up at a zoo with chimpanzees or at a children's park with water slides.

Brother asked me if I knew it was *kwang-bok-jul*, Independence Day. No. Of course not. I was a dum-dum. What did I think it was for? All those national flags flying on top of all the big buildings and at the doorways of shops and houses? They were celebrating the day light had returned to Korea. After thirty-six years of darkness under the Japanese. I could just imagine how that day the sky had opened up, parting like the Red Sea over Korea and light had poured down. A miracle. Just like that of Jesus standing freely among clouds bursting with silvery light on grandmother's wall.

◆　　◆　　◆

We laboriously climbed up the afternoon street as quiet as a grave. There, the road slanted up continuously toward Nam San, a dark green peak swelling in the middle of the city. The houses of red brick and granite crept along the hilly road with castle-like gradation. And over the high and long walls tumbled out vines of trees and red roses, dizzying our oxygen-deprived brains.

When we reached the spot where we could just see the bottom of the winding steps leading to grandmother's house, mother stopped us and straightened our clothes and patted down our hair as if preparing us for an interview. Then she herself took a deep breath.

Soon, the two-leafed wooden gate of grandmother's house came into view. It was closed tight and it made us hopeful grandmother wasn't home. But the sun-bleached side door opened and sister came out. She must have known we were coming and been waiting all morning. She hopped down the tumbling steps, her shiny black hair flying and her skirt ruffling up in the wind. Framed by the sky. Fourteen and no longer a child, she had the proud look of a peacock. And over the summer she had been away at grandmother's, her lotus-bud breasts had swollen to the good size of ripe peaches. They jutted out so proudly under her blouse and as she hopped down, they bounced like new, taut rubber balls.

As young as I was, I knew I would always remember the brief

moment of slowed-down motions: sister floating down the steps, looking so haughty and so beautiful in her pure molecule of youth. From then on, like an exotic tropical bird, sister would always float ahead beyond my grasp. Until the spring she peaked gorgeously and briefly like a cactus bloom that lasts for just a night. The spring when pollinated winds brought a feverish love to her.

It seemed to make perfect sense; why she should be mother's defiant child, a child, mother often said, she would never wish even on an enemy. (My very first memory of her, when she seemed to burst into a sudden existence, was her crying. She was a feverish, throbbing and unhappy thing.) For years to come, sister would always stand at the opposite end of an axis from mother and grab love and attention from the very people who gave mother heartache and misery. This brilliant and defiant child always tormented and puzzled mother. This child, the holder of father's smooth tongue and the keeper of grandmother's stubborn streak, demanded lasting loyalty and unfaltering love from mother. With audacity.

But for that miraculous moment, we melted into a family bound by an inexplicable pulling of hearts and walked up the steps crowding around mother: a tiger and her cubs. Momentarily oblivious of grandmother presiding like a lioness behind the gate.

Mother pushed open the gate and right away I saw her, grandmother limping out, in her exaggerated stilt, through the garden of old trees, red and yellow cannas and around a pond with goldfish and water lilies. How I felt like turning around and running away! I buried my face in the folds of mother's *chima*, the see-through summer muslin.

"*Aiigo, aiigo*, my legs! I'm getting old!" grandmother complained. "That long hair in this heat! Why don't you have it cut short?" grandmother whimpered as mother helped her back to the veranda floor. The old lady, grandmother's cook, cleaner and companion, tottered out from the kitchen and happily tottered back with the fruit basket mother handed to her.

"Come here!" grandmother suddenly commanded me, hiding behind the fold of mother's skirt. Her eyes seemed to shoot out sparks and I shrunk. "Why are you so afraid of your own grandmother? This old woman never devoured no child," she said while her hands wrapped around brother's shoulders.

"Why not? You always say mean things to her," mother said, pulling me closer to her.

"What mean things?" grandmother said pleading ignorance. She leaked a little smile between her thin colorless strip of lips.

"You tell her how we found her under the Chonggye-chon bridge abandoned among beggars and lepers on a snowy day."

"I wouldn't had she chosen a more fortunate time to come out to this world! A girl born in the early morning hour in the Year of the Monkey brings only bad luck," grandmother blurted out unapologetically. "Why do you think after she was born, your husband's business failed like a foiled coup and brought a mob of creditors to your doorstep? Believe me! Had she been born a boy, it would have been a different story."

"Please, not that old story again," mother said unhappily, letting go of me. Grandmother grunted and parted the bamboo shade. She climbed on to the floor. She looked like a big white bundle stuffed with well-kneaded flour dough. The old lady returned with fruit carved and arranged like flowers on a large blue plate. As we children slurped and chewed the fruit, mother and grandmother sat quietly, staring out at the summer garden bright with cannas. Silently, a huge wall drew between them and shut like a steel door. The air shuddered. We children knew. How, apart, the two women might pine for each other with compassion and pity but together, they collided loudly, chipping at each other's patience. Then they would part, their hearts broken, blaming their lashing tongues. Once again, they would swear to do it differently next time, to bear each other's way. But it never worked.

"Please have some fruit, *uhmoni*," mother pleaded with grandmother, fanning her again.

"I've had enough fruit. I've got this rheumatism and nothing tastes good anymore," grandmother said, an infamous hypochondriac and a voracious eater. "All summer, your dead father appears in my dreams. And the morning after I see him, my rheumatism flares up. He must be jealous. Jealous that I am still alive. So he tries to coax me away. To the other world. To keep him company, maybe. But how could he be jealous! I didn't have it easy. He left me a widow at the bright-green age of twenty-nine to raise four children all by myself. If it wasn't for my faith in the Lord, I'd be long gone.

"People tell me how lucky I am to have such successful sons, not one or two but three! But they don't know what they're talking about. It's no luck. It's the fruit of my blood and sweat. Not one person knows what I went through. Not even my own children. There wasn't a thing I hesitated to do. I'd sell rice cakes, going from door to door. By the end of a day, my feet would be covered with raw blisters. But hoping to sell one more rice cake, dragging my sore feet, I would make another round and then another. Until it got to be late in the night. After a year of that, I was willing to do anything if I didn't have to be on my feet all day. So I tried sewing. But sewing is no game, either. Try to sit hunched over a sewing machine all day and into the wee hours of night. Day after day. So tired, your eyes would begin to see double. I don't remember how many times, I sewed my own fingers. Before I knew it, the needle would go right through my thumb. All the way through! Go in from the top and come out the bottom. For years, I hadn't a day when one of my fingers wasn't infected or swollen or bleeding.

"Still, the worst was the winter when I sold *biji*, bean curd dregs. They called it poor men's meat. Some tofu factories would let you have it free-of-charge. But you had to fight for it. Tofu factories always worked overnight so they could get the fresh tofu out early in the morning to shops and markets and that was when they gave out the *biji*, too. So I would get up before dawn and walk half an hour to a tofu factory. It would be still pitch dark and freezing cold. Cold enough for your nose to freeze and fall off your face. If I got there too late, all the *biji* would be gone. So I would go there early and wait outside in line, shivering like a beggar! Pacing around to keep warm. I couldn't begin to tell you the humiliation and shame. It scalded me to the bone but I swallowed all that down. When your father was alive, I lived a life of luxury. If there was anyone more ill-prepared for that kind of hardship, it was me! But I never once felt sorry for myself. I had faith! It gave me all the strength I needed. I was never alone. Jesus was my constant companion. And when your brothers went to America, I prayed to God to keep them safe. Every night. No matter how sapped I was. I prayed, kneeling on the ice cold floor in the middle of deep winter. I didn't even feel the cold because the holy spirit would come down on me and keep me warm. So God answered my prayers and returned all of them to me safely. Does any one of them appreciate it? Of course not! If I wrote down the story of my life, it would easily fill a thousand pages and more!"

"So after all the sacrifices you made, why do you live alone?" mother retorted. "Why aren't you living with one of your successful sons? Isn't it time for them to take care of you?"

"I would be just a burden to them. They all went out, met and married modern, educated girls. It isn't like the old days. These days, no girl wants to be bothered by a mother-in-law. That's that. Anyway, who said that's what I was talking about? I was talking about your father being jealous when I lived such a harsh life after he drank himself to death to spite me."

"It isn't true," mother said forcefully, putting a piece of watermelon back down to the plate. "I wish you would stop saying that in front of my children. He didn't drink himself to death. He was no drunkard."

"That's the truth. I don't lie. How could I? God is watching from above. Do you really believe that it was his angry ancestors that took your father away?" Grandmother picked up the fan mother had put down and began fanning herself. She was determined to resurrect her dead memories.

"The twists of fate! Who knew he would die so young like that? Certainly I didn't. I was just seventeen years old when I was married to your father. It was an arranged marriage like all marriages those days and I had no say in that matter. But I couldn't have asked for more. Your father's family was wealthy and had a good name. They lived in a big house with more than a dozen servants and the whole village farmed their land. You'd think I was all set for life!" Grandmother snorted and laughed. "It was funny. How your father was tall and good-looking. Delicately built. Like a woman. And I was just the opposite! I was short and robust. Healthy as a cow, too, bursting with energy. I could never sit still. If I did, I felt itchy. I should have been born a man. Would have made a name for myself.

"So, I wasn't a typical shy bride and had to feign it for a while. They were the happiest days I ever knew even though my senile mother-in-law mistook me as the scheming concubine of her dead husband and ordered me around all the time. She was always sending a servant to fetch me to her. Just to give me a hard time.

But it didn't bother me too much. Your father was very attentive. And when I got pregnant, he made sure I had everything my fickle tongue desired. A pregnant woman's tongue craved the strangest food: summer watermelon in winter, winter pear in summer and cow intestines she never dared eat before.

"I wanted a son so badly. Every morning, I would get up before dawn and bathe and dress. Then I would take a bowl of the purest water to the backyard and offer it to the mountain spirit. I would pray to him to be blessed with a son. I also hoarded away the best shaped red peppers to hang out at the gate to announce the arrival of a son. I was no fool. A son always boosted a woman's status at home.

"But one snowy morning, my luck ran amok. I was returning from the usual prayer to the mountain spirit. I was very heavy by then, expecting any day. I must have looked like a turtle on its back. As I was coming back to the house, I heard a bird chirp loudly. I looked up. The bird was perched on a snow-covered tree branch. A crow was a bad omen. A magpie was a good omen. But because of the snow, it was hard to tell if the croaking bird had the white belly of a magpie. Of course, I later knew it had been a crow because what I gave birth to was a girl!" Grandmother looked at me and said, "That girl was your mother."

"But you were born a girl, too, grandmother," I said boldly. Grandmother looked surprised at what I said and pretended she hadn't heard me.

"I am sorry to tell you this," grandmother furtively said to mother. "But I was so disappointed. I refused to look when the midwife told me it was a girl. But your father! He couldn't be happier. Once he laid his eyes on you, he couldn't take them off. His mouth never closed. My mother-in-law was happy too because the scheming concubine had a girl-child instead of a boy. She sent in all kinds of delicacies for me. Six or seven months later, I was pregnant again. I was so sure this time I was carrying a boy. It felt different from the first time. So right away, I stopped feeding you my breast milk. Every morning, I took a fresh cotton swath and tightened it around my swollen breast. By noon, it would be drenched with leaked milk. I let all go wasted. It was wrong of me. I can see that now. But that was what I did. When your father found out, he was mad. To make sure you were fed enough milk, he got you a milk mother, a village woman who just had a baby. It was unusual. How he was beside himself over you. He doted on you like a delicate bud. I didn't know it but I must have been jealous.

"So it was a son. Two more followed him. I gave your father three sons but you were still his favorite. For every holiday, he had a new dress sewn for you. He used to send a servant all the way to Seoul so that your dress was made of the best cloth there was. On every Buddha's birthday, year after year, he took you to the temple, dressed in a new *hanbok*. He never took your brothers. It was always you he took. He would come in to the inner courtyard and wait for you to come out of the room. His eyes would light up at the sight of you. He would proudly ask the servants around him, 'Look! Isn't she so beautiful and graceful in her new *hanbok*! No girl carries a Korean dress more elegantly.' He would go ga-ga and every time, I felt like a fire was burning inside me. I didn't know why I felt that way but it rubbed me the wrong way.

"Still, I had nothing to complain about. When my mother-in-law died, I inherited all the house keys. I had all the servants at my beck and call. But that didn't last too long. The Japanese started a land survey. That was just an excuse to steal land from Koreans. When the Japanese seized a large part of our ancestral lands, your father was devastated. He blamed it on himself. He got what we called *wha-byung*, "anger disease." He took to drinking. He used to be sober as a monk. But once he started, he never stopped. He drank like a fish. Every afternoon, he would go up the hill to the pavilion and drink. Then he would come down at sundown, drunk out of his mind. His handsome face turned yellow and gaunt. Then one summer, he started acting strangely. One full-moon night he raced down from the ancestral hall, screaming and clutching his head with his hands. He looked scared out of his wits. He shouted his angry ancestors were after him. He had been chased down by angry ancestral ghosts throwing a black net over him. I didn't believe a word of it. I thought it was his drunken gibberish. I had known no angry ancestors. We had diligently tended their graves and never missed the daily offerings. No reason for his ancestors to get upset. It was all in his head: Your father was convinced that his ancestors blamed him for losing the land to the Japanese."

Grandmother swirled her fan as if chasing back her husband-ghost. She may have believed in the holy ghost of her God's church but she had never lost her shamanistic inclinations altogether. She sighed and sagged as she saw how her life became a long and lonely struggle after that.

"It was horrible. Your father was confined to bed all the time. His belly ballooned up and up. It eventually swelled up to the size of a big, ripe watermelon. It looked like it was ready to burst. The skin was distended tight and had the strange sheen of paraffin paper. Herb doctors came and applied moxa on his belly. It left ugly scars and when the weather turned hot, they got infected and started oozing. The room was filled with a stench. The servants would go in and run right out retching. It was that bad.

"I used to dread the coming of night. As soon as the sun went down, your father started hearing the ancestral ghosts marching down from the hill and later stomping into the house. His eyes would bulge with fear. He shook his head. 'They are coming! I hear them! I hear them!' He would howl and holler. He would roll around his bed with his hands over his ears trying to shut out the noise! Then he would bolt up from his bed and desperately hold onto the door to stop the angry ancestors from entering the room. But angry ghosts know no doors or walls. They would be inside the room with a black net of death, throwing it over his head as fishermen throw a fish net. He would flail his arms as if he were tearing the net away from him. Out of desperation, I tried to help him. I couldn't see the net but I pulled it away from him as if I could. When it didn't work, your father would kneel down and rub his palms together, begging the ancestral ghosts for mercy. This went on the whole autumn. Night after night. All the doctors I sent for came and just shook their heads. It was too late. That was what every doctor said. They said your father had already crossed the line that separated the living from the dead. I even brought in a famous shaman and had her perform *gut* to placate the ancestors. When I heard that a woman hanged herself on a tree, I sent a servant for the bark off the tree. I boiled the bark and had your father drink it. It was believed to cure any disease. But nothing worked."

"Of course, nothing worked. You were just practicing quackery," mother said, with a suggestion of scorn in her voice. We children giggled. Briefly, grandmother seemed at a loss for words.

"You look down on every old custom. What would you have done? A desperate person grabs at a straw. Anyway, one night, his ancestral ghosts stopped coming. Instead, in his dream, your father was visited by a messenger from the Yellow Springs. He came riding a gray horse. He opened the death book where the names of people called by Yum Ra Dae Wang, the King of Hell were listed. Your father's name was one of the names in the book.

Your father later told me how he himself had seen his own name. Before leaving, the emissary gave your father a fortnight to prepare for his journey to the other world.

"Do you know what your father's last wish was as he lay waiting for death? He wished for a mere crab apple. A lousy crab apple. Why couldn't he have wished for something like a turtle's liver? Nonetheless, there was no crab apple to be found in the middle of the winter where we lived. I sent a servant to Seoul who set out on a snowy evening. I anxiously waited for his return. I had a faint hope that it might even cure your father. One never knows. Five days passed and on the sixth day, it didn't look like your father would hang on another night and the servant was still nowhere. I was afraid that your father would die without his last wish fulfilled. That was when the servant hurried in carrying with him a box full of the most expensive crab apples money could buy. I hastily cut a slice and slid it into your father's mouth who was drawing his last breath. Just as he took a bite, his jaws froze. He died like that with a piece of crab apple stuck in his mouth. Such a dramatic death! Till this day, I can still see the slice of crab apple stuck in his mouth.

"When the funeral procession passed through the village, all the villagers, his tenant farmers, lined the road and wailed as if their own father or husband or son had died. Especially the sight of his three little sons trailing their father's coffin in hemp clothes and straw sandals brought tears to everyone. Your father was just thirty-five years old and no longer a person of this world." Grandmother slowly surveyed us with that superior look of hers in her eyes. In our impressionable minds, grandmother had succeeded in planting the mortal fear of incurring the wrath of the ancestors.

◆   ◆   ◆

Grandmother had to reluctantly end her story there as the old lady came and announced dinner. We happily congregated around the dinner table. But as we reached for the spoons, grandmother clasped her hands, closed her eyes and plunged into one of her infamously long prayers.

"Oh, our Lord in heaven," grandmother chanted, drawing deep furrows between her scant eyebrows. I pressed my eyes tightly and tried to imagine God sitting lightly in heaven, in the sky over the white clouds but all I could think of was my grandfather being chased by angry ancestors with a black death net and him lying dead with a piece of crab apple stuck between his frozen jaws. "Please accept our humble thanks for the abundant food on our table. Let it become our blood and flesh and enrich our faith in our Lord," grandmother continued, sucking the spittle of saliva that formed whirlpools at the corners of her thin, willful lips. Through my half-closed eyes, I could see brother longingly staring at the broiled mackerel on the table. Mother fidgeted and stared at the floor. Only sister's eyes were closed as tightly as grandmother's.

"Please, Lord," grandmother said in her extra-trembling voice that got everyone's attention. "Bless my daughter especially, a destitute soul without faith yet. Please bridle her wandering mind with faith and return her husband to her arms of compassion and love. Let her see in him only the virtue not his many shortcomings and faults," grandmother pleaded with God — she preferred God to Jesus for His fury and wrath — like a shaman cajoling a ghost spirit. As I wasn't sure what God looked like, I imagined heavy grandmother clinging to the thin, emaciated arms of Jesus. If grandmother clung to him any longer, Jesus would surely come toppling down.

"Let your love come down on her as sweet rain that breaks out of the sky with thunder and lightning after a drought and soak her faithless, harsh soul with your love. Open her eyes as once your beloved son opened the eyes of a blind man with his power of faith." Mother winced and sighed unhappily. Mother suddenly remembered her strange dream and was convinced that the Pumpkin Wife who had snapped the threads with a dagger was in fact her own mother. With her strange tales and ways, her mother was alienating her children from her.

Grandmother's litany went on and on, covering each and every child and grandchild of hers, her words forming a chain of oblique stories from the Bible — Jesus feeding a hungry crowd with a loaf of bread, his disciples washing his feet and the betrayal by Judas — inexplicably connecting these ancient incidents on the pages of the Bible to the well-being of her family. Where were the places like the sea of Galilee, Babylon, the mount of Olives, Jericho, Samaria and Gomorrah grandmother seemed to know so intimately and where she seemed to roam at will? Her prayers kept flowing out like a long choking river squeezing dry tears from her tightly pressed eyes. We children, starving and bored, half-listened to her words and waited impatiently for her prayer to be over. Then when she said her last word, we all blurted out a loud "Amen!" in a cheery chorus and hastily picked up our spoons and chopsticks.

Grandmother picked at her food and in between her chewing still mumbled on about grandfather.

"God knows what I went through after your father died!" grandmother whimpered. Mother pleaded with her to finish the meal first.

"I have no appetite," grandmother insisted. "You go on eating and I will go on talking. It's one of the few pleasures still left to me. And how often do I get to have all of you children with me? They should hear these things. They should know what their own grandmother went through in life. This is no old tale I make up. So let me talk about it." Grandmother readjusted her statuesque but somehow shapeless body. The only thing that hadn't lost its shape was her big "fist" nose. It punctuated the middle of her face wilfully and resolutely. Mother looked at us, exasperated. Her eyes smoldered with anger.

"You must remember,"Grandmother said, ignoring mother's silent protest. "I had to let go of all the servants after your father died. I handed over the remaining farmland and the house to your father's family and with all of you small children in tow, came to Seoul. I wanted my sons to receive a modern education. And your father's wealthy uncle promised me just that. That was all I cared about. Anyway when I arrived in Seoul, he immediately sent his aides and took all your brothers away from me. They were taken to his one-hundred-room estate with servants and private tutors. I rarely got to see my own sons. Whenever I went to see them, I was turned away at the gate. But I took comfort in them being well fed and clothed and getting the best education.

"The uncle was lucky to be born to a progressive Christian family. He was already a married man when his family, encouraged by an American missionary, sent him to America to get a Western education. After receiving a Ph.D., he came back to Korea and devoted himself to the struggle of independence from Japan. Later, he opposed Syngman Rhee's dictatorship. Everyone said he would become the president of this country. But he died of cancer before his time at the Walter Reed Hospital in America. So I had to take your brothers back and educate them myself. See how fate works? How it makes an unexpected turn? Whenever it became too much to bear, I opened my Bible to Matthew 7:7. 'Ask, and it shall be given you; seek, and you shall find; knock, and it shall be opened unto you.' God gives you everything when you ask, seek, and knock." Grandmother's bulldog face lit up with a triumphant smile. She looked as proud as someone who had just won a long and arduous *janggi* game, Korean chess.

"Mother, please! I know all that. What's the point of repeating the old story again and again?" Mother put down her chopsticks. "I have my own old grievances. If you want so much to talk about the old times, tell my children about them," mother said challengingly. Grandmother glanced at mother sideways and sighed.

"I know what you have in mind but I have nothing to say. Those days, not many people believed in educating girls. It was not like these days. What would you have done if you had gone to a university? A girl married and served her husband, his family and the children. That was a woman's place. Besides, we were living under the Japanese. It wasn't getting better. All over China and Asia, the Japanese were waging wars. We were their pawns. All the young and able men were taken away to fight or to labor in mines and war factories. Worse, they started plucking up young Korean girls like so many chickens. Shipped them off to Manchuria and God-knows-where to serve as whores for their soldiers. Called them comfort girls and put them to work at what they called *wi-an-so*, comfort stations. But they were just brothels serving soldiers. Lots of girls just disappeared, kidnaped off the streets. What mother would sit and watch that happen to her daughter? I did what I did for you. I was so worried that the Japanese might come and take you away. I had to marry you off fast. I wasn't the only one. It was the same for all Korean parents with young unmarried girls. And there weren't many eligible men around. You couldn't pick and choose. Desperate parents gave away their girls to cripples and widowers old enough to be their fathers.

"How could I have known that in just four or five months,

Americans would drop bombs and the Japanese would surrender? Even if I had known it, it wouldn't have helped. In a time like that, even a week is a long time. Anything could have happened in that time. You forget what it was like. It's easy now to blame your mother. Your poor mother," grandmother bleated with defeat in her voice.

"Never mind, *uhmoni*," mother said. "You ignored my protest. You went ahead and arranged a marriage to a man twelve years my senior, for whom I had no feelings." With sudden alarm in her eyes, mother looked at us children: she just couldn't believe the words she was spitting out in front of her small children.

"Why? Was there a man you had feelings for then?" grandmother asked back, blowing her nose.

"Even if there had been, you wouldn't have listened to me anyway. You were so taken up by him at first sight. True or not true? And ever since we were married, endless lies, debt, worries and pain, that's all he has given me. And whenever he's in financial trouble, he just disappears leaving me to deal with the mess. Where is he when I have to feed my children and send them to school? How do I explain this to my children?" It wasn't the story mother had told the Pumpkin Wife who pawed at her like a curious cat. I had heard mother tell the Pumpkin Wife that father was running a business somewhere, in a city so far away that he couldn't come home often. I looked at mother, confused, but she had already forgotten her face-saving story she had concocted for the Pumpkin Wife.

"Should you talk about feelings! What feelings?" grandmother asked scornfully. "For hundreds of years, every Korean woman married a stranger selected by her family. Why, I married your father, a total stranger. No marriage was decided by an individual. It was decided between two families. Nobody had it differently."

"It's a backward custom. You should know that yourself if you had it so badly with father," mother said, irritated.

"I was a backward woman who followed backward customs. But that was all I knew. I was myself in the dark about the world. You can't blame me for that. Anyway, your husband had everything going for him when I arranged the marriage. He was a good catch. From a prominent old Confucian family. And handsome as a devil. Oh, my, what a glib tongue he had, too! He could talk and I believed every word that tumbled out of his mouth. I would have believed him if he had promised me a jade mountain. After all these years, I know he can still persuade me all over again. He can walk into the room right now and make me believe whatever he wants me to believe. With nothing but his own silver tongue! He said I would never regret giving him my daughter. I thought I had found the best son-in-law in the world," grandmother hooted.

"But he never told you that it was his second marriage," mother said. "How his first wife died during her labor. And how he had a son of his own blood growing up somewhere." It was as if a sudden beam of lightning bolted down from the clear sky and struck us children. Mother, who chided the Pumpkin Wife's improper words and resisted her persistent attempts to pry out a story about father, had just casually let loose the most shocking secret in front of us. All of our eyes were fixed on mother. But mother sat erect and didn't even blink an eye. She looked like a woman warrior who had been seeking a final vindication and found it.

"No. I didn't know," grandmother mumbled, dropping her eyes. Her body sagged into stacks of soft pleats.

"All of his family were in on it with him," mother went on. "Every single member of his extensive clan. And I had to find out in the worst possible way. At a family wedding feast. She was just several months old," mother said, looking at sister who had left the dinner table and joined us crowding around mother. "I had sat down for a bowl of wedding noodles when a short old lady came over to my table. I figured she was one of the village women who came for the feast. Do you want me to tell you who she turned out to be? His first wife's aunt! And she was bold enough to show up at the family wedding and tell me all this in the presence of my in-laws. That wasn't all. My husband's own flesh and blood, the son I had never known about, was playing shuttlecock right there in front of my nose. Running around in the courtyard! The old lady pointed him out for me. It was unmistakable. The boy had the same high-cheekbones and deep-set eyes of his family. I could have picked him out in a crowded marketplace. Do you think it was just an accident that they were there? Think about it. And the old lady was dying to see how I reacted to the news. I didn't want to give her the pleasure but I couldn't help it. I was caught so off guard. My heart was thumping. And my face must have turned red. She couldn't have missed it. And then she long scrutinized my flushed face and said how she was pretty too, the first wife. 'Your husband was inconsolable for a long time after she died,' she said. Until then, I had tried to make the most of my marriage but right at that moment any feelings I had for my husband just went cold. Had it not been for the sake of my children..." Mother's voice trailed off. Her eyes were tearing. Shocked into silence, we stared at mother. All this time, I had believed mother was perfectly happy with her children behind the blue gate house of ours. That we children made her happy and she needed nothing else.

"Forget what might have happened before you married him," grandmother said cautiously. "Obviously he wouldn't have married for the second time if he was still grieving for his first wife. I know he *is* a good man in his heart. Anyway, I didn't hear you complain when he made all that money and had a half dozen houses and buildings in his name. Why does he have such chains of bad luck?!"

"You say bad luck! It is his first wife's curse!" mother snapped, surprising us with her sudden spurt of anger. Her usual gentleness had vanished without a trace.

"How do you know that for sure? You shouldn't say all this in front of your own children," grandmother said, smacking her lips.

"How do I know that? A fortune-teller told me. That there is a jealous woman's spirit that doesn't want me to be happy."

"What fortune-teller? *Aiigo*!! *Aiigo*!! My Lord! You are saying that you have been frequenting a fortune-teller's house when I tirelessly pray to God day and night to guide you to the house of the Lord?" Grandmother turned to the wall and made sniffling noises. "It wouldn't be enough even if the whole family pushed in one direction. But I am pulling this way and you are pulling that way! In this muddle, what will your children see and learn?" Brother, who rarely took anything very seriously, giggled, covering his mouth, and sister pulled his ear to silence him.

"I didn't go to have my fortune read, if that's what you mean. The policeman's wife begged me to go with her. All I did was sit there waiting for her while the fortune-teller did whatever business she had with the policeman's wife. Then, out of the blue, the fortune-teller pointed at me and started screaming and hollering. She asked me how I dared to bring that spiteful spirit to her house. 'It stinks my room! It's rotten and vengeful!' she screamed. I didn't know what she was talking about. The fortune-teller was blind. Not only couldn't she see me but she knew nothing about me. I hadn't uttered a word in front of her. But there she was, screaming and shouting. She pulled out a folding fan from the waist and jabbed at the air and said a woman who had died at a young age in a painful circumstance remained vengeful and jealous. I knew right away whom she was talking about. The fortune-teller wasn't doing it to get a few bills out of me because she refused even to look at them let alone touch them when I later tried to give them to her."

"When was this? You have never said anything about it," grandmother said, and let her dog-eared Bible slip from her hand as if it had lost all its power.

"It was when he was making more money than he could handle and before he squandered it all. When he could satisfy every bit of his vanity. With a whole closet full of the best suits, shirts and shoes money could buy. He isn't a good-looking man for nothing. He had women all over too. I never confided to anyone and bore it alone. It may have been an arranged marriage but I had feelings and pride."

"All men are the same, you should know that by now. There isn't a man who would mind ten, twenty and even a hundred women if given a chance. Anyway, you are his wife. You should be able to hold on to your husband. When in trouble, he disappears. I can't help it. You can't blame that on me. I've paid for my own mistakes. I've been carrying your blame all this time. I forgot the old saying, you save a drowning man and he demands your bundle. I should have learned that lesson long ago." Grandmother raised her crouched posture and her eyes came alive with renewed confidence. "It's spilled water. What is the use to sit and complain? Do something. What's stopping you from going out, grabbing any work and supporting your children? I did that. I was suddenly a widow at twenty-nine, at the peak of a woman's life. I could have remarried but instead I devoted myself to raising my children.

"Throw out all your pride and shame. It's your father's fault. He raised you like a princess. I knew it was wrong to raise a girl like that, a flower in a greenhouse. But I had no say in that matter when he was around. He wouldn't hear it. He fell in love with you the very moment you came into this world. He used to tell everyone that he would send you to Tokyo Women's University. He wanted to make you a modern, educated woman. What did that do? Make you just full of regrets and broken dreams." Grandmother clicked her tongue. The clicking and clucking of her tongue conveying her disapproval, unhappiness and pity and anger all at once. "You are just like your father. He was a noble man descended from noble people. He had never fully rooted himself in this harsh world under the Japanese. You and him, two noble creatures. Too delicate for this world! Always above the rest!"

♦   ♦   ♦

The Independence Day fireworks began over the top of the peak against the night sky. We sat on the veranda floor and watched big sparkling umbrellas, a drizzling colored rain of yellow, red, pink and purple, explode in successive thunderous bangs and fizzle down over the mountain slopes. Then, it was quiet all over again. Sister and brother sneaked away to their beds. I lay on mother's lap. Silent, grandmother and mother sat shapeless, swallowed by the darkness. I could hear the murmuring of their unhappy past, quieted by the thumping sounds of explosions, come alive again. Boiling and whispering in their hearts. Their unfulfilled past, resurrected by each other's presence, hovering like a ghost unwilling to go away to the Western Paradise. Too much regret, too many unfinished relations and too much attachment to the living.

They each stared out at the insect-gurgling garden, shadowed by the mountain, in search of answers. They watched the old trees, those nameless hundred-year-old trees, drip purple over the moonlit ground, poisoned blood from broken hearts, continually shifting like restless ghosts and knew there were no answers but reflections.

"*Aiigo!*" grandmother broke the silence in the dark. "Just think how one lives so long in this world! It could be hundreds of years ago when I lived with my family before I got married," she whispered in a nostalgic tone. "Life is no one spring day's dream as they say. It goes on and on and on."

Grandmother's whispering voice flew by me into the dark night and mother's caressing hand on my head gently carried me away to the deep valleys of dream. In my journey, I became a summer star. I traveled back over four thousand years when bears and tigers roamed on Mount Sublime Perfume in the mountainous north of Korea. The time when the mountain was carpeted with virgin forest and whirling majestic clouds enveloped the summit in silvery veils. The time when the son of the king of heaven alighted on the majestic mountain and went in search of his bride.

One day, the son of the heavenly king came upon a she-bear and a tigress. He gave each twenty pieces of garlic and some mugwort and sent them into a cave where they were to stay one hundred nights. Inside the dark cave, nights and days passed ever so slowly. A few nights later, the tigress got restless and bored and left the cave for her enchanted forest. But the she-bear endured those dark one hundred nights and emerged as a beautiful woman to marry the son of the king of heaven. I had seen the beginning of the Korean people.

Those thousands of years shifted restlessly and tumultuously as I slept. I saw how Korean women, the descendants of the she-bear woman and the son of the king of heaven, lived in the folds of history, laughing and wailing, as spirit-cajoling shamans, wise queens, poetry-writing entertainers, tear-hiding wives, bosom-bracing mothers, dutiful daughters, scheming concubines, ill-treated daughters-in-law and fire-breathing mothers-in-law. Their lives sweeping through, season after season, flowers after snow, rain after drought.

Finally, there I was standing in front of mother. I had become her sorcerer. I had seen mother's history. Her very own history, a legacy of a river full of the hopes and dreams and despair of women before her. I tell her it is her turn now to continue the journey on her own. I will stand by her until there is no more time to write it and I will be the next carrier of her hopes and dreams when I become a woman one day.

CHAPTER 3

A MAN ON THE ROAD

*L*ong ago Prince Siddhartha traveled roads studded with secrets, human secrets, and everywhere saw the results of fates' foul play: suffering. Later people read the tales of the wise man — concoctions of fiction and nonfiction, of myths and fantasies — and learned lessons about living. But knowing and practicing the knowledge were two different matters. Ordinary souls found how hard it was to forsake pleasure and to withstand temptation. How little room their hearts held for compassion and mercy. How insatiable was their greed and strong was their desire. How easy it was to prolong hate rather than love. Thus long after the wise man was gone, temples of worship proliferated, and yet human conditions remained the same as in the days of the wise man's roaming.

But I saw in those tales — the tales of Prince Siddhartha who forsook *the pleasure of his palace and the fig tree garden to become Buddha, the Enlightened One, He Who Knows, The Only One — a man's failure and betrayal. He was a man who had left his home and family never to look back or to remember their sorrow for having been abandoned by their son, husband and father. A man who selfishly reached Nirvana for himself, the place of eternal happiness and calm where the cycle of rebirth was stopped, but who couldn't save the rest from sorrow and suffering. His teaching — give up thirst so that there would be no sorrow, suffering or dissatisfaction — was lost on ordinary men. Ordinary souls constantly faltered from the middle course they were taught to follow. It was not an easy task to shake off all the ills inherent in flesh: Imagination that rose out of Ignorance, thus Self-consciousness, Name and Form, Thought, Contact, Feeling, Craving, Attachment. All that made ordinary souls mortal.*

For so long, I thought of my father as a wise man on the road, having abandoned his family, searching for his kind of Nirvana. It was easier that way. But father returned again and again, as an ordinary man who faltered and wavered. A man with good intentions but who couldn't shake off a mortal being's weakness. Later, when I grew up I understood that he had no more control of his fate than any other man. That he struggled like any other soul to reach his mortal moment that came to everybody. His rebirth guaranteed: to suffer, to falter and to struggle all over again.

There is a particular evening in my memory when the purple dusk came violently. I was a child of seven. A gentleman in a fedora hat walked in through our gate, the blue gate that hadn't let in any man for a whole year. He walked in against the shifting light of the dusk, tailed by an old man pulling a cart full of fruit. He walked without hesitation, in his double-breasted beige suit, past the flower bed along the wall where summer flowers had gone and only some chrysanthemums stood, waiting for the first frost to flower.

The stranger walked into the house of ours he had no claim on and called our names. As if touched by lightning, brother and sister rushed out and held on to the stranger's arms, calling him "*apa*." Father! Without a tinge of shame, they claimed the stranger as their father! I watched him squeezing them in his arms and messing up their hair with his hands. Then he finally looked at me, hanging onto mother and said, "She must be my baby girl!" I stepped behind mother's skirt. "She's now ugly seven, *apa*," brother said, explaining why his baby girl, a little Miss Korea, wasn't as pretty as he had remembered. Father nodded and smiled.

Mother hung back, by the kitchen door, silent and awkwardly fingering her hair, swallowing millions of words that were trying to push out of her throat. Instead, a look of reproach in her eyes replaced all the words. Here is a man, a husband of mine and father of my children. A man I didn't choose, yet a fate of mine. I will ask no questions because this man, a husband of mine, has always come and gone as he pleases. A man born in the Year of the Horse with galloping feet. A man born with a destination of his own. I, an ascending dragon, and he, a galloping horse, have as much marriage affinity as a mouse and a cat.

When he looked at mother, it was half-mumbled words father let out. Mother responded with her own half-mumbled words, while her eyes glanced at us children. Uncertain. Hesitant. They stood. Like two trees standing apart. There were no embraces or touches. If there had been some gestures or body language of affection or intimacy, a child's eyes missed them.

I looked and looked at the stranger who was said to be my father. A gentleman with a graceful body, looking like a millionaire in his snug-fitting double-breasted suit. Handsome as an actor, a suffering hero in a black and white movie. His voice resonated low like the bass notes of a piano and his diction was that of a scholar. But he was no longer the dashing young man in the pictures I had seen in the family album. The album with a green leather cover brother often sneaked out as if extracting a secret, from the deep folds of clothes inside the chest. There, I had seen him among the piles of many yellowing black and white pictures; in immaculate suit and tie in professional studio portraits taken on brother and sister's one hundredth day birthdays. The ones with the chirpy springtime scenery of a hill in the background. Father and mother, young, skin taut and their cheeks touched up in the same shocking pink of the azaleas blooming on the hill. I had seen him standing on a rock by the seaside, in his swim trunks, with waves breaking behind him. He was laughing raucously in the picture, about to fall off the rock.

But still he stood in front of me, a mystery man. So, I stared and stared at him. He was the man in the stories sister idolized and cherished. He was the man in the arguments between grandmother and mother, dethroned and vilified. Who was he?

The day father returned as a stranger, I started keeping a secret. It was a secret because it was never to be told to anybody: father was the gentleman with a fedora hat I had seen earlier on the street playing with other children. He was the gentleman who had asked an old lady for directions. He must have asked her where so and so's house was. Father and I had been just a few feet away. He must have seen me. His own baby daughter. With his nose, eyes and high cheekbones. Yet, he had failed to recognize her. Such a long time had passed since he had last seen her. She had just started walking.

It had never occurred to me then that the gentleman could be

my own father, such a rich looking man. Just a little envy for the
gorgeous summer fruit of primary colors piled in the cart. I
wondered, only briefly, who were those lucky children who would
get to devour that fruit. So later when he walked into our house,
and brother and sister called him father, what I felt was shame. A
child who couldn't recognize her own father. A father who couldn't
recognize his own daughter. I never told this secret to anyone. I
understood that a secret was a secret because a secret was shame.

◆　◆　◆

The night father came home, we children lay in the dark and heard
mother and father arguing in their room. Mother's unhappy voice
droned on as a monologue before father's flat voice replaced hers.
We listened to their arguing voices in anxiety. We were afraid that
mother's unhappy words would drive father away. Afraid that
we would wake in the morning and find father gone again.

Already one evening with father had turned me into his admirer.
I found the stranger who came home through the dusk light a charmer.
How smoothly and easily he enticed me to his court! No apology or
explanation was needed. He was already forgiven. We were impressed by the title on his fancy business card — black letters embossed on white paper showed him as a president of a fire insurance
company — and a picture taken to celebrate "the start of business."
How important and dignified father looked in the picture, surrounded
by his staff in front of his office, an old two-story wooden building —
the very kind susceptible to fire, mother had pointed out — in his
immaculate suit, with a single carnation on the lapel! We found to
our delight that a freshly painted and just dedicated sign on the building — "The First Fire Insurance Company Limited" — matched the
company name on his business card.

"*Umma*, here look at the picture!" Sister, a staunch supporter of father, enthusiastically pushed the picture to mother who wouldn't look at it.

"It's O.K. Let your mother be a doubter for a while. But when your father becomes a big success, she won't be able to stop herself from smiling. Then you remind her how she never believed your father," he said, convinced he was in one of the brightest future industries.

Their arguing — a tug of war with words — continued on and off through the autumn. We would go to bed each night wondering if the sun would rise again the next morning. But in the morning we would wake up and find mother and father in puzzlingly good moods as though all the demons had been exorcized overnight. We would have a happy morning and send him away with a cheerful "*Apa*, please return safely." We would wave to him as he walked out of the gate in his snug-fit suit and freshly starched and ironed shirt and tie with a kerchief in his breast pocket, uncertain that father would indeed come back at the end of the day.

It was a little miracle each time father appeared around the corner of the street in the evening. He would return home mellow after a few bowls of rice wine. From his hand dangled a package of still steaming dumplings or seaweed biscuits we loved. A bait for his talk. He liked to gather his children in front of him on such evenings. Mother would tease him for gloating in his fatherly glory. His three children bashfully sitting on their knees, ready to listen to him, made father truly happy.

Once father opened his mouth, words flew out effortlessly in a seamless river. He was an exciting and gifted talker. He could turn a simple plain story into an epic. And transform a scraggly hill into a legendary landmark. An uncut stone into a sparkling gem. In his words, old obscure Oriental literature and philosophy became tangible and entertaining tales that held his children in thrall. But father most enjoyed telling us about the family history that rolled back more than a thousand years. The fierce pride he took in his old family roots was infectious. He would make it easy for us to imagine our grandfather of seventeen generations back who had led a triumphant war against invading Yeojin tribes and had built nine castles in an area that was now a part of China. Father told the story in such vivid detail that our ancient grandfather came alive right in front of our eyes. A fearless general on horseback, with a sword and arrows and a bow, riding high along the spines of rugged mountains.

Each night, we eagerly anticipated these story sessions. By the close of autumn, we had learned all the stories of the queens and scholars and ministers that father's family had produced during the Yi dynasty. About the power struggle among the families. About the schemes that backfired and the blood that was shed. About the years spent in lonely banishments. Father used to conclude these stories with lessons we should learn as he tended to become philosophical and brooding at the end.

Father was a Confucian. He looked down upon material things and valued loyalty, learning and honor more than anything else. That became his teaching to us. We were too young to perceive the ironies. We children didn't understand the bitterness of a man who had spent the first thirty-three years of his life struggling under the Japanese, and who had lost the opportunities to become the man he would have liked to be: a scholar instead of a businessman. Yet he still dreamed of leaving his name behind. There were many examples for him: illustrious kings, heroic generals, revered scholars or great poets. He wouldn't be content just with his children carrying the family name. Father always said, "A tiger dies to leave his skin and a man dies to leave his name."

This ambition of his became an obsession. This ambition of his became his worst enemy and when he was just at the throne of financial success, he threw it away in his grand attempt to leave his name behind. And there were always people more than willing to exploit his grandiose dream. The candle he lit burned constantly and he was always running out of time to achieve his goal.

Had he only known that his children wished for just an ordinary father! A father who left for work in the morning and returned home in the evening. A father who was there for us. To encourage and to support and even to discipline us. And had he known that mother wished for just an ordinary husband! A husband who was stable and steady and constant. A husband who fixed door hinges and blown-out fuses.

◆　◆　◆

Before the spring came, father was gone again. There was a strange let-down among us children but no one talked about him. We carried on as if nothing had happened. Nobody asked where father had gone. The desk plaque from his now defunct fire insurance company, the black lacquer with father's name engraved in mother-of-pearl, was pushed around from corner to corner in the house.

In the mornings after father was gone, when dawn came to the window panes in a faint silver glow, I would wake up to the sound of a tofu vendor's bell passing by outside the street and to the holler of an oyster seller, "Fresh oysters here. Fresh oysters!" and remember the fleetingly short autumn and part of the winter with father. I would remember the mornings when father used to wake us at dawn and herd us out into the dark of the morning. Remember the way streets were faintly mapped out in the blue-gray mist of early morning and the way we shuffled after father, half in slumber, each of us carrying an empty jug and a towel. And remember how we had passed the streets that had no names, sputtering white fog from our mouths, vaguely happy and slightly disturbed by the sudden bliss of father's presence.

Everywhere there had been the same faint sounds of the dawn: brooms sweeping the streets and the tofu man's bell slicing the stillness. Every morning at the exact spot in the street, we would come across the silhouette of the tofu vendor turning the corner, slumped by the wooden tofu panels stacked high on his A-frame slung around his back. At that exact moment, he would clank the bronze bell in his hand. The "clink clank" metallic sound was always followed by the oyster seller hollering into the quiet morning, "Fresh oysters here. Fresh oysters!" Exactly in the same pitch. His voice would come as close as around the corner only to get fainter and fainter along with his footsteps. Now with father gone, the sound of the tofu vendor's bell and the hollering of "Fresh oysters here. Fresh oysters!" sounded inexplicably sad in the morning.

Often, lying in bed, I would close my eyes and follow those same streets again, weaving in and out of block after block, and turn to the lane lined with pine trees and bushes, clumped dark against the mauve blue space. There the road gradually climbed up all the way to the spring, tucked under clumps of rocks. Huffing and puffing, we labored up the lane after father, past old men trudging down from the spring, carrying their jugs filled with ice-cold spring water. They always came preceded by the sound of their footsteps and of spring water slopping from side to side in their jugs. I could hear all over again father's voice greeting them through the fog. I remembered how, just for a second, the old men's smiling faces had poked out from the dark as they passed us. And the way the old men had cackled pleasurably with the pride of runners who had won a race.

Warm and out of breath, we would reach the spring where the first sip of the ice cold spring water jolted our still soggy brains. One by one, the jugs were filled with trickling spring water and we did our morning exercises, perfunctorily swirling our arms, stretching our legs after father who practiced strange movements he had learned as a youngster from his own father. Then in single file, we would start down the footpath where sunlight cast dizzying smithereens after filtering through the dense pines like gold dust.

Some mornings on our way down from the spring, father would take us to a goat farm at the edge of the pine tree hill. There, the owner, a scraggly old man, would bring out his fresh goat's milk in a wooden scoop. Father, standing under the morning sun, would urge us to gulp down the goat's milk at once to the last drop. His laughter at the sight of us drinking goat's milk, holding our noses and creasing our faces, would spread through the light of the air and the goats would join in with their indiscreet cries.

Now the sad sound of the tofu man's bell and the oyster man's hollering also brought back the promises father made us children on the way home from the spring. The promises he had made us, in his morning lucidity, now echoed like bells from remote fairy tale lands. There was no guarantee, I knew now, that father would come back, like a knight on a horse, to fulfill his promises.

I could vividly picture the house father had said he would build for us one day. A garden of red peonies and bamboos and a pond with lotus flowers and stone lanterns. A garden so aesthetic, the mere view of it on a summer evening would turn an ordinary soul into an inspired poet, father had said. I could hear him all over again, not with the same excitement but with an ache, promising us an exciting future, making our wings flap and soar.

Each of us children carried his promises like jingling marbles in our pockets, always remembering and never forgetting. It mattered little if the promises were so far-fetched. For father, the future was always something realizable. Even more certain than the present. He made it so tangible. He could not see a hurdle anywhere. Reach for the stars and the moon. He believed his children were irrevocably special and gifted and all that we needed to do was to become incorrigible dreamers like him.

Father's vague promises always turned specific for sister, his favorite child, a terrific singer, the owner of a divine voice. He used to repeat to starry-eyed sister how he would one day send her to the famous Julliard Music School in New York. After Julliard, he would tell her, there would be a triumphant soprano debut in Carnegie Hall. Good logic. Why, father had asked us, can't you almost hear the cheers of the enchanted crowd at Carnegie Hall shouting, "Encore! Encore!" for sister. And the newspapers hailing sister as the next Renata Scotto or the next Anna Moffo or Maria Callas. It seemed an unspeakable sin to doubt all this. Father had never imagined that there might come a moment that his children would come crashing down, wings clipped and dreams broken. And blame him.

So we came home each morning trailing father, inspired and ready to conquer the world, and ate heartily the breakfast mother had prepared. Food melting down like sweet honey on our tongues. Mother couldn't help but smile watching us children inflated with hopes and dreams. Her children acting like cocky monkeys sure of their skills and talents. Whatever doubt mother had, she never warned us that even a cocky monkey falls from a tree once in a while or reminded us of the gullible rabbit who was lured away to the bottom of the sea by the promise of treasure. The rabbit arrived at the Dragon Palace riding on the back of a cunning turtle only to lose his organs to cure the illness of the Dragon King.

CHAPTER 4

MOTHER AND CHILDREN

In the New Year, mother put up a calendar on the wall where I would see it upon opening my eyes in the morning. Each page carried a number. Blue for week days. Red for Sundays. Monday was also Moon day. Tuesday, Fire day. Wednesday, Water day. Thursday, Wood day. Friday, Metal day. Saturday, Earth day. And Sunday, Sun day! Each morning, as mother watched, I would totter out from the bed and standing on tiptoe, tear off a page. "Twenty-two more nights. You're going to be a proud school girl," mother would say.

Page after page, number after number, my anxious hand pulled off to March and I went to school in a gray pleated skirt and a red sweater. I took with me the fond memory of an afternoon when brother's teacher had let me sit in his classroom which had been

71

converted from a chicken shack after the war. I remembered the light that had shafted in through the windows as yellow strips of dancing motes and the fragrant smell of chicken droppings that had floated up from the creaking floor. And the happy sing-song chorus of the children reciting a story from textbooks. The fidgeting children had been like so many chickens that had once twittered about there. I remembered how the bell had rung so cheerfully just like in a song and how each child had come over and patted my head like a patronizing adult.

But as I trotted after brother through winding alleys and plunging steps to school, I grew anxious. I walked reluctantly like a cow heading to the slaughterhouse, swept up by the stream of screaming and laughing children with running feet, wet cowlicks and jingling pockets of knickknacks. I walked timidly, carrying a book bag mother had sewn from an old wool coat, turning it carefully so that my name mother had embroidered so large for anybody to see wouldn't show. Then as we gained the distance and the school gate appeared in sight, a strange urge to pee seized me.

Every morning, I pleaded with brother to walk me to my classroom. Then as soon as he gallantly marched away through the echoing hallway, I broke into tears. I was a child mortified with fear.

All morning, I sat hour after hour, tortured by a constant urge to pee but when the bell rang and children stampeded to the bathroom, I remained glued to my seat with a full, throbbing bladder. I feared the school bathroom where rows of doors banged constantly and howls and cries of children ghosts echoed. Then children returned from the bathroom to confirm the stories of ghosts of children who had been sucked into dark holes over the years.

In the afternoon, I hurried home alone, tottering like a pregnant duck, with a bladder ready to burst. Accompanied by the noise of broken pieces of crayons in the cardboard box rolling inside my book bag, I rushed toward home, counting the seconds. When I reached the well in a little square just around the corner from home, I let go and peed in my pants.

Mother waited outside the gate of our house for her baby girl to return from school and saw a miserable little girl hurrying in her still steamy soaked pants, carelessly dragging her book bag on the ground. Each time, mother looked surprised, as if that was the last thing she had expected. She laughed as she hurried me inside. "My poor baby girl. How you must have suffered all morning!" There was always a certain festivity in mother's voice when she stripped me down. I squatted inside the bath jar and let mother's soapy hands wash away all my fear. Then mother, oblivious to the torture her child was going through each day, happily talked away: how much she used to enjoy bathing us children as toddlers. How she used to scrub our soft limbs and buttocks with such joy. The joy that had included her hopes and dreams as well.

My peeing continued despite the remedies — jump across the doorstep three times forward and three times backward every morning or sleep with arms stretched upward or drink water through the side of the mouth — and the Pumpkin Wife finally came up with a smart idea. She told mother to boil some earthworms in water and have me drink up the soup to the last drop. She said that would cure my aberration. Mother eagerly took to the idea. She took an empty can to the flower bed and dug soil looking for earthworms. She would hold up a wriggling purplish worm on a stick and then ask me how I would like it in my soup. It was a ploy that worked.

I eventually learned to cope with my fears. I didn't know then that they were the fears of leaving mother's fold, the fears of coping on my own. That they were the fears of a child stepping into a new world for the first time. That they were not simply fears of dark school corridors, banging bathroom doors and howling winds and cries of children ghosts. And I also learned what brother and sister had learned: what it meant to have a father like ours. A father who came and went as he pleased. A father who easily made promises and as easily broke them. A father who encouraged you to dream but who was nowhere to back you up. It meant I spent lingering hours in the stationery store near the school, admiring and fingering those spanking new coloring pencils, plastic-covered notebooks, box-full of thirty-six color crayons, vanilla-scented erasers, a hand-held easel of Vanier with a snap clip and thick sketch books but came home empty-handed, knowing enough not to spell out my desire to a mother with an empty purse. It meant I carried the cloth book bag with shame but deferred the dream of owning a leather one until father returned with his success. It meant I passed by the food stall where children rushed with their sticky coins for the fish balls on a skewer dunked in hot soup and learned not to desire them. It meant I went on romanticizing holding a marvelously misshaped aluminum bowl filled with steaming fish-ball soup. It meant I heard children bragging about their fathers and pretended not to have heard them.

I learned to carry on. I learned to cope with fears and shame. I learned how to walk with my back straight and chin high like my sister. I learned to strut along like my gallant brother who with bravado and cheer coped with his shame and fears. I learned and learned. I was a good child even then. A child who instinctively understood mother's pain at not being able to provide everything her child needed.

◆　◆　◆

Every late afternoon, on the way to the marketplace for her vegetables, mother passed a linen shop at the corner wedged between a shoe store and an oil house. It was a popular corner that pulled women like a magnet. Women dropped their sesame seeds to be pressed into oil and headed to the linen shop next door. As the machine pressed the roasted sesame seeds and dark brown liquid slowly trickled into green bottles drop by drop, women sat at the linen shop, fingering and marveling at the newly-arrived cloth. Then carried away by the sweet smell of sesame in the oily wind, they always spent more money than they had intended, buying cloth they could barely afford. Later, happily ballooning their nostrils, they returned to the oil shop to pick up the warm oil, bottled and ready. It wasn't until they were far away from the corner that they realized they had spent far too much and started to worry.

Once a week, mother stopped at the linen shop and asked for a look at the newest arrivals. As she waited to be attended, mother fingered the rows and rows of beautiful cloth, rolled around wooden poles and stacked high to the ceiling. Then finally the rotund woman who ran the shop greeted mother, laughing and bowing, adjusting her glasses on her flared nose.

Mother's eyes widened as the rotund woman pulled out the rolls of newest cloth and quoted the price by the yard from her head. The wonderful names of cloths rolled out from her tongue like puzzles. Foreign names turned into Korean with stuck tongues. Names that couldn't be found in dictionaries but sounded wonderfully modern and fashionable. The names that reminded one of foreign ports and cha-cha-chas and tam-tams, mambos and tangos and romances in movies.

"I tell you this is the newest rage, now. It's going so fast I can't keep it in stock. Every woman wants it. Take enough for a summer *hanbok*, Young Wife. As they say, clothes are your wings," the woman said, pulling out just an inch of the newest rage for mother to examine.

Each time, mother was tempted. The thought of draping herself in the newest rage made her heart terribly light. It was like somebody promising her a new identity. She could become one of those carefree women who trotted mambo steps in a ballroom. Or a woman in a light-winged summer dress, sipping aromatic tea in a musty tea room. The airy ballroom opened to a tropical port of Indochina. Or a woman in the tea room of old Shanghai where a ceiling fan turned dreamily all day long. She could hear wooden shutters flapping in the wind carrying an afternoon storm. Often, vivid images like these alarmed her. Where did this imagination of hers come from, she wondered. Only a loose girl with a questionable reputation would have such time and freedom. Mother never forgot that she had always been a good girl. But just a little dreaming wouldn't harm anybody, mother decided. She didn't mind if the thought of a new dress carried her momentarily to a port in a foreign land where everything was exotic!

She even felt proud of her wild imagination. She looked around at the ordinary housewives, clutching their worn purses, pulling at cloth and doubted they had such flights of fancy. These women didn't see anything beyond what their eyes saw. The same ordinary thing. She was sure none of those women, strapped with daily worries and children always pleading for this and that, would guess that a woman right in front of her nose had once dreamed of living in Turkey. They probably hadn't even heard of such names as Turkey or Istanbul.

It now made mother blush though for having once believed in such a preposterous idea. When father had told her that they might move to Turkey with his business — he was forming a business venture with Turkish officers in the UN team stationed in Korea — she had thought Turkey was a promising land, like America from where her brothers returned with airs about them. Why not? She didn't know better. Father had told her Turkey had once been an old glorious kingdom, a flowering culture, not unlike the Shilla Kingdom of Korea that had once flowered dazzlingly with artistry and Buddhism. And he had described an Istanbul full of beautiful mosques and bazaars and gold trinkets. There in that mysterious old city, father had told her, they would be whisked around in a shiny black sedan. She would have a Byzantine garden with strange, perfumed flowers and a spewing fountain. The rooms would be decorated with beautiful kilims and the floors would have mosaics of colored tiles. And every afternoon, a servant in a white uniform would serve her tea in the finest china.

Father himself probably had no idea what he was talking about. He himself had never been farther than Tokyo. Later, he ended up being swindled out of lots of money by his Turkish friends who had vanished to their far-away home with father's money and his dream of Istanbul.

The incident became the butt of jokes among our American-educated uncles. They told mother how lucky she was after all that she didn't get to go to Turkey or Istanbul. That Turkey was a Muslim country where women were not allowed to go out without covering their faces. But mother still liked the idea of living somewhere strange and exciting although she wasn't too sorry that it had ended up just a dream. She couldn't imagine what she would have done if father had abandoned the family in a foreign place.

Even now, sitting at the linen shop, when the owner mentioned those wonderful sounding names of cloths, she fell into her habit of imagining the strange place called Istanbul she had never reached; the tea rooms, bazaars and domed mosques. In a foreign quarter, a woman like her might be free to go to a tea room and listen to mellifluous songs on the radio. The voice she imagined was that of Ella Fitzgerald although she had never heard of her. The carefree woman who drank tea in the tea room had the sultry charm of Lauren Bacall. And the cool romantic man standing nearby watching her would, of course, look exactly like Humphrey Bogart. Not that she had seen them or heard of them. Anyway, little difference it made now. All she wanted was several yards of new cloth which she would bring to a dressmaker with a design she had in mind.

Mother sat there, forgetting everything around her, calculating in her head how much it would cost to buy the newest rage. Adding and subtracting. It took her forever to make up her mind as she sat glued to the floor, touching the cloth again and again. The rotund woman eventually turned her attention to somebody else.

Mother continued to take in all the pros and cons of her new purchase. She thought of her dresses and *hanbok*, dozens of them, all laundered clean and ironed and folded and tucked away in her chest with mothballs. She thought of the magenta velvet one she had since her wedding. Barely worn. She had carried all of her beautiful clothes to the south during the war, bartered some of them for food and lugged the rest back to Seoul. She regretted not having gotten rid of them then. How hopelessly out of fashion they were now. And the light blue one with white polka dots. Her brother had brought the cloth from the States — the sensation at the time — but the seamstress had cut the *jeogori* too long and now nobody wore *jeogori* so long these days. She went on this way, reasoning and justifying the purchase of the new cloth.

Then gradually, her thoughts carried her back to the days when her father had been alive. Her father used to love to have her dress up in a new *hanbok* on Buddha's birthdays, harvest festivals and New Years and accompany him to Buddhist temples. Before each of those holidays, her mother and servants used to gather in the inner room and sew for days. The newly sewed *hanbok* of *jeogori* and *chima* was then laid out all ironed and flowing for her to put on and step out into the courtyard where her father was expectantly waiting. She could hear him complimenting her on the graceful way she carried herself in traditional dress. That was a long, long time ago.

Then, her far-fetched dreams and unjustifiable reasoning would be jolted by her child's begging to go home. She hadn't noticed that her child, bored to death waiting for her mother to decide, had gone around the marketplace and returned. It always surprised her that it was almost dark. She had to hurry home to make dinner.

Most of the time, mother returned home empty-handed with just vegetables. But once in a while she would make a big purchase and hurry home, holding the new cloth, wrapped nicely with reddish brown paper and neatly tied with brown strings, happy and excited as a hunter returning from gaming. She would hurry in and spread it on the floor to make sure she found it still that same tempting thing. (Remember the tricks a magician could pull! An apple in his handkerchief later came out as a flighty dove.) Mother wanted to be seduced all over again. And find it still irresistible. Mother would stand in front of the mirror with the cloth draped over her. She would laugh for no reason and ask us children how it looked on her. But she would soon sigh and fold the cloth slowly. The newest rage would end up inside her chest together with her rarely worn dresses and piles of cloth.

Years later, when these cloths and dresses were long gone out of fashion, mother would attend weddings, birthdays and our graduation ceremonies looking strangely demure in her impeccable but out-of-fashion dresses. One year when one of our uncles left for Vietnam, mother went to Kimpo airport in her now old dress made of the newest rage. In the snapshot taken that day, mother stood by the weed-infested airport's fence, puzzlingly sad in her dress next to her modern sisters-in-law who donned themselves in white gloves, pastel-colored Western suits, high-heels and beehive hairdos. Each of them held a parasol overhead. Mother held hers in her hand, unopened. Exposed to the sunlight, she seemed to be fading. Already. Into the memories.

CHAPTER 5

SUMMER

*T*he house had been built in the days when there were no streets around, only fields and a hill. Half of the hill behind the house was a cherry orchard and the other half a graveyard. The family who had built the house buried their own dead on the hill.

There had been many deaths in the family over the years. Men died of old age, illnesses and wounds inflicted by the war, but women mostly died of han: broken hearts, unfulfilled love and regrets. So when they were buried on the hill, the ghosts of these men and women came down to the house at night to protect or to haunt the family. Men died to become mostly benevolent ghosts, with no ill-wishes for the offspring; but women died to become suffering ghosts still trying to mend old wounds, to avenge an old betrayal and to correct the wrongs done to them.

There was one particular woman ghost of the family still trapped deep *in the well. Years had passed since the girl, a beautiful and curious one, had drowned herself in the well that stood in the back yard, unused and moss-covered. The cause of her drowning was lost over the years. People suggested a scandalous love affair that brought shame to the family or abandonment by her lover. Her bloated body had been pulled up and buried by the family on the sunny side of the hill. A shaman had been called to release her trapped soul but the soul remained unappeased.*

During the quiet of midday, the family women heard, through the sloshing of the water in the well, the young woman's moaning. At night, women walked to the well to draw water and saw the young woman ghost floating up from the well, her hair down and her white dress dripping. The family covered the well with a wooden top and nailed it shut permanently. But the ghost persisted. On rainy nights of summer and snowy and windy nights of winter, her weeping sound crept in through the gates, door sills and eaves and haunted the family.

After the young girl's drowning, the family's fortune dwindled steadily and their children were stricken with mysterious illnesses. Not long after the war, the family moved away. They left the family graves behind, meaning to return and claim them later. Years passed and the graves remained on the hill, their round mounds covered with weeds and their weathered tombstones felled. Rats and other animals dug holes through the mounds and pulled out pieces of rotting coffins and bones. The only proof of the existing souls were the flowers that came in spring in front of the graves. Some pasqueflowers — spirits of old women — and some China Pinks — spirits of young women. When in the spring the cherry trees blossomed white and scattered their petals over the uncared-for mounds, their sweet scents calmed the spirits. Then the quiet and peaceful spring would turn to summer and the spirits became restless in the fermenting ground. They would turn vile and rancorous again and whoever lived in the old house inherited the family ghosts from summer to winter.

Mother stood in the middle of the emptied room and took one last look. The bare room looked desolate and cold like a deserted waiting room at a railroad station after the departure of the last train. Then, we all walked outside where the June rain drizzled like church-whispers. In the rain-soaked flower bed along the wall, red and white balsam buds were pushing through their sepals. "*Umma*," sister said, "this summer we won't be able to have balsam dyes on our nails." Mother just nodded which meant neither yes nor no. Then for the last time, we walked out of the blue gate of ours.

The truck, piled with our belongings, rattled away, sputtering water into the mist. The tearful Pumpkin Wife saw us off to the end of the street making slapping sounds with her rubber sandals and wiping her tears. Mother held the Pumpkin Wife's hand and comforted her. "Please, don't be sad. There's a time to meet and there's a time to part. That's life." Then we walked away, mother and children. Mother walked resolutely, never looking back, but I couldn't help turning my head again and again. The baby blue of our gate, now rain-streaked into sea-blue, kept shrinking into the distance until it looked like the size of *wha-too*, a flower card. One day, father would come and knock on it only to find us gone. How would he find us? What would guide him back to us? Would he be sad? He would become a man without a family.

Hesitantly, the children next door, my best friends, straggled after us a few feet behind. Their hairs curled in the rain and their lips turned blue. Then at the corner before the canal, they stopped and stared at us, sucking their fingers in the rain. Eventually, I could see no more of them. Faint in the drizzling rain, just an empty street where we used to play jack stones and hopscotch and down which father had come one evening as a stranger.

The haunted old house must have been all mother could afford.

The wooden gate with a tiled roof opened with a sharp squeak and we stood in the cemented courtyard shaded by moss-covered walls, swirling roofs and drooping eaves. Along the brick walls, summer flowers bloomed in passionate hues among tangled vines. Suddenly, we children knew the safe, sparkling and bright world behind the blue gate was gone forever.

There is little memory of the autumn and winter that came and went. In the spring, we relinquished the main quarter to a family and moved to the back quarter, connected from the main quarter through a flimsy, single-leafed gate. That was also where the haunted well stood, a moss-ridden stone tube, holding forever sloshing water at the bottom.

An Oh family moved into the main quarter we vacated. Their family name "Oh" had the same sound as when we count "five." They were a family of four pretty females and one absent man. Of a majestic handsome woman and her three very pretty daughters. The woman's husband and the girls' father, we heard, managed a hotel in Pusan, the southern port city.

With the arrival of the Oh family, the spring seemed to skip ahead. After school, we ran around, shrieking and singing, playing hide and seek around the house. Then one evening just as the blue shadow drew across the courtyard, the gate opened and in strode the handsome woman's brother-in-law, cutting a striking figure. Tall and skinny as an electric pole, he carried a face that was as pale as white soap and lips that were redder than an iodine stain. Down his cheeks ran thick side-burns, each neatly trimmed in the shape of an ax. And his pomade-greased hair was a dome of thick wavy hair. If I had known Elvis then, I would have thought he was fashioning himself after him. But it was his two-toned leather shoes below his mustard yellow polyester pants that really caught my eye. After he disappeared into the inner room, leaving his two-toned shoes on the stone step, I remember, the shoes sat there with a strange allure all evening.

After that evening, the brother-in-law often came by, bringing with him a drum full of live eels from Pusan. He'd fill a cement tub in the courtyard with water and release the dark, slithery eels into it. There, fascinated and revolted, we would hunch over and watch the eels swim. Later, the slithery eels were chopped and opened and dressed in spicy *gochoo-jang*, red pepper paste and garlic and were barbecued over a charcoal brazier in the middle of the courtyard. In the jiggling sound and the whirling smoke from the roasting eels, dusk turned to night. We ate them as soon as they were off the charcoal. They were hot, spicy, tender and chewy. They were most delicious.

Then, the summer rolled in, ripe and thick as a sun-beaten juicy peach. Everything around us turned shades deeper and darker. The petals on flowers were fervid. The sky was textured and layered. The wood of the gates and doors and beams was moist and dark. Through the cracks of the cemented courtyard and brick walls, thick green moss crept and spread. We children became preoccupied with ghosts and endlessly told and retold ghost stories to one another. In the dark unused room in the back, we discovered broken bits of this and that: a cracked mirror, an old piece of stained silk, an embroidered leather thimble among mildewed pieces of furniture. We looked at these things and our feverish imaginations immediately invented ghosts. So preoccupied with ghosts were we that we wouldn't sit with our backs against any doors, drawers or openings. The snatching hands of ghosts were very real.

One evening, braving a heavy rain, sister went to a neighbor's fence to pick some pumpkin leaves. (We used the leaves to wrap our fingers for balsam dye. Mother added crystal pieces of alum and tobacco to the crushed balsam petals and leaves. They gave our nails that deep red dye we coveted but they also made our fingers throb all night!) A while later, the gate was flung open and there sister stood framed by the rectangle blue, dripping. In the gleaming, blue liquid light, she was the ghost of the well we had so many times imagined. Then behind her, lightning broke in white jagged bolts, plucking her out of the blue gloom. We covered our eyes and ran screaming.

At nighttimes, in bed, we heard doors creak, gates squeak and women ghosts weep. On stifling afternoons, we climbed up the hill and roamed around among the abandoned graves, picking China Pinks that flowered there and peeking into the upturned, rotting coffins and weeded tombs. We came back home carrying the soiled part of a jaw or a cracked hip bone, russet colored and porous as sponge.

Braving the blurry summer heat, we children went to places of suicide and accidents and tried to decipher these on our own. One scorching afternoon we hiked up and across the cherry hill to look at the body of a woman who hung herself on a pine tree. She killed herself because of "unrequited love," one of the pretty Oh girls said, pushing her curled bangs away from her cream-colored forehead. The two words, "unrequited love" were so tantalizing and so provocative that we went on repeating those words for days. If love called for death! Suddenly, any kind of death, death by fire, death by drowning or death by fever, seemed possible and so close at hand. Death spoke to us children so intimately and sweetly through every tree, flower, breeze or drizzle. All these souled things constantly rattled in and heaved out of our imaginations.

All through the summer, women gossiped in whispers about the fat handsome woman and her tall and pale brother-in-law. He was often seen in the morning, in his striped pajamas and tussled wavy hair, brushing his teeth and shaving by the garden. He and his sister-in-law slept in the same room, the women said. The rest, better left unspoken.

One sweltering afternoon as we played hopscotch in the courtyard, the front gate opened and the brother-in-law's fiancée walked in, feverish and swollen-cheeked from the mumps she suffered. She looked as wholesome and lonely as a moonflower in her white blouse and pumpkin-colored, long, flaring skirt. She had come to claim her *ai-in*, the person of her love, from his sister-in-law. The handsome woman, though, sat on the floor, beautiful and massive, and didn't even blink an eye.

That afternoon, mother confined us children to the back quarter. Hopelessly caught up in that mystery we barely understood, we tried to catch every little noise coming from the main quarter. Never before had the little gate that connected us to the main quarter looked so mysterious! After what seemed like hours, the gate finally opened and the brother-in-law's fiancée walked in. She melted down on our veranda floor and broke down into a shuddering sob. She told mother how she had become an "old miss." She would never be able to take back the years she had wasted waiting for a man. Blinded by love. She had always believed that he would one day marry her. If only she waited patiently. She waited and waited. And it was her last resort. To come here. It took every bit of her courage. It was now all over. Her eyes were finally opened. She could see that his sister-in-law would never let him go. She contemplated throwing herself into the well to become another weeping ghost.

She didn't.

Instead, death came that summer somewhere else. Down the street, in the house behind a varnished wooden gate. There lived a childless old couple. The woman hated children. Like the pitiful giant in the story we had read in school: in his garden, flowers never bloomed and birds never came to sing because he hated children.

It was always around dusk when the scattered children would gather on the street in front of her house. There, the street was level and wide and if children wished they could play shuttle-cock, hide-and-seek and roll marbles into holes all at the same time. Children ran around screaming and laughing until the dusk progressed to a stifling summer evening. Then just as the faces disappeared into the dark, the lamp light on the electric pole would suddenly flicker on, sputtering orange haze.

At once, children's voices shot up an octave and punctually, the varnished light brown gate flung open and the woman who hated children stepped out, carrying a tin bucket full of water.

"Why can't you go some place else to play!" she yelled at the children. "How many times did I tell you not to play here?" She must have been well over fifty. She had the skin of yellow squash and sunken fox eyes with dark half-moon circles. But she had a young woman's jet black hair which she wore in a bun, steadied with a long traditional silver pin. Children hated and feared her. Once or twice, she had made good on her threat and dumped a bucket of slimy dish water onto the scampering and screaming children. But children returned again and again to the same spot at dusk. To play well into the night.

One day, a sudden rumor traveled up and down the street: the mean, hollering woman had committed suicide. In the blue and purple light of dusk, we stood at a corner of the street like a bunch of grapes and watched a coffin go in through the gate. After the coffin went in, the gate shut. During the night, someone came out and hung a lantern, announcing a death in the house. It cast spooky, spidery shadows on the varnished wood. Children abandoned the spot and went home early. Her death lingered stealthily through the summer. Children claimed to have witnessed the dead woman guarding her varnished gate at dusk. She was bleeding from the corner of her mouth. And the blood was black, not red. And the dead woman's husband, who was rarely seen outside, was starving himself to death. So helpless a man was he without a wife.

One rainy afternoon, the gate opened once again. Just wide enough to let in a pudgy woman, carrying a bundle on her head. She came as a new wife to the dead woman's husband and started running the house as immaculately and efficiently as any woman. She was so frugal that she didn't let a grain of rice slip through her fingers, women said. It wasn't a compliment. It was scorn. Soon, though, the new plump wife wasn't so plump. Her health suffered a steady decline. She was like a waning moon. Her once rosy cheeks turned ashen and ghastly circles gathered under her eyes. It was the jealous spirit of the dead woman that deprived the new wife of sleep. Night after night, the new wife tossed and turned in her bed. During the day, she was like a zombie.

One evening, through the thick of mist, all the children rushed after their mothers and for the first time walked through the varnished gate into the courtyard as guests to witness a *gut*. In front of the offering table stacked with fruit and colored candies and rice cakes, a shaman read the rice trails and declared in her scratchy voice that the dead woman's spirit wasn't ready to go to the Western Paradise. In her fluttering garb of red and yellow and blue, the shaman danced, jumping and whirling. The bells rattled in her hand and the sword gyrated. Thumping rhythms of gongs and drums filled the sticky, breezeless summer night. In the mist of frantic swirls, the shaman was transformed into a *Pari Gongju* — Rejected Princess — and descended into hell to rescue the dead wife's soul. When the shaman collapsed in her trance, some terrified children fainted into the arms of their mothers. Through the shaman, the dead wife's spirit returned — as a hungry ghost — and devoured the food like a savage animal. From the courtyard, the women yelled and chastised the wife's jealous soul and the shaman cajoled the spiteful spirit to fly away to the Western Paradise. The plump new wife, no longer plump, crouched in a corner in fear of being attacked by the jealous wife and the dead woman's husband hunched sheepishly outside the kitchen door, drunk with rice wine. It was near midnight when we children went home down the quiet street, purified and cleansed of the dead woman's spirit by the shaman's pine branches.

The summer went on and on. After the rainy season, we children took to bed with fever. In our afternoon delirium, from the sickbeds, we heard songs on the radio, women spilling out their broken hearts. Mother had lost her appetite in the heat. And she was restless. But the Oh sisters looked prettier than ever. Their beautiful, massive mother grew more massive each day. The eel drum stood empty in the corner of the courtyard, rusting. Summer flowers withered away on the stems. The sun dipped to the west earlier and earlier.

◆ ◆ ◆

Toward the end of August, I accompanied mother to a town where we were strangers. We got off the bus at a busy terminal and followed a sweating tarmac that shortly branched out into dusty lanes. After a marketplace and a narrow and shabby commercial street, we were soon in an altogether different part of the town. Mother suddenly seized my hand. "Don't look," mother warned and pulled me after her, propelling us past a row of bars and clubs with English signs. Over the whole length of the street, the air hung thick with the smells of stale whisky, salt, oil and perfume. At the doorways of the bars where music thumped in a monotonous beat, young women with made-up faces and tight dresses lounged about, languid and unruffled, smoking and chatting and laughing among themselves. Now and then, they scanned the hot, deserted street up and down. And when they spotted an American in a checkered shirt and crew cut, they all hurled strange-sounding words at him. "Hullo, G.I.! Hullo!" They giggled through their puckered red lips.

But before long, we were out in the open country. All around, it was just rice fields and empty sky, uninterrupted golden yellow of the ripening rice pressed by the unblemished blue of the sky. Mother took a single graveled lane meandering toward clumps of houses below the squatting hills far away. As we walked, the heat increased and over us, the traveling sun swelled in size and flared into a large flaming disk. And now and then, raising red clouds of dust, green U.S. army trucks rumbled by, temporarily blinding us.

Mother opened the parasol and patted her face with her white gauze handkerchief, crocheted in blue around the edges. The gravelly road, its shoulder dotted with tiny wild flowers, stretched on like a rubber band. Mother stopped and looked through the blazing sunlight, to the houses far away, blurring like a mirage in shifting distances. All around us, everything was hushed and still and breathless in the noon sun. It was like we were standing in the middle of a painting.

Mother sighed and took out a piece of paper from her black vinyl purse. She peered at the address, scribbled in leaking ball-point pen. Later, on the village houses, mother could find no numbers or name plaques. We walked from house to house calling but no one responded. The foot-packed roads sat empty too. A yelping brown dog followed us halfheartedly through the heat and turned away bored after a while. When finally mother located a house at the far end of a road facing the rice paddies, the sun had reached the center of the sky.

Mother pushed through the little twig gate between the bush of thistle and entered the yard. A young woman looked out from the *maroo*, veranda floor, and greeted mother in a smoky voice, full of sleep. Mother gave father's name and asked her if he lodged in the house. The young woman nodded and pointed at a rice-papered door, secured with a rusting lock. Mother walked to the door and clinked the door handle a couple of times as if trying to be assured.

"He won't be back until evening. Please make yourself at home if you would like to wait," the young woman said pulling her long, bleached hair into a pony tail. Mother and I settled at the edge of the veranda floor where red peppers were drying on a straw mat. The acrid smell tickled our nostrils and soon mother and I were sneezing, "Achi! Achi!"

The young woman laughed and disappeared into her kitchen slapping in her see-through sandals and came back with two glasses of cold barley tea for us. "Your husband never mentioned his family in Seoul," she said to mother, patting me on the shoulder with her red-nailed fingers. "He only sleeps here and takes his meals in town. An old lady comes and does his laundry," she said as if to reassure mother.

She returned to her veranda floor and turned on a transistor radio. The afternoon floated by as the sputtering radio played a long *pansori*, Korean talk-singing. The story of *Shim Chong*, a dutiful daughter who sacrifices her life for her blind father. On a tumultuous journey to a wild sea *Shim Chong* hurls herself from a boat, her head draped with her billowy *chima*, to save her father. Then, the sun finally tipped toward the west and still there was no sign of father. Mother sat still, plant-like, her eyes on the twig gate. The *pansori* went on, unyielding and sad, and the shadow of a persimmon tree drew longer and longer on the courtyard.

The young woman excused herself and disappeared into her room. Mother said she reminded her of another young woman she had known in Pusan. That was during the war. The woman lived with an American G.I. in the upstairs of an old Japanese-style house. Every evening, the G.I. would come home and put a record on his gramophone. Mother used to love that mellifluous sound of music that floated down to the quarter where she lived crammed with several families. It always made her momentarily forget the harsh life she was living in the midst of war. In fact the two most vivid memories she kept from her refugee days in Pusan was the gramophone music that laced the evenings and the fish smell the wind carried in from the sea.

One day, though, the G.I. learned he was being sent back home to America. The music suddenly ceased. The American man with the smiling face became a mean beast and started beating the young Korean woman. At night, as mother was in bed waiting for sleep in the dark, she would hear sudden, ear-piercing screams. Every time, it made mother's heart flutter with strange fear. She used to swallow down the fishy breeze to calm her palpitating heart. Sometimes, she would lie awake long after the screaming and crying stopped, unable to go to sleep. Then in the morning, mother would see the young woman and her bruised and swollen face. Mother couldn't bring herself to ask about the night, the beatings and screams and cries. This went on until the American sailed back home aboard a ship.

It was only after years had passed that mother could guess the reason the G.I. beat her. It must have been to sever the *jong* that had formed between them while they lived together. *Jong* is a feeling that bonds two people after a long passage of shared time. If love is fickle and erratic, *jong* is steadfast and dependable. Love is a tramp and *jong*, a loyal servant. One cannot sever the feeling of *jong* overnight. And often it's because of *jong* that a man and a woman stay together even after all the love is lost between them. That was why the American beat the young woman. To sever the *jong* between them. To spare her from the suffering. So she wouldn't long for him and yearn for him. It was a strange logic.

Mother told the story as if it were a perfectly proper subject for her nine-year-old child. The Pumpkin Wife had been right. A girl is never too young to know what it is all about. And after all, it was at the end of a summer when her children had been exposed to all sorts of things they shouldn't have been exposed to: adultery, betrayal, unrequited love and suicide.

The sky was turning into a vast magenta and purple curtain when the gate opened and, instead of father, a tall, freckle-faced American walked in. He was so young that his pink face still had baby fuzz all over. Mother stood up and sat down again. She felt dizzy at the smell of a Western man; after-shave and deodorant. (Later, my uncle returned from Vietnam to tell us how the Vietcong could sniff out American G.I.s from miles away because of the after-shave and deodorant they wore. He wondered if that was why America lost the Vietnam War.)

The G.I. playfully shooed away chickens loitering in the yard in his strange language. The young woman, now all made up, came out of her room laughing and the G.I. embraced the giggling girl in his extra-long arms, bushy with reddish hair. Mother didn't know why but she felt ashamed to stand there and watch the young woman tickle and paw at the young American boy like a cat.

We walked out of the twig gate and stood on the road. Mother didn't seem to be able to decide which way to go. She looked up and down the dusty road and at the rice paddies, burning gently in a golden blaze, stretching into the horizon. A dark American jogged by in his running pants and waved his hand at me. Mother and I laughed in the dust his feet kicked up. The dust smelled like a cinnamon stick.

"*Umma*. There's *apa*!" I shouted, pointing at a slender figure walking toward us through the phosphorous and dusty light of the setting sun. His skin was tanned brown by the country sun and his suit and shoes were filmed with red dust. (In this desolate countryside, father still dressed in a double-breasted suit, white shirt and tie.) Father came toward us, not hurrying, squinting his eyes and looking flustered. Without a word, mother resolutely turned around and walked away from him as if she had never intended to come and as if running away from the whole world. Mother had guessed that father was down on his luck from the rusting lock and rain-stained rice paper on the screen door of his room. And now the sight of him smothered even a smidgen of hope. It would have been better if she hadn't come.

Finally, father caught up with us and walked abreast in awkward silence. Mother didn't look at him. Not even once. She resolutely kept her eyes to the coming night in front of her. Finally, when father talked, it was to ask if we had been waiting long. Mother wouldn't answer. Father looked at me and I nodded, looking away. In my childishness, I felt disappointed. By then, I was mother's child. A flower nurtured by her care.

Father paused and wearily took out his cheap cigarette and placed it between his lips. Suddenly he was seeing his dust-covered suit and wrinkled shirt and mud-caked shoes. With his fingers he brushed his hair and shook the dust off his jacket and stood in despair with the cigarette burning in his mouth. He looked around in a futile search for a place to hide from his humiliating loss of face.

Father took us to a food stall in a corner of a shabby marketplace and ordered two bowls of noodle soup and pancakes for us and a green bottle of *soju* for him. He poured the drink into a small grease-filmed glass and emptied it at once. Then he poured himself another one and another one. When the food came out, mother didn't touch it. Father pushed all the food in front of me and urged me to eat. I slurped the noodle soup and father patted me on my head a little bit too long.

For a while mother just watched me eating and then asked father if he even knew his baby child had started school in the spring. And the house was gone. We even had to move to the back quarter at the new place. That wasn't all. The children had all been sick during the summer. Father sighed and said of course he knew all of her worries and troubles. How could he not? That was why he was running around day and night, trying to get his business going. His nights were sleepless. His mind, so full of worries. For a man, each day spent away from home and his family was a day wasted, he said.

Mother shook her head and looked at him in exasperation. He still knew how to talk his way out. He kept his tongue well oiled. Father laughed for the first time. It was a short guffaw that said: I know, I know. Not to worry about the house, he said reassuringly. If everything went well with his project, he would buy her an even bigger house. It was a promise. And he would see to it that the children got the best education in the world. That was what he lived for. For the children. Soon, buoyed by his own talk, father's mood picked up. His mind was again racing to the future. But it was the present that always held him back.

"What project?" mother asked skeptically. She could hardly believe there would be anything going on in this dusty nothing of a town.

"I don't blame you for being skeptical but there's a huge

development project going on not far from here. Finish your meal and I'll take you to look at the site yourself," father said, his words trailing off.

Later, mother and I made our way across the farm fields after father. The sky was sweeping purple and pink. Crickets were getting noisier in the bushes. We stood in the middle of tall summer weeds at the edge of a scallion field and saw a green hill cut through in half, showing an ugly scar of turned-up red soil. There was no sign of recent activities; only a mud-caked crane and a bulldozer idling in the fast fading sun. The dirt drying and cracking in the heat and dust. Mother could see father's developing project, his newest business venture, was going nowhere. One more day of an idling crane and a bulldozer costing him money. Mother didn't say a word and turned away.

Father wanted to walk us to the bus terminal but mother wouldn't let him. Before we left, father said he would be home soon, as if assuring himself rather than us. Then he peeled off several red mud-smeared bills and handed them to mother. He stood a little hunched as we walked away. When I looked back, he was still standing in the same spot. All alone with his loneliness.

It was fast getting dark as we walked. When we were far enough away from father, mother stopped in the middle of rice paddies and started sobbing. In this open country, she was trapped with no place to run. "*Umma*, please don't cry," I pleaded. "When I grow up, I will make you happy." Mother took my hand and looked down at me with a wan smile. "Don't worry. Your mother will never cry again," she said, and dried her eyes with her handkerchief.

◆   ◆   ◆

One night in October, father came home, tanned ever deeper and smelling of rice wine. He woke me up from sleep. In my drowsiness, I heard the voice that always seemed to come from the realm of hopes and promises. I stirred up from the bed, rubbing my sleepy eyes. Father eagerly said, "Look! Can you see what your father brought for his schoolgirl!" He impatiently tore open a box and pulled out a beautiful leather book bag with shoulder straps. Father proudly held it up for me. On its flap was embossed a Korean tiger and a lily inside an oval circle. The best kind money could buy. Father urged me to try it on. When I stood in front of him with the straps secured on my skinny shoulders, father's face broke into a big smile.

"See? Your *apa* didn't forget his baby girl," father said. He saw that I didn't believe him. "Tell your *apa* how many fingers there are," he said, spreading his fingers of his right hand. "Five. Right? If your *apa* bites each one of these five fingers, each one of them hurts. Just like that, your *apa* loves each of his children equally."

That night I slept with my book bag at my side. Dreaming, in the fragrant smell of the new leather, of the next morning when I would head for school with a new book bag.

In a matter of days, father was gone again like the monsoon that comes every summer with a sweeping wind and rain to ease the thirst of the parched earth. The beautiful leather book bag father had brought turned out to be too big and cumbersome for me to carry around. I went back to my cloth bag.

CHAPTER 6

WORKING MOTHER

Winter came and from Monday to Saturday, mother woke up at dawn while we children moaned and giggled through dreams. She hurried through the blue morning of the winter, adjusting the collar of her thin, wool coat against the chill. Each morning, the pang of leaving us children behind followed like her own shadow when she hurried toward the bus stop. The street that stretched ahead of her showed no way out — just another turn to another road to be walked and hurried down to reach nowhere.

After a grueling journey on two different buses across town, mother picked her way through icy streets and soiled mounds of snow to the gray cement building next to a lumber yard. She quickened her steps, no longer sad. She imagined us children rushing through breakfast and heading to our schools and felt proud of us. This job of hers paid her a small salary and gave her much humiliation. But each day, she went through it, putting on a brave face because she never wished us children to know the same humiliation. She gave a last push to her feet that were growing more numb with each step as she trod through frozen streets.

She passed through an iron grill gate and into the courtyard, out of breath and her throat feeling dry. She stopped briefly in the middle of the courtyard to catch her breath and couldn't help but smile at the sight of a stream of middle-aged women marching like children to a song that blared out from a speaker above the courtyard. The saccharin girlish chorus urged everybody to walk as it was a beautiful morning. Even when it was a cold and dreary morning, the cheerful song bombarded the courtyard.

Mother didn't know that right at that moment, her own children were marching to their classrooms across the school playground where the same cheerful song blared. The whole country was swept in the "New Village Movement." In the black and white news reels they showed at movie theaters before a movie, she'd see President Park cutting ribbons at the site of a new expressway project, breaking the ground with a shiny shovel at a new dam site and cutting rice in the rice paddies. The whole country was pushing forward and often the air seemed to throb with hope. Mother wasn't certain how she fit into this picture. Mother slowly climbed dark narrow steps to the third floor, feeling already exhausted.

All day, mother sat at a small desk stuck in a corner of the large and stuffy room and cut cloth samples in zigzag patterns with a pair of heavy pattern scissors. Each hour when the large clock on the wall struck like a gong in a temple, she thought of us children in school learning something and got down to her repetitious labor with renewed hope. She cut pattern after pattern, paying no attention to the women with kerchiefs on their heads who gossiped and laughed all day long as they worked by the noisy machines, that clicked and clacked in ceaseless motion, churning out wool cloth for men's suits.

At lunch time, mother joined the women at the long lunch table. She washed down cold rice with scalding hot barley tea. The women laughed and gossiped around her. When a bawdy joke was told, mother blushed like an innocent girl. Mother often felt as alone as an island among these women. She was an alien who by a strange twist of fate had ended up in a foreign land. Mother had come out in the world and found herself hopelessly prim and proper, incapable of breaking through the shell of her early upbringing. Each day, she was hurt, appalled, repelled and yet fascinated by the world she encountered outside home.

We children saw quickly how desolate and cold home was without mother. In the afternoon, we returned from school hoping against hope that somehow mother would be waiting for us at the gate. Every time, we were disappointed. We would push the gate open and rush in calling out, "*Umma*, we're home!" But there would be no answer from her. We missed mother's festive welcome. Her ringing voice. Her warm, comforting presence.

We picked up the coins mother left in the morning for us on top of the dish cabinet. For the rest of the afternoon, we roamed the streets like lost sheep. After all our friends went home for dinner, we walked up and down the plunging steps shivering in the cold, our purple and blue hands in our coat pockets, past the snow-packed slopes, sniffling through half-frozen noses.

"Are you hungry?" brother would ask me whenever we turned the corner to the comic book store.

"No," I would answer, shaking my head, although I longed for hot fish soup and a steaming bowl of rice.

"I am," brother would say as if he were disappointed with my less than honest answer.

"I am too. But not much." Then I would hand him my coins. Together we walked into the comic book store where they sold hot soup with fish balls. We sat side by side on the hard wood bench and drank our soup, feeling our frozen limbs melt in the warmth of the furnace.

Then through the darkening street, we would rush to the bus stop, worrying that we might have already missed mother. We were no longer cold but happy. We would pass stores decorated with Santa Claus cutouts with snow-white bushy brows and cottony beards and a record store playing Christmas carols that hurried people unintentionally. All winter, we would hurry down the same street, often through a pulpy mess of melting snow, to wait for mother at the bus stop.

We always planted ourselves outside the display window of a jewelry store where the store lights formed a little pool of golden mist. Mother would be able to see us right away. As we waited patiently, one smoke-belching bus after another would come to a lurching stop and spit out a crowd. In the fast-scattering crowd, we would search for mother's face in vain. It would get dark and colder and the toes inside our frozen shoes would grow numb. Then, always like a miracle, we would spot mother's face among the bobbing heads coming off a bus. We would leap toward her and grab her arms. Both of us taking mother's hand, we then headed home.

On the way, we would pass a bakery where they sold hot red bean cakes with crushed walnuts inside. We would look up at mother with pleading eyes. Every time, mother found her resolve melt away fast like snow in the sun. Mother would relent and enter the bakery, feeling her purse inside her overcoat pocket. She always ended up spending the money meant for the week's vegetables and fish and walked the rest of the way home confused with happiness and worry.

At night, the happy glow would return home while mother cooked, washed dishes, ironed clothes and mended holes in our socks. We children argued and laughed in the safety of home. We did our homework and often raced to crowd around her to have her settle an argument or to report the events of the day. It was only after we children went to sleep, half finished with our homework, that mother lay unable to sleep. Her mind led her astray, back to each little event during the day at work.

When spring returned and school started again after the winter break, we no longer trod through the empty streets missing our absent mother. We were as free as wild ponies. Every afternoon when my class was over, I would hurry over and wait for brother outside his classroom. Then finally the last bell would ring out and brother would be one of the first boys stampeding out of his classroom. Together, we would rush to the comic bookstore around the school corner and spend the rest of the afternoon turning the pages of comic books. Or together, we would hike to the craggy hill where we could find lizards that made their home among the rocks and gather them in a bottle to release them later in sister's desk drawers. Or we would walk all the way to the street of our old blue gate house and visit the policeman's children. Often the Pumpkin Wife would treat us to dinner before she sent us away.

Brother's friends always teased him for taking his little sister in tow. Boys played only with boys. They couldn't understand why brother always brought his sister along. Why does your sister follow you around like a shadow? Couldn't your sister go play by herself? Ah, you must be a sissy! They hoped their teasing would shame him. It took them a while to accept that so and so's little sister went wherever and everywhere he went. So every afternoon, I would sit in a sunny corner of a street or a playground while brother and his friends pitched and rolled marbles into holes in the ground, whipped their crayon-colored tops into spins and kicked and chased shuttle cocks. They played until the last daylight was gone. Then into the darkness, their faces began to disappear one by one. Reluctantly, they gathered their things and brother was finally ready to go home. Proudly lugging his loot, brother pulled my cold hand into his chapped one. That was the happiest time of the day when I walked home with brother.

That spring, mother was summoned to school which forced her to miss a half day at work. Mother, looking demure in her polka-dot *hanbok*, sat in front of brother's teacher, Teacher Koo who had a big, bulbous red nose mapped with purple blood vessels. Mother was embarrassed for him as she sat across from the rosacea-afflicted nose that demanded and screamed for attention. Teacher Koo showed mother brother's textbooks and notebooks, every available margin filled dizzily with his drawings: mostly tanks, planes, guns and soldiers. (Every Wednesday evening, with the coupons he had won in one game or another, he would go to the comic bookstore to watch the much-waited latest episode of *Combat*, stirringly dubbed in Korean. Vic Morrow was his hero.) Mother apologized profusely to Teacher Koo. It was all her fault. This neglect of supervision. She promised him that she would be more vigilant from now on. Teacher Koo nodded in agreement. It made mother think that her ordeal was almost over. But Teacher Koo ceremoniously flipped to the back cover of one of brother's notebooks. Mother was staring at a drawing of Teacher Koo with his exaggerated "strawberry nose." Brother had him surrounded with a dozen "strawberry-nosed children," peeking out over his shoulder. Still, Teacher Koo had to admit brother was a talented drawer.

Brother gallantly moved on to other mischiefs. One sleepy afternoon, during a dictation test, I heard my name being whispered outside my classroom window. I looked out. Brother was crouched in the flower bed among cannas and gladioluses. I could see the round top of his closely cropped black hair bobbing among the leaves. He peeked at my paper — his head bobbed in and out of the window very fast — and pointed out my spelling mistakes. Every time I looked at him, he scratched his head, signaling that I had made yet another mistake. In the ensuing confusion of frantic erasing and rewriting, I was missing the rest of the lines my teacher was dictating! Soon, it was distracting the rest of the children around. They got up to look out the window to see where the whispering voice was coming from. You could see the children dangling out the window, their heads like so many bunched up coconuts.

The same spring, brother went on to launch my brief literary career. It was a story of a dog that dies from choking on a fish bone. I wrote down the story word for word as it effortlessly flew out of his mouth and took it to my class. I was profusely praised by my teacher and was chosen to represent my school at the upcoming national composition contest. Mother, unaware of our conspiracy, proudly took me to a shop and bought me a blouse printed with strawberries and a red skirt for the contest day.

I remember mother waving and wishing me good luck as we left the school yard. We followed our teacher to the Secret Garden, a palace ground of great beauty. (The Japanese had turned a part of the palace into a zoo to insult the Koreans, our teacher said.) I sat by a pond under a cherry tree in full blossom with writing paper and a sharpened pencil. It wasn't true what father had once told us: in the midst of natural beauty, any ordinary mortal soul couldn't help but become a great poet. Time flew. The cherry blossoms drifted down, their petals blushed in faintest pink. Birds of great color dipped to the pond where lotuses blossomed. But I couldn't think of anything to write: neither poetry nor prose.

Soon it was noon. I opened the lunch box and ate the *kimbab* mother had rolled for me with seaweed and rice and eggs that morning. For the rest of the afternoon, I forgot all about the contest and roamed around the ground watching monkeys and peacocks and hippopotamuses. When my teacher found me outside the peacock cage, it was too late for me to write anything coherent. I hurriedly wrote down a few messy, eraser-crossed lines about my ghost mother — father's first wife who was supposed to have died at childbirth — and handed it in.

A month later, when our principal announced the prize winners in front of the whole school, my name was naturally missing. Mother took it in stride but brother was very disappointed; his literary protégée had failed him miserably. But all too quickly we forgot the conspiracy and moved onto others.

CHAPTER 7

WAILING WOMEN

On a summer afternoon under the pelting sun, brother and I hurried after mother, spattering through the puddles left by a shower. We carried two little bundles mother had packed with our clothes, summer homework and books. The books we had read many times but mother didn't feel right to send us away without them.

Ahead of us, the steamy street throbbed and shifted as though in a mirage. And the buildings behind the gauzy curtain of thick mist were opaque shadows. We already missed our cool veranda floor in the shade and the cold pieces of watermelon we used to slurp lying on our stomach. But mother seemed determined to send us away.

We reached the intersection and clambered up the steps on one of the octopus legs of the "cloud bridge." In the middle of the overpass, mother stopped and pointed to the sky. We looked up and saw a huge rainbow arched over a hill that was giving way to matchbox houses with verandas and rusty rails. "Look!" mother said and happily declared that the rainbow was a good omen for our travel. Brother cocked his head and looked up at her. Wasn't mother sending us away because we had become bad? As a king would banish his disloyal subjects to remote places in the back country? And mother seemed glad that she was able to banish us with a good omen.

At the bus depot, mother took us inside the dusty depot store and bought us a bag of roasted peanuts, a pack of bubble gum and dried squid legs.

"Be good," mother said, releasing us from her hugging arms. Her voice broke a little. "And don't forget to go straight to Big Mother's home when you get off the bus." After brother, carrying my little bundle, I climbed onto the bus and took a seat by the window. I looked out at mother who stood alone on the steaming pot-holed tarmac. Mother squinted her eyes and craned her neck to catch a glimpse of our little faces through the dust-streaked window. She smiled and waved her hand. For a moment, she looked oddly unfamiliar. And we must have to her, too. Ready to fly away from her. Mother hurried over and tapped the bus window with her fingers. My heart leaped! But right at that moment, our bus rumbled and lurched out of the depot. We looked back: looking forlorn and with her arm still frozen in mid-air, mother stood in the swirl of black smoke.

The bus traveled fast, pulling back city streets and winding up sheets of landscape paintings. After hills, bridges, towns, farm fields and trees, the bus rolled into the terminal and disgorged passengers with crumpled clothes, bundles of luggage and fatigue.

As soon as we got off the stuffy bus, we no longer remembered mother's words though. We trotted after country women and men into a marketplace. Before long, brother and I were ambling along in the company of farmers, passing mounds of summer vegetables and fruit, sad cows and flapping chickens, yelping goats and steamy food stalls. Where a crowd gathered, brother and I pushed our heads through, craning our necks and poking our noses. We watched a pig being swapped for dried ginseng roots and a chicken for a poplin dress, cucumbers for a hand mirror, tomatoes for a jar of face cream.

The afternoon sunlight shifted over the soggy, straw-strewn market lanes. But we had become helpless captors of a medicine man who commanded a large, enthralled crowd around him. With a conductor's baton, he pounded at the propped up colored pictures of worm-infested intestines. As the sunlight glinted off the charts, the worms in the pictures seemed to wriggle. Those worms inside us were sucking away all the nutrition even as he spoke. He stirred up clouds of fear with his pebble-crunching voice. We would shrivel until we were just bones, he declared, unless we got rid of those worms. He personally knew a girl who almost died from worm-infestation. The girl complained to her mother of the stomach pain. Do you have children who sweat at night, toss and turn in their beds and even pace around the room like they are possessed? They are not possessed! He slowly surveyed the crowd. I tell you what happened to that little girl next. Slowly like a tree in a drought, her limbs shriveled away until they looked like dead twigs. And her tummy ballooned up and up like that of a pregnant woman. Ha! What did her ignorant mother do? Hoping to cure her daughter's illness, she squandered all her precious money on a *gut*! Invited a money-hungry shaman to her home. It kills me, he said pounding his chest, every time I hear things like that! If you love your children, don't go out and spend money on candies or clothes. Buy these little pills. You have never used your money so wisely before. Look, he pointed at a picture, when a doctor finally opened up the little girl's tummy, this is what he found inside. At least a hundred fattened worms packed together like a big ball! We shivered and gasped.

He then opened his tattered black vinyl bag and took out clear bottles holding various-sized ringworms and tapeworms in alcohol and passed them to the awe-struck crowd. The strangest excitement seized us. We eagerly waited for our turn to hold the bottles and examine them closely. But before we had our turn, he took the bottles away. They disappeared back into his vinyl bag. Disappointed, brother picked up our bundles and got up. It was time we headed for Big Mother's.

Then, at the rear edge of the marketplace where fortune-tellers read palms and moles and faces of country women who hadn't had much luck in life, we came to an old man with a straw hat, funny-looking glasses and a basket full of squirming puppies. The puppies had sad little faces and soft ears. Their fur, light and dark brown. We squatted next to the puppies and forgot the afternoon flowing by. The old man laughed and said we could have all the puppies for two chickens. We had no chickens, brother told him. Ha, I could see that, he said. Farmers stopped on the way to their villages and asked the old man how much he wanted for the puppies. Two chickens, he replied, holding up his gnarled fingers. Two chickens for three puppies. They shook their heads and went away. When all the farmers left, leaving empty stalls and drunken men, the old man got up with his puppies in the basket.

The old man went his way with his puppies, yapping and whining. We went our way through the rice paddies. Brother picked up a tree branch, tied our bundles at each end and carried it across his shoulders like a night soil collector. As we walked, the sky sank lower and lower and, before we went far, rain blew in as thick as bamboo sticks. We slipped through the muddy lanes along the water canals. The bundles mother had packed for us turned fast into a shapeless mess like sacks of mashed potatoes. Brother carried them like a martyr, his skinny shoulders pressed down by the weight.

"Hurry up, we are almost there," brother yelled at me, chugging along behind him. "You see the chestnut field over there?" he asked, pointing at a dark amber mass ahead. "After that, it's as easy as eating a rice cake lying down." I looked at the crouching forest once and got scared. "Don't be scared. I've walked through it before. Just stay close next to me if you don't want to be bitten by a snake. I can hear snakes miles away," he said boastfully.

"Are you ready?" brother yelled at the edge of the chestnut field. He tossed the tree branch away and went ahead into the forest, dragging the bundles. I followed him, holding my breath. The wet leaves sagged mournfully under my feet. As I pushed through the dark space, each strand of hair stood up on my skull as stiff as a needle. Somewhere a wet branch fell with a dull thud and birds flapped away. We paused and pricked up our ears. Like rabbits. We were now standing in the middle of the forest without guideposts or a trace of a footpath.

I was no longer scared, though. The forest was soft and gentle and fermenting. The crisscross of branches formed a looping canopy over us. The dripping rain hooted like mischievous horned goblins who made their homes in forests. Any minute, I expected to hear the sound of their magic clubs banging with "thump," "thump," as they commanded: "Come out silver! Come out gold!" Those horned goblins were known to play tricks on adults but were friendly to children. If I were to meet those horned goblins, I was ready to ask for two chickens or better for the little puppies in the old man's basket. Or who knew if we might just come across wise-cracking hares who came there for fallen nuts? Or suddenly find ourselves standing in front of the beautiful house where an old witch was said to entertain stranded travelers with old tales and delicacies that human tongues had rarely tasted before. The possibilities seemed limitless. I could forever roam through the forest, eating the nuts and sleeping with the leaves as cover.

Brother pointed toward the blue and gray light that shifted in between the chestnut tree trunks. He said all we had to do was to walk toward the light. He walked kicking the wet leaves, chasing the light and singing. I was sure all the noises he made scared off any goblins, wise-cracking hares and the witch.

"After the chestnut field, it's as easy as eating a rice cake lying down," brother had said. But after the chestnut field we stood in front of a roaring river. The little stream that ordinarily flowed gently like liquid marble around the bend of the chestnut field had turned into an angry river. We stood staring at the muddy river tumbling down, cascading and spinning. We had heard where water made a swirl, there waited a water ghost with a snatching hand. Waiting for its sacrifice. So it wasn't the water we were afraid of but the ghost's snatching hand. Brother looked at the sky quickly disappearing into the darkness of colorless dusk and sighed like an adult.

"Wait here," brother said and with a stick he went down the bank, holding on to the wet summer weeds. Cautiously, he pushed the stick into the tide. Immediately, the river yanked away the stick like an angry mother snatching a toy away from a bad child. Brother scratched his head and looked at me with a sheepish look. He swallowed the wet air filling his lungs and this time pushed his skinny leg into the stream. He quickly lost his balance. His arms went up and he yelped, "*Aiigo!*" Soon, brother was being swept fast down the stream! His flailing arms looked as though he was frantically waving good-bye. I quickly covered my eyes with my hands. When I pulled my hands away, there was no trace of him in the muddy water plunging down fast to nowhere. All that was left were the soggy bundles lying in the puddle.

I remembered the story of a disobedient green frog who buried his mother by the river bend obeying her last wish. Alas! But the mother frog had expected her disobedient son would bury her on the mountain instead, because he had always done the opposite of her wishes. So, when the rain came, the mother frog's grave was washed away and the green frog cried by the river bend, "*gaegol*" "*gaegol*" for everybody to hear. What was the lesson of the story? Never bury your mother by the river bend? Or be a good child and listen to your mother while she's alive? I started crying, competing with the roar of the river. Then I saw a village man returning from his field. He hurried over.

"*Tzt! Tzt!*" he clucked his tongue when I told him about brother who had disappeared down the stream. He looked at the noisy river and said, "Every summer in the rainy season, it swallows up a boy," he said, not without satisfaction. Better a city boy than one of their own. He squatted down lowering the A-frame on his back. I climbed onto it and sat perched like a bird. He stood up, took off his white rubber shoes and waded into the river with his strong, muscled legs. All around us, brown wavy water tumbled down, roaring and roaring. With my eyes shut, I clung desperately to his wet A-frame. When he came out at the other side of the river, he cleared his throat and carried me all the way to Big Mother's house.

The villager pushed through the wet gate, calling out to Big Mother. All our relatives — Big Mother, three cousins and a cousin's wife — ran out. The villager put me down and explained dramatically what had happened at the river as if he had witnessed it himself. The women immediately fell to their knees, wailing. Their wailing so wrenching and beautiful, it would churn any listener's stomach.

"*Aiigo! Aiigo!*" Big Mother bellowed. "*Aiigo! Aiigo!*" Big Sister and female cousins followed in unison. "How can we face your parents again! They will blame it on us." Big Mother pulled my hands, wailing. I joined the wailing women. Our wailing sound spread through the rainy dusk as a haunting melody. Big Brother, Big Mother's son, and the villager stood shaking their heads, mumbling and dry-coughing.

Suddenly, the women stopped wailing all at once and looked toward the gate. A rain soaked man walked in carrying brother in his arms like a prize. Brother lay slumped unconscious, his water-filled belly mountainous.

"Ha! In my fifty-year life, I have never pulled out a boy from a river!" he said proudly. "Not an ordinary day for an old man like me!" He put brother down on the floor and Big Brother knelt over and worked on brother's swollen belly with his palms. Brother spat out gulps of water like a spastic rabbit and Big Mother clapped her hands and the cousins cheered him on. Gradually his belly plummeted and through his purple lips, a loud cry shot out.

Big Mother gathered him in her arms and triumphantly carried him into the room. "What havoc you city children are causing!" Big Mother said, not too unhappily.

◆   ◆   ◆

"Mother, your grandchildren are here from Seoul," Big Mother shouted at grandmother who sat on a silk futon looking as ephemeral as a wisp of cloud. Grandmother was a fine-brushed still portrait in a scroll painting, fading ever so slowly with age. Her fine silver-white strands, swept back in a traditional *chok*, gleamed like metal as did her eyes that could not see.

"Go closer," Big Mother commanded pushing us toward grandmother. We moved reluctantly, a little scared at the sight of her bullet-grazed eyes, an inch forward and a half inch back. Then startling us, grandmother's small face poked out from the dark and we saw how father shared her beautiful high-cheekbones and oval face.

"You better be happy your grandson's alive. He almost became a river ghost on the way," Big Mother said, smacking brother's shoulder.

"What, my grandson became a river ghost?" grandmother asked, turning her half-deaf ears.

"Never mind, *uhmoni*. Ghosts or no ghosts, here they are in front of you," Big Mother shouted again.

"*Onya. Onya.* You don't have to shout. I can hear fine. Let me see how big they have grown," grandmother said, holding out her tiny hands. Brother pressed his eyes tightly as if swallowing a bitter medicine and let grandmother's small hands grope him all over. "Such a strong arm!" she said, rubbing and squeezing his skinny arm. "A head general," caressing his big head. Then she cackled, creasing her small nose. "Now where's my grand-daughter?" she asked.

"Don't be afraid," Big Mother said, pushing me again toward grandmother. "She's your grandmother. You share her flesh and blood." I moved with my knees and sat shuddering as grandmother's ancient hands groped and poked and patted and rubbed.

"Your grandmother was a famous beauty when she was young," Big Mother said reassuringly, shouting out each word so that grandmother would hear her compliment, too.

"What are you telling my grandchildren?" grandmother asked, widening her gray pupils as a cat would in the dark.

"I was telling them what a beauty you were in your younger days!" Big Mother said, shaking her head.

"Oh, I know. It's true; I see nothing but shadow lines," grandmother said and laughed. "And I am almost deaf, too. But that's no excuse for you to make up stories and to shout at me."

"Never mind, *uhmoni*. I'm leaving you with your grandchildren," Big Mother said and got up.

"Now you may leave me alone with my grandchildren," grandmother hooted, waving her hand. Then grandmother pulled down her gray silk tobacco pouch from the wall. After much groping, her hand produced a couple of honey-colored cinnamon candies from the pouch. We immediately put them inside our mouths. The candy had a tangy taste of cinnamon and tobacco leaves. We sat in front of our blind grandmother and busily rolled our tongues, separating tobacco leaves stuck on them and slurping as loudly as we could to indicate how we enjoyed her candies. Grandmother laughed happily, her bullet-grazed pupils staring nowhere.

Grandmother continued to dispense two cinnamon candies out of her tobacco pouch each morning. No more, no less. I wondered where the candies came from. Every night, her tobacco pouch was filled with new candies while we slept. She probably had a magic wand as mother used to.

"Now let me have my pipe," she would say after dispensing the candies. Brother and I would take turns and fill the tobacco leaves into her long bamboo pipe, packing them with thumbs. When it was all ready, she would tap it a couple of times on the rim of her bronze furnace and suck it like a fish with her little mouth while brother held up a match for her. Then out of her mouth, floated out and up three perfect rings. Bubbles out of a fish mouth. They were so perfectly round, we could almost hook them with our fingers. We called it "chasing a dragon" because when the three perfect rings disintegrated and floated away, they looked like ascending dragons.

Then for the rest of the day, until Big Mother and the cousins returned from the field, grandmother, blind and half-deaf, stayed home alone with a barking dog. We children spent the day picking wild berries on the hills, or dog-paddling or chasing fish in the stream.

Sometime in the afternoon, we'd return home with crushed wild berries in our pockets or rice paddy locusts for the dog and find grandmother alone inside the *anbang*, inner room. Sitting still on her silk futon, her little, slender frame just a shadow. Often looking like an emaciated Buddha reaching Nirvana, with her silver hair on fire in the sunlight that filtered through the rice-papered door. In her hand, she always held a *yum-joo*, a Buddhist rosary. With her fingers, she pushed the prayer beads around and around, one at a time, counting one hundred and eight, the number of evil lusts of the flesh. Counting the beads, we learned, was her way of gaining merit, of getting rid of desires, of stilling her suffering, of severing the ties of the flesh, and of bringing the unresolved past to a resolve. A meditation. The way of Zen.

If our grandmother back in Seoul waited for such a great phenomenon like the Second Advent of Christ, our grandmother at the farm waited only for news of her son, father's older brother, our Big Father. It was a long time to wait for someone. As it was in 1943 when grandmother had last seen him being taken away by the Japanese. She still didn't know his fate and for that she still suffered.

Big Father was only twenty-eight years old when the Japanese had taken him away. He was already a husband and father of one boy and two girls. He was also grandmother's number one son who was responsible for the ancestor worship and the tending of the graves.

It was right after the harvest. A beautiful autumn day with the river blue sky and crackling sunlight. Big Father was one of a dozen or so village men the Japanese took away that day. Grandmother still couldn't believe how all she could do was watch. The Japanese didn't even let them hand him the bundle they had hastily packed. She stood helplessly with weeping Big Mother and her children and watched him get smaller and smaller through the rice paddies. In the sunlight, the white of Big Father's clothes seemed to shimmer and seared her eyes to tears. The memory of that day never faded. It made grandmother its prisoner.

Grandmother didn't know she would never see him again. Without Big Father, time passed ever so slowly. The autumn turned into winter. Winter into spring. So on. Until the year the Japanese lost the war. Grandmother eagerly waited for her son. Her neck stretched a mile like that of a crane. Trickle by trickle, other men returned home ravaged but alive. But her son never returned. He became one of those countless lost people. Neither living nor dead.

Her suffering was such that grandmother eventually lost her sight and went blind. So it wasn't true that a grazing bullet had taken her sight during the Korean War. Anyway, after she went blind, the world around her was like a black cloud. Floating and shifting. All she could see from then on was the past. It came back to her, rushing in living colors and forms and lights and sounds and grew even brighter, clearer, sharper and louder as time went on. The past claimed her like an old master with proof of an uncleared debt and never let her go.

It was now only in dreams grandmother got to meet her son.

But in the dreams, Big Father always appeared as a man without a face. It was a sign of anonymous death. Of a wandering spirit. He had met a man's worst fate. To die away from home and become a forever hovering ghost. Even a little bird returns home when it's time to die.

In Grandmother's ceaseless dreams, Big Father, faceless and voiceless, always stood at the other side of the milky way, the Silvery River, where grandmother suspected the dead dwelled. Grandmother and her number one son, separated across the Silvery River, unable to hear each other or touch each other. Our hearts went out to her. Obviously, grandmother hadn't the luck of Kyon-u, the herder, and Jik-nyo, the weaver. At least once every year, on the seventh day of the seventh moon, Kyon-u and Jik-nyo were reunited. Perhaps, the magpies and crows who gladly lay themselves across the Silvery River for the lovers' reunion, didn't find grandmother's story sympathetic enough. Grandmother cried and wailed in her dreams without a voice or tears. Her tear ducts had long since gone dry. Perhaps, it was true, the story of a grazing bullet. It had sealed her tear ducts off. Without tears, grandmother had no proof of her sorrow to show. Magpies couldn't hear her silent cries, either. So grandmother was just one of the million separated lovers, husbands and wives, mothers and children who crowded across the Silvery River in her dreams. Her story none sadder than the others.

It was just as well that only Kyon-u and Jik-nyo got to cross the Silvery River. Their tears of joy and sadness come down to earth as sweet rain. Just an adequate amount to soak the parched soil and wet thirsty paddies for the joyful harvest. The tears of the lovers put nutritious food on the tables. That was the irony of life.

We asked grandmother: if all these separated people got to cross the bridge once a year and cried all at the same time, in joy, wouldn't the whole of Korea be flooded and disappear? Then, in that flood, there would be more people separated from their loved ones. And just imagine, what a mob they would create fighting to cross the Silvery River once a year. Poor magpies and crows. They would return all featherless after enduring a million stampeding feet! Grandmother agreed it was a good speculation and sucked on her bamboo pipe. Her city-born grandchildren were smart.

So in her nightly dreams, grandmother never got to cross the Silvery River to meet Big Brother. But she knew her day would come. She lived and waited for the day. The day when she would close her eyes for the last time and in her last journey, she would cross the Silvery River to join Big Father on the other side.

Finally.

CHAPTER 8

BRIGHT BIJOU

Big Mother's baby daughter, no longer a baby, had a beautiful name and just that. Her beautiful name, Young-ok (Bright Bijou) never fooled anyone. She had the long narrow face of a horse and the eyes of a frisky monkey. Her skinny limbs were too long and her supple feet were too broad. That summer we spent at Big Mother's home, we often heard Big Mother call her "a thorn in the eye." Big Mother's husband, Big Father, was a good-looking man. "As good-looking as your father and taller," Big Mother didn't forget to tell us. "And as graceful as him if not more."

So where did she come from? Young-ok couldn't wash dishes without jangling them with her clumsy hands and couldn't walk by haystacks without causing them to topple with her striding feet. Big Mother worried and fretted: it was said girls at her age bloomed like an opening lotus rising out of the mud under the beaming moon but Young-ok had none of that blooming beauty about her. What man would marry her?

But Big Mother had never encouraged Bright Bijou to be anything but a plain farm girl and that was what she was. A simple plain farm girl. She carried herself as empty as the blank sky. Her mind flowed like nature from season to season without a flicker of turmoil or confusion. Big Mother often warned her: life at the farm was too busy to hone thoughts or tend to complicated emotions. Too much thought always disturbed farm girls and then they wanted to be somebody else. Girls with too many thoughts would look beyond the rice paddies and cucumber fields to a world where they didn't belong.

There had been girls who had dared to look beyond the farm fields. Big Mother knew what had happened to them. One still looked like a child when she went out to a city where she met a smooth-talker and got into a heap of trouble. She came back home one winter to give birth to a fatherless child. Still, she was prettier than Bright Bijou. Had the skin of a city girl. As pale as a pear blossom. The only kind of trouble Big Mother expected her daughter to cause was an occasional mishap: breaking a dish or two or forgetting to close the latch to the chicken coop. The kind of troubles that could be easily mended.

♦   ♦   ♦

A day at the farm started with the first belching cry of a rooster that cracked the dawn in half. It was then Young-ok reluctantly would pull herself out of bed. In sleep, we often heard her outside the back door of our room, slowly making her way to the chicken coop, grumbling and shuffling her feet. Then with a loud clank, she would unlatch the hook to the chicken coop. Right away, a commotion erupted: the chickens flapped and squawked as they scattered away from her. Protesting hens she ignored and gathered the newly laid eggs, warm and white and perfectly oval.

Afterwards Young-ok would return to the house, smelling like the inside of the chicken coop, feathers flying from her hair. "Wake up! Wake up! You lazy city cousins!" she squalled like an emissary of a rooster. Soon we were being marched out to the well, like two squirming puppies under her grabbing hands. Brother often managed to free himself of her pulling hand and run away. Each and every time, Young-ok eagerly chased him around the house, to the backyard, to the cow stead and to the chicken coop. There, laughing, she stomped around and triumphantly plucked him out from among the bellowing chickens and marched him back to the well.

"*Tzt! Tzt!* Just like a boy!" Big Mother would look out from the kitchen and cluck her tongue. Her mother's clucking tongue Young-ok would ignore and go on scrubbing us children with harsh homemade soap and a hemp cloth until our skin turned bright red. What a good start of the day we used to have!

Later in the early afternoon, exactly when the sun reached the top of a tall jujube tree, Young-ok loaded the fresh-cooked lunch into a wooden bin and set out for the fields. I would accompany her through the poplar-lined roads and rice paddies and across the stream. Carrying with me an aluminum kettle full of cooled barley tea, I would hurry after her. She walked ahead dancingly in big strides, whistling an old-fashioned love song. How perfectly Young-ok balanced the lunch bin on her head while her long arms dangled at her side! She even managed to turn her head to yell at a mangy dog trailing us from behind.

At night, after the dishes were done, Young-ok would join us on the mat spread in the courtyard. She helped Big Mother peel and slice the melons for pickles, grind dried potatoes in the stone drill or empty the insides of old pumpkins. She never once looked up at the star-freckled sky where a honey-colored moon hung. The floating melody of a distant bamboo flute that often laced the summer nights never inspired her. The hooting sounds of night birds stirred up no emotions inside her. She worked slowly without thoughts, yawning without covering her mouth. When the oil in the kerosene lamp had all but burnt and the flame started to flicker, Young-ok would succumb to her fatigue and stretch her arms.

◆ ◆ ◆

One night toward the middle of summer, the army brought a cinema to the village. In the evening, Young-ok and her sister, Young-mi (Bright Beauty), changed into their outing dresses — sleeveless poplin with floral patterns.

"Watch out for your sister," Big Mother warned Bright Bijou as they left for the clearing next to the chestnut field. Big Mother fancied her older daughter, Young-mi, a great beauty. All the eligible young men in the village — she counted six — were secretly dying to marry her. But Big Mother was holding off all the marriage offers. For now. In fear of losing out on a better one. But she knew: even the sweetest melon has its day. Got to be careful not to hold onto it a little too long. A ripe melon bruises easily and then it stinks. She constantly fretted.

It was a balmy summer night, pitch dark in some places and transparent dark blue at the edges of hills and the center of the sky. They walked to the clearing arm in arm, scaring themselves with tales of carnivorous tigers and foxes. They arrived at the clearing and joined the excited villagers outside the makeshift tent.

After a while, a young soldier came around to usher the villagers into the tent. Young-ok looked at the young man in a smart khaki uniform, lined as sharp as a blade. He had an exquisite face. A fine jaw, romantic eyes and a subtle smile that seemed to spill out from his mouth and soon disappear like a vapor. He was the very type of man Young-ok was supposed to shield her older sister from.

When their turn came, Young-ok boldly looked straight into the young man's eyes. She couldn't help herself. The young soldier's eyes were like two deep dark bottomless pools. They locked her eyes and pulled her into them. She was falling and falling. And floating and floating. So light. Like a willow leaf! The briefest second stretched on like forever. When her sister, Young-mi, saw Bright Bijou staring and staring at the young solider, alarmed, she pinched her baby sister's skinny arm sharp and pulled her away. Young-ok moved on reluctantly, blushing deeply although she had never been known to blush.

After that, she felt like a spelled chicken in a cock fight. She stared at the make-shift screen, creased by the breeze, carrying images of love, betrayal and revenge, but only saw what had been burned into her mind: the young solider's eyes.

Later, Young-ok walked back home through the moonlit country remembering nothing of the movie but a young man's penetrating gaze. She went a gawky, simple farm girl and returned a girl with a secret. She went without looking up at the sky speckled with so many stars and a velvet-smooth full moon and came home under the spell of them. She went with a heart that had never fluttered and came back with a strange ache in it.

After that night, Young-ok carried her secret with her wherever she went. In the morning, she climbed the hill behind the house to pick mushrooms and sat glued under a crooked pine as the beautiful country opened below like a painted folding fan in rising mist: rice paddies and the chestnut field against softly undulating hills. She sat bracing herself with her arms and trembling as if she was cold and hot at the same time. Her secret came tumbling loose and unleashed inside her the most hurting and pleasing feeling at the same time.

Baffled and tormented by these strange emotions, Young-ok wondered if this was what her mother was talking about; this strange emotion aroused by her secret was as dangerous as looking beyond the rice paddies. And this secret made her for the first time ashamed of her plainness. A plain girl didn't deserve to keep a secret or harbor a dangerous thought. Sometimes, she would take her hand and feel around her bony face. How did she look? She didn't know.

She would then notice that the mist below had all but scattered away and she would reluctantly get up. She could almost hear her mother grumbling about her delay. She hurriedly picked mushrooms in the shady feet of pines: Black Trumpets, Morels and Oysters. Often she would spot beautiful poisonous ones; huge orange, pink or red umbrellas with white dots. Poisonous like beautiful women, she would tell herself, as if that thought helped her any.

She dreaded it and longed for it, the shifting despair and elation that visited her out of the blue while she worked in the field or carried the lunch bin. Often on the way back from the field, she stopped and stared at the clearing by the chestnut field where the movie tent had been set up that night. There was no trace or proof of the brief strange romance there except a few grazing cows and heat-burned weeds. She then walked away from it, imagining herself traveling to the town where the army was stationed. If she passed by the barracks, she might just run into that mysterious soldier. But she knew she wouldn't know what to do next even if she did. She doubted the soldier would even remember her. Limited by her inexperience and ignorance, she was suspicious of what her intuition was dictating to her.

When pink dusk dyed the country in the evening, Young-ok went to the village well and instead of drawing water, she stared at the dancing image of herself reflected on the sloshing water at the bottom of the well. The broken image of her face swelled up and down. It was ugly. She hurried home, spilling water all over herself. She knew her sister-in-law always hid a small cloudy hand-mirror between her bedding. She sneaked it out and took a look at her face. The face in the mirror disappointed her. She sighed and put it back, never intending to take it out again. But over time, the face in the mirror would gradually fade away in her mind. It became a fuzzy-edged moon. A blurry smear. And she would feel an urge for one more look in the mirror. She remembered the way the young soldier had looked at her and how she had felt beautiful then. The next time she pulled out the mirror and looked into it, she might be able to grab that beauty that had eluded her scrutiny.

◆   ◆   ◆

"Kyung-a, my little cousin, could you keep a secret if I told you one?" Young-ok asked me the afternoon we walked home along the water canal that fed into the rice paddies. Young-ok steadied the lunch bin on her head and looked down at me with her bee-stung eye that had become just a slit on a mound. Young-ok waded into the dusty weeds on the side of the road. A locust jumped out and Young-ok slipped. The dirty dishes inside the bin jangled. Young-ok put down the bin and flopped down on the weeds.

"I'm going to tell you a secret and you have to promise me

that you won't tell anybody as long as you live," she said. I readily promised and we hooked our baby fingers and shook them. Young-ok pulled up a bunch of grass in her hand and loosened them into the breeze. It was as if words had been lodged in her throat and wouldn't come out. I couldn't imagine what secret she was about to tell me. I wondered if it was about the ghost mother. Or father's secret son. I thought she might know all about that.

Young-ok then started telling me about the young soldier she had met at the cinema. About the man who had locked her eyes so tightly that she still couldn't let go. I understood it was secret but not why. Young-ok and I raced home for the rest of the way like two flying geese; I, proud to be a secret keeper and Young-ok, giddy for having finally parted with her secret.

Young-ok pushed through the twig gate surprising the shaggy dog that brother was feeding with locusts. Young-ok quickly unloaded the dirty dishes in the kitchen and came out, laughing with her bee-stung eye and pulled me to the backyard. "Can you really keep it a secret?" she asked me in an excited whisper. I nodded my head vigorously, more than necessary.

Young-ok said nothing and went sprawling down on the mat in the shade of a pear tree. She lay motionless, her arms as pillows, staring at the blue sky. Breezes came and stirred her hair. In the bushes up on the hill, cicadas cried noisily. Then, very slowly, Young-ok raised herself and walked to the twig fence where Blue Sapphire Bells cascaded like a million stars. She cupped a flower — a perfect blue lantern enveloping a white stamen — between her fingers and snapped it. Then Young-ok pinned the flower behind her ear and tiptoed around in bare feet. Slowly first and then fast, she gyrated her feet on the mat, her arms stretched and her head turned to the sky. She faltered as the sky spun out of control. Giggling, Young-ok staggered toward the twig fence and stood in front of the cascading bell flowers.

Then with sudden savageness, she began snapping flower after flower. Between her thumb and forefinger, the purple blue lantern petals popped with soft explosions: "pop," "pop," "pop." The breeze died down and the shade shifted as Young-ok chased her demons, strewing the mat with crushed bell flowers. When there was not a single flower left to pop, Young-ok crumpled onto the straw mat. She was no longer smiling. Her eyes that Big Mother had accused of smiling too easily like a loose girl were now mismatched slits. And she had lost that fever and shiver — a shaman out of a trance — and she was again just the plain farm girl everybody expected her to be.

◆　◆　◆

The next summer, brother and I returned to the farm, taller and skinnier and city pale. We traveled on a rickety bus that carried boisterous farmers returning from the town drunk and happy. A jolly woman propped me on her lap and when the bus reached Big Mother's village, hurried us off the bus with a belly laugh and waving.

Young-ok was waiting for us at the village's tutelar tree, a five-hundred-year-old oak worshipped by shamans and sterile women. Young-ok strolled toward us, smiling with her eyes and pulling a curl of hair. It had been cut short and permed in a mass of ringlets. They sat on top of her long bony face like a lamb's wool hat. But she was still the same plain country girl with flat chest, horsey teeth and giggles. She led us through the front yards of farm houses, carrying our bundles.

"I hope you city kids are hungry. Big Mother made pumpkin

porridge for you. And Big Sister's pregnant. She throws up every morning and sends me out to town for dried persimmons and pig feet," Young-ok said, rolling her eyes.

As soon as we entered the gate, with great festivity Big Mother ushered us to grandmother's room as if she had been waiting the whole year for that.

"I'm fluttering away like a butterfly at the end of a summer day," grandmother said, after groping our limbs and faces and after dispensing two candies from her tobacco pouch.

The summer went by just like the previous summer. We swam in the stream, caught locusts and dragon flies, hunted for eggs laid by Korean crow tits in the rice paddies, witnessed vultures sweep down and snatch away chickens, chased a loosened bull across the fields, and witnessed a village boy climb up a jujube tree and catch a stork from its nest. We often accompanied the women from village to village for birthday and marriage and funeral feasts where we sneaked sips of rice wine and returned home drunk with the merry women. We never once thought of mother.

At night, we sat out in the garden on the same straw mat and read books taken out from the village library. Just like the previous summer, there were a million stars embedded in the sky and from the hill came howling sounds of foxes and soft hooting sounds of night owls. Young-ok sat next to us, opening the pumpkin seeds. Under the frisky curls, her tanned face registered only the simplest of emotions. Her secret had faded away like a distant star and the promise she had me keep was forgotten as well. She missed her sister, Bright Beauty, who had married that spring and gone away. She was already pregnant and everyone wished for a boy. When she had her baby, Young-ok hoped to go see her and the baby. And her new brother-in-law, the man Bright Beauty married, was a village official, skinny as a bamboo stick. She said this and that and then started dozing.

When the summer was half over, an old woman, a matchmaker, began coming around with small, black and white snapshots of men. Each time she tottered in through the twig gate, Young-ok would grab my hand and run to the backyard where the summer before she had popped open and crushed all the bell flowers. She would wait there as she was expected to, until the old woman left with the snapshots of mystery men, black and white, corners rounded by so many fingers.

Big Mother pored through those finger-smudged pictures as if picking up a secret or two, but she could never tell anything from one picture or another. She picked up no clues from them. Timid and half-suspicious, Big Mother wavered like a willow tree. Young-ok saw none of those pictures. She knew nothing about men. All she had experienced was the locking of eyes with the young soldier. Those eyes no longer brought her shudders and ache. Now she even suspected that the eyes were of a demon's that once so clouded her head and confused her mind.

At dinner time, Big Mother described each and every prospective groom she had seen in the worn pictures the matchmaker had brought. She confused the details and family names. She exaggerated bad points and good points. Big Mother basked in the glory of deciding her child's future. She might have been blind to let her son marry that stocky, stubborn girl who was now her daughter-in-law but this time she was determined to do it right. She knew she had not much negotiating power. A mother of a plain farm girl got as much attention and respect as a stray dog. In fact, each time she took out a new picture of a man, the matchmaker always told Big Mother, "Choose a man who's equal with her. Simple and humble. Why would a handsome, educated and rich man look for a farm girl? It would spell trouble, if he did. Something wrong with him." Big Mother couldn't agree more. She wished for only one simple good man for Young-ok.

◆   ◆   ◆

Shivering with fever and prodded by rain, I clung to Young-ok's bony back, slipping up and down as she struggled through the flooded country, soaked and drenched to the bone. The ringlets of her permed hair streamed down her face, dripping rain. Field after field of corn stalks and bright green vegetables smudged and blurred and we made slow progress; fifteen *ri* of walk ahead. Young-ok prodded me, trembling and moaning on her back. She hummed through the rain.

"*Kyung-a. Kyung-a. My little cousin. Did you swallow the bad soul of a water ghost? Be frank but don't be cranky. You have a bad fever but not hay fever,*" Young-ok sang. "*Kyung-a. Kyung-a. The brave one, my little cousin. Be ready for the doctor's magic needle. That will sting but not stink. Be ready for the sting of doctor's magic needle.*"

Big Mother had grumbled when she put me on Young-ok's back. The sky had sprung a leak. Rain day after day. Too old to take me to the doctor herself in this rain. Already lost several nights' sleep escorting the child back and forth to the outhouse. Take her to the doctor. He will give her a shot. Afraid she might die on us. Don't want to take the blame.

By the time Young-ok traveled through two small villages and hills and streams and rice paddies, I had become a shriveled growth on her hard back, barely glued. I heard Young-ok huffing and puffing through the rain. Her bony back became harder and harder.

Young-ok pushed through the door to the doctor's office. She carried her half-dead cousin in her arms and asked to see the doctor right away. She forgot her soaked clothes and dripping hair and carried her cousin into the doctor's room. There, she put her cousin down on the table and let loose a sigh of relief.

Young-ok stood in the stuffy room, out of breath and exhausted from all that walk in the rain. When the doctor — a round man with a slightly balding head — came in, Young-ok greeted him in mumbling words and anxiously waited for the doctor's magic needle to appear. She imagined a doctor always carried a magic needle in hand. Ready to stab the behind of any sick person who walked into his office.

It was only seconds later that she saw the doctor's roaming eyes follow the contour of her body through her rain-soaked poplin dress and rest on her breasts. Young-ok followed his eyes and saw her small breasts sticking up under the blouse, dark circles and nipples for the whole world to see. She blushed, dyeing her cheeks persimmon red and put her arms across her chest that was pit-patting away.

That was the second time Young-ok had experienced a man's wicked eyes. Eyes that could shake her to the roots and make her ashamed. Later, Young-ok returned home through the muddy field, mindlessly pushing her dirtied feet in rubber thongs, flipping and flapping. She had half-forgotten her cousin on her back, sound asleep. She felt like she now knew something about men. The doctor's roaming eyes brought no pangs and aches like the young soldier's. Just a little stirring and murmur and shame. She felt violated and yet felt like a woman. A woman who knew all the goings-on, shameful or not shameful. Things that she expected to happen only in the world she would enter with her marriage. She felt a letdown. She had a hunch the world she would enter would be a harsh one. No romantic fluttering of hearts she expected. She expected a stony husband and suckling children and the unkind words of in-laws. That was how life had been for every country woman. All she could do was ready herself.

◆   ◆   ◆

The matchmaker returned at the end of the summer. Her words were, "He's a very nice man. I wouldn't say this if I didn't know for sure." She unwrapped a picture of a man from her yellowing white cotton handkerchief and pushed it under Big Mother's nose. Big Mother examined the broad forehead and the calm eyes and convinced herself that the man in the thumb-sized picture was nicer than the other ones. The kind who would pay attention to family. The kind who would be satisfied with his wife and who wouldn't lust after another woman. The kind who wouldn't drink too much or entertain grandiose thoughts. A simple farmer who would faithfully worship his ancestor ghosts, respect his elders and cherish his wife and children with calm indifference as a respectful man should.

"He's the only son from an old *yangban* family," the matchmaker said.

"An old *yangban* family doesn't feed rice into mouths. I know, we used to be *yangban*," Big Mother rebuked to gain some leverage.

"But you will like to hear this. Besides his mother, he's got just two younger sisters. Your daughter doesn't have to work hard. And the mother is all any girl would hope for in a mother-in-law. You marry your daughter to this family, you won't regret it," she said matter-of-factly. Big Mother asked to keep the picture and showed it to anyone she could find and asked for an opinion.

Young-ok saw the picture herself and felt nothing. No emotions or fluttering of heart. When Young-ok half-heartedly wondered whether he was a tall man, Big Mother said, "You saw his nose and eyes and mouth are where they should be. What would you do with a tall man?"

The old lady took with her Young-ok's birth date and time and her one and only snapshot. Big Mother consulted male relatives, old books and a fortune-teller and picked a wedding date. Young-ok vaguely looked forward to the marriage, just a little more than she would look forward to a New Year or a trip to town. But not much more.

After the harvest and full moon festival, Young-ok had her first egg pack on her tanned face, got the same advice Big Mother had gotten from her own mother three decades earlier, wrapped and unwrapped the silk cloths — presents from the groom's family — to show the villagers who streamed in with insatiable curiosity. Some suggested the silks were of cheap quality. They said the cloth had the unnatural shine of fake silk. Some even suggested they were not silks at all. But nobody could do anything about it. A present once accepted was a present that could never be returned.

◆ ◆ ◆

At dawn on her wedding day, Young-ok woke up for the last time in her room at the rooster's cry and sobbed at the sentimental thought of leaving home. When the sun floated up and brightened the screen door of the bridal room, women relatives put bridal make-up on Young-ok's plain powdered face: three red dots, one on the forehead and one on each cheek, and helped her put on her flowering wedding gown and a head coronet piece.

Sitting stiffly, Young-ok looked around the bridal room decorated for the wedding night, with lanterns and silk beds and pillows embroidered with a pair of mandarin ducks and folding screens depicting the ten symbols of long life. Young-ok felt a little smile sneak onto her face: for the first time she felt almost proud to be a girl. She couldn't remember when all this attention was paid to her and she was the reason for a feast. She listened to all the commotion going on outside. The voices of congratulations, teasing and laughing. She felt so happy that she worried she might burst into giggles during the ceremony or get caught smiling with her eyes. The villagers would gossip for days!

From then on time passed excruciatingly slowly. Slower than the most monotonous summer day out in the hot field. Her legs were going to sleep and she felt confined in the wedding gown. Her thoughts raced to that night when she would be left alone with the bridegroom, a stranger she had never met. She shuddered with fear. The mystery was almost too much to bear.

Then, as if she'd lost her hearing, everything went absolutely dead outside. As if the world ended in the midst of all the bustle and fuss. She thought she had heard a woman gasp before all the noises ceased. It was so quiet that she could hear the batting wings of a swallow miles away on its migration to the south. Young-ok wondered what had happened. But nobody came in to tell her what it was. Gradually, the noises came alive again outside but they had a different mood and tone.

Young-ok fidgeted and fidgeted to free her sleeping legs under her ample gown. The screen door slid open and Big Mother entered, with her eyes cast down. Her mouth that had not closed for almost a week was drawn tight. Big Mother tumbled down and adjusted her daughter's wedding gown, sniffling away as if she had a runny nose. Young-ok was touched by her mother's sadness: it had just hit her mother that she was giving away her daughter. Young-ok felt like comforting her but she remained silent lest her mother indulge in a full-blown wailing.

Young-ok felt her mind go blank when she was helped out to

the wedding court. She stood still in front of the ceremony table, across from the bridegroom. She stood, her head lowered, without any idea that the bridegroom who had come bearing a wooden goose as a sign of marriage fidelity was much older than in the picture and walked with a limp. She stood without an inkling that beneath his blue wedding garb, he hid a leg deformed from childhood polio. She stood in front of him, her arms raised inside the cascading sleeves and her eyes cast on the broom-swept ground where the traces of broom still remained. She stood surrounded with many symbols of marital happiness and blessings: the red and blue threads on the bamboo lantern — the coming together of Yin and Yang, of a woman and a man; soy beans and red beans for many children to come; chestnuts and dates for sons to carry on the family name.

When night drew up at the end of the wedding day, there was only silence. Outside the bridal room, there was no gathering of giggling women. No wet fingers perforating holes in the rice paper door to the bridal room. No jostling for position to peep through the holes. No roaring laughter in the guest room where the male relatives gathered for marriage wine. The pale crescent moon crawled up and across the sky. Somebody started playing a bamboo flute. The notes threaded the night in long trembling waves.

The next morning, Young-ok emerged from the bridal room, her eyes puffy and dressed in her bridal dress; yellow *jeogori* and red *chima*. Young-ok stood on the veranda floor and surveyed the forlorn compound where the wedding had taken place only the day before. Her life had turned an irreversible corner. A day had changed everything. Young-ok decided to leave for her new home that very morning instead of spending the traditional three nights in the bridal room.

After a half-eaten breakfast, following her limping husband,

Young-ok left carrying her meager belongings. Young-ok resolutely passed through the twig gate, her swollen eyes looking at no one, leaving her wailing mother and sad family behind.

The women relatives who had spent the night comforting Big Mother trailed silent Young-ok to the opening of the poplar-lined road, quietly clucking their tongues. Male relatives with hangovers stood behind the twig gate, dismayed and still feeling cheated: they had passed up the traditional ritual of hanging the groom upside down and eliciting the confession of the wedding bed.

Young-ok walked away, holding her bright gown that shimmered in the October light. The bridegroom limped ahead, instead of riding on a horse. Young-ok followed him in her big strides, instead of being carried on a palanquin. Young-ok went away without ever looking back or stopping at the tutelar tree at the entrance of her village. She heard her wailing mother and hastened her feet. She felt she owed no lingering tears to her family who, to save face, had gone ahead and married her off to a much older limping man.

◆　◆　◆

Three autumns later, grandmother passed away — she went out in her sleep, we were told, like the last flicker on a burnt candle — and we traveled to the farm for the funeral. Young-ok came with her two suckling children, one strapped on her back, one pulled by the hand. She looked older than her twenty-two years. She was now a plain country wife.

Young-ok strutted in where the mourning table was set up and went down wailing. The chorus of beautiful and synchronized wailing of other women, women who shed no tears, buried Young-ok's real sobs. Young-ok let out all her pent up feelings and regrets and wailed with an ugly sound of a wild goose. When other women stopped wailing, she couldn't stop. She cried, gurgling and wiping her eyes with the back of her hand.

When grandmother's funeral procession left home for the family mountain, Young-ok stood outside the house, watching grandmother's coffin being carried away by men in hemp hats and arm bands and straw shoes. She stood with her children as the wailing of the mourners became fainter and the coffin covered with paper flowers floated up and away into the distance. The long streamers fluttered in the wind like streamers on the hats of dancing farmers celebrating a fall harvest with gongs and drums.

Finally, the procession passed the tutelar tree and turned around the corner. Young-ok no longer heard the wailing but only the beautiful sound of a bamboo flute. The sound of a bamboo flute that had once so sadly embroidered the night of her wedding. She pulled her children to the folds of her *chima* and smiled a smile of the Suffering *Bodhisattva*. Of the *Bodhisattva* who had forgone his Nirvana when he heard the cries of suffering people. Of the *Bodhisattva* who extended his compassion and charity to all the suffering ones.

CHAPTER 9

SISTER

Sister grew to be a haughty and proud girl although, as I heard it, when she was a little child, she used to tell anyone who cared to listen that she would marry father when she grew up. As I also heard it, when she was a child she had very much wanted a penis which she called *gochoo*, "a pepper." That she used to beg mother, in the midst of war, to take her to the *Jagalchi Shijang* at the harbor front to buy one for her. One could buy anything there. Even a penis.

Mother often told those stories in a joyful relish but the stories convinced me that sister had to be a peculiar thing. For one thing, I never wished to marry father even if I grew up monstrously ugly. And it had never occurred to me that a "*gochoo*" was something to covet.

Over the years as his silent absence extended, father, sister's brilliant star, seemed to fall from his orbit. Her blind faith in him vacillated. Then one day when our handsome Third Uncle came to see us on his first leave from the Military Academy, sister casually swore off her first love. She fell helplessly in love with Third Uncle, so dazzling and princely in his splendid cadet's uniform. Sister vowed that one day she would marry him. No one else.

Brother and I were then still children running about the streets. Sister was already sixteen. With her jade-smooth skin, she was a blossom bursting open on a yulan tree. Resplendent. In the afternoon, when sister appeared on the street coming home from school, children playing on the street froze like cocks caught in a spell. Mouths gaping, they stared at her as if she were a princess on an outing. In her sailor-collared white blouse and blue skirt, sister was the picture of all that was pretty and pure. No, she wasn't a milky, dreamy, soft pink cloud kind of girl. She made you think of the bluest water, of sharp autumn sunlight and of white virgin snow. Unapproachable. Cool. She was a cold whiff of wind. A jolt to a soggy brain. As sister approached, children silently made way for her. And the way she walked past us children, never giving an eye, it was terribly clear that she had no taste for us straggling and sniffling things, tugging and screaming like monkeys in a zoo.

We were lucky to claim her as our sister. Brother and I often enjoyed privileges at her church. Like mother, brother and I were part-time Christians. We went to the church on Easter and Christmas and attended its summer school. One Easter Sunday, brother and I were bribed with extra moonstone blue, cherry red and straw yellow eggs by a high school boy who entertained us little children with stories of miracles at Sunday School. As soon as we were outside the gate of the church, we cracked open the eggs and wolfed down every single one of them. We came home with stomach cramps and violent hiccups and forgot all about the letter we were carrying from him to sister.

That same year on a snow-falling evening near Christmas, we spotted a crouching boy toss something over the wall and dash off into the dark. The package mother picked up from the bed of wet snow was wrapped in beautiful paper and addressed to sister. We sat expectantly, surrounding sister as she fished out a pencil box with a Mon Ami fountain pen and a pair of leather gloves lined with pink-dyed rabbit fur. Inlaid on the purple enamel cover of the pencil box was a single long-stemmed white lily. That and the pink rabbit fur-lined gloves were the most exquisite and beautiful things I had ever seen. Mother said they were very expensive things. More than a high school student could afford. So we imagined him as the son of a wealthy family. We also thought it was an extravagant, foolish gesture because the boy sent the presents anonymously. Didn't it seem perfectly natural though that sister should deserve a lofty devotion?

At another time, a boy boldly appeared on the cherry hill behind our back gate. He wore a red carnation on the breast of his black school uniform. On his head, his brass-buttoned black school hat sat in a cocked angle. (Boys who wore their school hats at cocked angles, we understood, were bad boys.) All afternoon, the Oh sisters and I stood around the well and watched him pacing back and forth in a circle up on the hill. We were spellbound by his theatrical presence. He pretended he wasn't seeing us gaggle of little girls staring at him.

How he must have hoped and hoped that sister would come out. Only if she did, she would surely notice him. With that red carnation, who wouldn't? He could not have known that sister wasn't home. After a long, long while, long after the bored Oh sisters abandoned the well post, in the falling dusk, all I could see was the blazing red of the carnation against the black. Finally, the disappointed boy took off the carnation and walked away.

But sister was an unhappy thing. Inside the flap of her spiral-bound diary book, I once read: *Poverty is not a shame but only an inconvenience. (Schopenhauer)* It made me think of skinny-legged children in ragged clothes foraging in a smoldering garbage dump. They carried frayed brown burlap sacks flung over their shoulders and long pickers that looked like eyebrow tweezers. They were poor, poor orphans. That was my picture of poverty. And we couldn't be poor. Our ancestors were queens, scholars, ministers and generals. We were royalty — father had implicitly made us believe — living in temporary banishment.

But our temporary banishment more and more looked like a permanent one. And sister chafed. She was deprived. It constantly demeaned her. I remember one time when mother brushed lime over the blue-cloth of sister's shoes to turn them into summer shoes. I thought it was ingenious of her. It didn't occur to me that sister might prefer a new pair until I saw her crying the next morning as she stepped into those stiff, bleached shoes.

Feverish in discontent, sister often argued with mother. She always had a lot to say, mother said. And she was so eloquent. Like her father. She could kill just with words. So contentious and unhappy, she was like an enemy. An enemy for no reason. Like a poisonous snake, she bit and bit. This child tormented her and drew blood from her. Could it be true, mother wondered, that this child of hers was the reincarnation of the jealous ghost wife the fan-wielding fortune-teller had once told her about. That her child was a puppet of this vengeful soul. And where was he? The man who promised his child the moon and the stars and wings to fly and soar. It was about time for him to come and be accountable. She couldn't bear it alone.

◆　◆　◆

The summer mother sent brother off to the farm at Big Mother's, sister ran away. Also that summer, mother met a man she referred to by his full name only. (I never forgot his first name though, because it sounded like "Sang-uh" which means "shark.")

It was on a rainy night, mother met him. She was returning home from her brother's and got caught in a heavy downpour. He was the kind stranger who offered mother shelter under his black umbrella, wide but not wide enough for two strangers. In the night rain, mother must have looked young and demure; he thought mother an unattached woman, a "miss." That night, going out of his way, he walked mother all the way home. And they must have chatted. Mother found out he was a lonely bachelor, over thirty years old. Inspired, mother volunteered to be a matchmaker for him.

All through that summer, he often stopped by after work. Each time, he and mother sat by the window across from each other. Separated by a small fold-and-carry table. They hardly talked. Mother seemed bashful. And he, resting his thick elbow on the desk, smoked one cigarette after another. He had the kind of hard-to-remember face that made a child distrust him. And each time he brought with him an opaque aura that he'd leave behind, to linger like the smoke from his cigarettes. Although mother always kept the door wide open during his visits, I sensed the room was off-limits as long as he was there. With him, mother seemed to exist in a whole new realm of the world.

Seared in my memory of that summer is a picture of him and mother sitting by the window buried in the thick swirl of blue smoke. In the late afternoon light streaming through the window, they were as still as two people arrested on a camera lens. Fuzzy and grainy and mysterious and immobile.

One night on the way home from somewhere, mother and I stopped by to see him at his office inside a long building of cinder block. It sat at the edge of a big, fenced factory yard. (He was a factory manager and was often on night duty.) We might have stayed just for ten minutes or as long as an hour. Inside his office, time stopped moving. Mother and I sat across from him separated by a big steel desk. The metal chair was low and hard. The orange light was dim and sometimes all I could see was his black-rimmed glasses. They grew and shrank away and grew and shrank away. The entire time, he spoke no more than a few words. Mother, hardly a word. And we left.

After that night, he came by just one more time. He wasn't wearing the black-rimmed glasses. His face looked like a white china plate in the bright afternoon light. He stayed only a little while. He didn't sit by the window at the fold-and-carry desk. He didn't even smoke. And for the first time, he gave me a light pat on the head.

After he left, mother said he was getting married. I was glad. It must mean that he would stop coming by. Mother didn't sound excited or happy for him though. Instead, she seemed lonely and even a little sad. Mother often looked a little sad and lonely anyway in the evening when the sun set. It was because, she once told me, the sun-setting sky made her remember things she didn't want to. It made her nostalgic. I wondered if nostalgia always made people feel sad and lonely.

◆　◆　◆

The afternoon she ran away, sister sat at the same fold-and-carry desk by the window writing away furiously. She was hunched over — her hair fell around her opaline face in glistening jet streams — and half turned away from the window. Outside, the summer afternoon stood still in an uninterrupted slumber. Once in a while, in my feverish head, I imagined hearing the electric hum-hum. But it was the sound of the pen in her hand, scratching its way in a hurry across the paper, that filled the room. It sounded like a leaf skipping in the wind. It made me feel cool.

It was a long while before sister finished the note. I watched her carefully fold it into a neat thumb-sized square with a tail and place it under that lily-inlaid pencil box. About then, the freckled face of sister's friend popped into the window frame.

I knew the girl, sister's new, unlikely friend, lived with her father at the other side of the cherry hill. On a late afternoon, on the way to a shop to fetch a bottle of soy sauce for mother, brother and I had passed by their house. We couldn't help noticing the beautiful strange flowers, brilliant and deeply hued, that were blooming in their fenceless front yard. I had never seen opium poppies before. People called them Yang-gui-bi. Yang-gui-bi, Lady Yang, was one of the four great beauties in Chinese history, the cherished concubine of the Brilliant Emperor, Ming Huang of the Tang dynasty.

It was one of the old stories father used to tell us; lessons to learn from history. In *Jang-han-ga*, the "Song of Everlasting Sorrow," the famous poem written by Po Chü-i, the Brilliant Emperor favored only Lady Yang although there were said to be thousands of ladies of great beauty in his court. The emperor spent all of his time with Lady Yang, indulging in elaborate feasts and endless merrymaking. And as spring nights behind the "hibiscus curtains" were so short and Lady Yang, rose so late, the emperor eventually stopped holding his morning court. Lady Yang grew to wield such influence that every one of Lady Yang's siblings held a title. And the Yang clan attained such glory, throughout the empire, every parent began to wish for the birth of a girl instead of a boy!

In the end though, resentment toward the Yang clan erupted in the An Lu-shan rebellion. The Brilliant Emperor and Lady Yang had to hastily abandon the Forbidden City and flee from the capital of Chang-an. Alas, when they reached the lonely Ma-wei slope in Shensi on their way to Szechuan, the emperor's own soldiers rebelled. They demanded the death of the despised Lady Yang. The emperor was helpless to save her: all he could do was cover his face as the soldiers led her away. Lady Yang was then strangled with a silken cord. When her hair ornaments of green and white jade and yellow gold scattered on the ground like falling autumn leaves, "no one picked them up."

The moment brother had whispered the word "Yang-gui-bi," I knew there was something illicit about those beautiful flowers. The freckled face of the girl brought back the memory of the bright poppy flowers in the yard and the story of Lady Yang. One of the lessons father had thought we should learn from that historical episode was that one has to be careful in choosing his or her associations. The freckle-faced girl spelled trouble. She wasn't the right friend for sister.

Breaking the stillness of the afternoon, the freckle-faced girl tapped the window with her fingers and scurried off. Soon, the back gate opened with a squeal and she was at the door, kicking off her shoes. She was carrying a small bundle with her. She must have been running. On her freckled nose, sweat beads were popping. And each time she loudly sucked in the air, her ball-bearing breasts heaved under her tight pink T-shirt. She quickly glanced at me with her big brown eyes that spoke of future wickedness and slid her bundle under the desk. She was a conspirator; she bent over and whispered to sister. Sister reached for the piggy bank on top of the bookshelf — a red glazed apple with a green leaf and a stem — took it down and smashed it open on the desk. All the coins jangled out. The freckle-faced girl went down on her hands and knees and chased after the scattering coins. One by one, they disappeared into sister's white vinyl purse. A few minutes later, sister and the freckle-faced girl were gone, slipped out through the back gate.

What sister last said to me was, "Listen to *umma* and be a good girl," as if relegating all her daughterly duty to me. "Also don't forget," she warned, taking her cool hand away from my sweaty forehead, "a crying child keeps parents away from home." As soon as she was gone, I cried. I cried so loud, I imagined it was my voice that chased the sun behind the clouds and stirred up the wind that rustled the leafy plants in the flower bed.

♦ ♦ ♦

In less than an hour, sister and the freckle-faced girl were at the Seoul Station, buying two one-way train tickets to Pusan. With the tickets, they hurried down to the platform and boarded the first car. Anxious, sister sat in the idling train. With every passing moment, her resolve was fast crumbling. Next to her, blowing bubbles with gum, the freckle-faced girl happily chatted away.

Finally, with a long-drawn yawn and halting jolts, the train started pulling out of the station yard, a vast ground of crisscrossing tracks overrun with summer weeds. From the sky that had suddenly turned dark, thunder cracked. Soon riding the winds, rain came down in thick wavy sheets. The rain streamed down the windows. The world outside the window turned into a blur.

Gradually, the train picked up speed. The wheels roared and whined. The steam engines hissed and coughed. The freckled girl hummed a song, something about a sentimental journey. Soon, overcome with emotions, sister was crying. The rain. The song.

The splash of summer green on the train window. They made her melancholy. She wondered if mother would look for her. Even cry? Regret every unkind word she had ever said? Did she ever love her? One day she and mother would pass each other on a street like two strangers. How sad that would be! In her head, sister kept writing and rewriting a long-drawn, full-blown family saga as the train carried her farther and farther away from home.

Evening was turning into night when the train reached Pusan, "the San Francisco of Korea." Sister and the freckle-faced girl walked out of the station into the streets of the southern port city. The balmy August night teemed with heat. The damp breezes carried smells of the sea, salted fish, and seaweed. Sister and the freckle-faced girl were quickly swallowed up by the crowd. They didn't fail to notice how the women talked in excited sing-song accents and how the men had an air about them of the unstable sea.

Like fish caught in a tide, sister and the girl went drifting among the moving throng down a busy boulevard. In the distance on the hillsides, lights twinkled as if beckoning them. They were excited. The port city with hills and harbors seemed so exotic. And the tall trees, the wide boulevards and the unfamiliar sights and sounds gave them an overblown sense of freedom.

After a while, where the boulevard ended, they crossed into a narrow street lined with outdoor food stalls. There the city seemed to have made an about-face. There, tall street lamps were replaced by bare bulbs strung along over the food stalls. Under the dim orange light, men sat in groups, their red, sea-weathered faces partially shadowed. The girls scurried by the stalls through the thick cooking fumes, clutching their bundles. Men dropped their conversations and chased the girls with their blood-shot eyes. The freckle-faced girl giggled. Sister, alarmed, pulled her friend's hand

and unwittingly turned into an alley dotted with pink and red neon signs that blinked incessantly. There, in front of the two girls stood a world that had been unknown to them so far. It was a world of adults, of lonely men and "sell spring" girls. Where pleasure was bought and sold like combs and mirrors and finger-greased bills ruled the night. Sister pulled the hand of the wide-eyed freckle-faced girl who was in the mood to linger and turned another corner. There, every alley seemed to connect to another, a mishmash without an exit. The heat seemed to swell around them like a choking river as they hurried through, passing drunken men and cheaply made-up women. A man staggered out from a door of a drinking house and hollered at the girls. The girls skittered away leaving the man behind with a satisfied guffaw.

By the time they found their way out to a deserted boulevard, sister was scared. She was no longer the unhappy girl who had dared to leave home. But a little sheltered girl lost in a big, strange city. And the city was fast lowering its lights and fewer and fewer cars passed on the road. Sister nagged the freckle-faced girl to call her aunt. The freckle-faced girl reluctantly went to the phone and summoned her aunt to fetch them away into the safe world.

Sister and the freckle-faced girl spent a few days taking in the sights of Pusan. They took a walk along the waterfront and watched the fishermen returning from the sea, their wind-beaten, salt-eaten flags announcing "full vessel." And at the port where ocean-crossing ships from faraway places dropped their anchors, they saw foreign-tongued sailors and shipmen come and go, releasing their tobacco smoke and whiskey-laced breaths into the air. The girls envied the freedom of the men who traveled through the sea from port to port, landing in the strangest lands with strange customs. How the freedom they had paled beside that of the men! Had they only been born boys. Free of those invisible shackles and chains that bound them. Now they could see that, no matter how far they ran away from home, those shackles and chains would remain with them like birthmarks and beauty spots and crooked smiles.

One morning, the girls woke up before dawn and went out to Haeundae, Sea Cloud Beach. They stood facing the vast, empty and dark ocean, stretching far into the blackness of nothing. From that black nothingness came waves, rolling and undulating to the curved shore as walls of cascading water. Then the sun bounced up and rose over the ocean. The sea shimmered in flaming red. And like the scholar who had carved the name "Sea Cloud" on the rock, all they could see was the sea and the cloud above. The breathtaking vista had inspired many poets before them. But as if they were the first ones ever faced with such wondrous beauty, they held their breaths as they stood on the half-moon beach.

They didn't forget to tour the famous Pebble Beach Market where, sister had once thought, they carried "peppers" for a little girl like her born without one. There, they saw all sorts of strange looking creatures scooped up from the sea: sea cucumbers, shrimp, devil's aprons, octopus, crabs, shark fins, turtles and hard-shell mussels and varieties of fish and shell fish. Live eels and turtles swam in seawater tubs. Gigantic fishes hung on cords from the ceiling. They squealed and giggled through the aisles throbbing with the pungent fishy smell.

After a few days though, the city turned mundane. Its mystery fast peeled off like scales on a rotting fish, and revealed itself in dust, hustle and noise. The aimless freedom that took her nowhere began to tire sister. Her worried mind brought her dreams of weeping mother. She was homesick. She saw how people were so busy making a living. How her coming or going mattered so little to them. She had thought she would be happier away from home. But she wasn't happy at all. She remembered what mother had often told her. About happiness. Happiness is not something one grabs out of the air and rubs all over like honey. One had to strive for and work for it. Deep inside, sister had always known that it was not all mother's fault. If only she could, mother would have given her all that she desired. Even with her life. She had thought she hated mother for not understanding her shame. Now, she pined for the comfort of home and family from which she had so much wanted to run away.

After a week in Pusan, sister left the freckle-faced girl behind and boarded a train for Seoul. She would always remember the city, she told herself, and most of all the fragrant live sea cucumbers she ate at an outdoor seaside stall with vinegar and hot, hot red pepper sauce. So hot, her eyes had turned watery.

She wasn't sorry either to leave her friend behind. The freckle-faced girl had found the city of passionate women and excitable men to her liking. There, she had found her heartbeat well tuned to the coming and going of a city where the gates opened to the world through the sea.

◆　◆　◆

After sister was gone, mother always left the back gate ajar. To spare her from the shame of having to knock and call. Lest people would hear her and see her and gossip. Mother waited for her day and night. Every little noise outside startled her hope to life. The tension and worry made mother shrivel like summer weeds burnt by the heat. Mother couldn't eat because her daughter might be starving somewhere. Mother couldn't sleep because her daughter, her very first child, might not have a roof over her at night. Worries made her insides rot. Mother told no one and worried alone. It was a secret we all had to keep. To save sister from shame when she returned. And when she returned, no questions would be asked and no explanations would be sought. Mother just hoped and hoped that sister would return, slipping through the back gate as if nothing had happened.

It rained like a drumming song the night sister returned. All evening, mother kept checking the clock sitting on the desk. The green luminous hands hardly seemed to move. But in the dark, it ticked and tocked on without ceasing. Sometimes, wind hooted by, rattling things. When mother looked at the clock again, the hands were almost touching each other. Soon the siren announcing the midnight curfew would bleat. And it seemed the wait again had been in vain.

Then mother heard something moving outside the window that faced the street. Mother jerked the window open and pushed her face out. There, in the rain, sister stood, hunched and dripping. Her hollow eyes, shiny with fear. Humbled and matured, she had come back. Mother rushed out into the rainy night. Softly calling sister's name. Suppressing her bursting joy, lest even a ghost would hear. Mother grabbed her wet child into her arms. The rain tapped on. Mother and sister clung to each other and quietly sobbed.

CHAPTER 10

MATCHES AND SOAP

Whenever something bad happened to us, mother always told us that it happened to forestall something even worse. We were lucky, she said. Something could always be worse. You cut a finger with a knife? You are lucky, you didn't lose the finger. You could have sliced it off. You got a bargain. So a man who breaks his leg in a traffic accident is still lucky! He is still alive and breathing. By breaking his leg, he might have averted death. As a result, it was a sense of fatalism that ruled over us children: something bad was bound to happen in life and if indeed something bad happened, we still felt fortunate that it wasn't something worse.

Grandmother didn't share such sentiments with us. Grandmother, a Christian, a puritan, a Confucian, a moralist, believed in self-sufficiency. She loved success, improvement and moving up. That was why grandmother came to visit us less and less and when she did, she and mother always ended up arguing. Although after each time we moved — to a smaller place and farther to the outskirts of the city, to her dismay — grandmother came for a visit with the customary box of matches and cakes of soap, hoping our wealth would spread like fire and multiply like soap bubbles in our new place.

But a quick look around was always more than enough for her. Her eagle eyes missed nothing. It always made grandmother unhappy to see the new place we had moved into. Often she didn't bother to take off her shoes. Instead, she sat on the narrow veranda floor and seethed. She was a dragon spewing fire. Then the anger would boil over and she couldn't hold it in any longer. In her low, nagging voice, she started to complain. She'd ask mother why she didn't go out and do something, anything to support the children. Instead of staying home like a noble creature and eating up whatever was left. One day, we would end up in a shack with a leaky roof, she claimed in her mean voice. "Why so noble? You are not a queen!" She knew mother tried but it was never good enough in her eyes. Just like the time when mother attempted to sell seaweed from door to door.

Once a woman with a seaweed shop in the market offered to supply mother with brown seaweed — the stiff and long kind used in birthday soup — without taking a deposit. On the morning of her first day as a seaweed seller, mother took the seaweed all the way across town. She didn't want to happen upon someone she knew. That was very important to her.

After getting off the bus, she walked until she came upon a residential section. The shop woman had told mother to walk around shouting, "Seaweed here!" to draw potential customers' attention.

"And knock on gates." But mother who had never done anything like it before couldn't for the world pull out those two simple words. The words were stuck in her throat. When she tried, it was only a mosquito's voice she could squeeze out. She choked on the words. And she was too shy, too inhibited to knock on a stranger's gate. She couldn't remember how long she walked up and down the same alley lined with traditional Korean houses that looked more and more like fortresses behind stone walls and wooden gates bolted shut. All the while trying to find the courage to shout and knock. And as more time passed, more imposing the closed gates and sturdy stone walls looked. They became fortified castles.

Then, suddenly, rain drops started coming down and soon it turned into a heavy downpour. The rain became so thick, drops so big, the street in front of her soon began to disappear into a fog. Clutching her seaweed, mother ran and sought refuge under the eaves. She was soaked. She had no choice but to wait until the rain stopped. When finally the rain let up into a drizzle, she came home with the soggy, ruined seaweed. She hadn't sold a single sheet. Never came close.

That was the end of mother's brief career as a seaweed seller. When mother told us the story that night, she laughed. Her lack of the knack to be a simple seaweed seller had seemed funny even to her. Grandmother, of course, didn't see it that way. Mother hadn't tasted enough hardship yet, she said. Not poor enough or desperate enough. And as usual, she blamed all this on mother's faithlessness. "If you believed in Jesus, you wouldn't feel shame!"

◆　◆　◆

It was soon after the day of "Enter Spring," that we left the old, haunted house at the foot of the cherry hill. Spring is the season of change, of a new start. People wait for the spring to get married, move to new places, change schools and start new jobs. And we moved "up." Moving "up" in that section of Seoul meant your fortune was "down." But we were lucky. Some families ended up out on the street.

Our house stood at the end of a narrow street clinging onto a cliff. The street was one of the many identical streets that crept up a hilly plateau, ring upon ring, all the way to the summit. From afar, the hill looked like a badly scarred snail shell. And there was nothing pretty in the scenery except some acacia trees, castor-beans and shrubby greens that spotted the plateau in small green bursts.

These identical narrow streets all poured out to a single steep road that plunged rapidly toward the lower land. In the winter, it turned into a huge snow slide where boys formed a long train and slid down together at hair-raising speed screaming and laughing. And during the rainy season in summer, it turned into a muddy rapid. Down and up this slope, once in the morning and once in the evening, adults and children traveled like marching ants to work and to school and back home.

After we moved this time, grandmother didn't come for a visit at all. She couldn't walk up the hill. Her legs were old. Grandmother just couldn't stand to see us "living up there in the company of clouds." We deserved better.

Mother and we children knew also right away that we somehow didn't belong to the street. Mother, composed, shy and quiet, stood out like a sore thumb just as she had among the gossipy, garrulous women in the textile factory. And to the women on the street, we children seemed haughty and even vain. Sister was proud and unapproachable. "Your older daughter!" they said to mother. "When she passes by, it feels like the chilly wind of winter." And in the street of polyesters and nylons, we children dressed in stiffly starched cotton. We always turned up on the street spanking clean. Even to play in the dirt. Our nose tips shined as if waxed! They snickered and wondered where we were hailing from.

But right away, brother and I were among the children who gathered on the street in the afternoon. We ranged from a tottering three-year-old to a fifteen-year-old with a faint shadow of mustache. They were the three children of the Fat Wife: Piggy, Skinny and Bamboo Stick. The only son of the roofer, Sparrow, with patchy crew cut hair. (Every so often, his mother wielded a rusty pair of tooth-missing scissors on him lest lice build nests there.) And then there were the five children of the newspaper typesetter — one boy and four girls. The four girls shared light brown eyes and freckled simian faces. So children called them Monkey Sisters although they looked more like spotted cats. The sisters were hoarders. They saved everything: used envelopes, wooden spools, pieces of cloth, spent ballpoint pens and plastic bags. They kept them in their separate boxes, each labeled with a number.

Out on the street, the children formed a hierarchical society by age and sex and played in harmony. Each child knew where he or she stood in rank and each followed a leader's order. But then a rift would occur and these same children would turn vile, calling names at one another and insulting each other's parents. Like the women, they constantly jostled for a respectable position.

For mother, there wasn't a place to hide. During the day, the street was the territory of the women and the children. And every afternoon, the women hurried through the street with little children in tow and congregated on the floor of the fat woman's house. And one of them would push her head out through the window facing our yard and ask mother to join them.

When summer came and schools closed, all afternoon those

women sought refuge from the heat behind the bamboo curtain on the cool wooden floor at the fat woman's house. They sat around and crocheted the edges of white gauze in blue and red threads — it was piecework they did for money — and gorged out all kinds of stories from their spiteful mouths. Often the stories they churned out were as wicked and steamy as the heat throbbing outside. The women whose lives were the results of their men's whims and blunders and vanity and condescendence bared their intimate secrets with zeal matched only by the summer heat. The children hovered around the women and occasionally interrupted them with questions like, "*Umma*, what's a 'womanizer'?" "Auntie, what's 'adultery'?" The women answered these questions casually and carelessly.

Then dusk came down and settled in the shrub of castor beans and the men began to return to the street. The tall, rugged roofer with his wooden tool box and a broken pencil behind his ear. Dominating the narrow street with his big gait and the smell of sour sweat. The dapper bureaucrat at the Agriculture and Fisheries Department with his slicked-back hair. In suit and tie. Finally, the typesetter of the evening newspaper. Pale and small. Shrinking under the weight of five children and a sickly wife. He always carried, tucked under his arm, a fresh copy of the evening edition.

As soon as the roofer disappeared inside the gate, the roofer's son came out carrying with him an empty aluminum tea kettle to fetch rice wine for his father. Along the way, he collected little children who followed him down the plunging steps to the wine shop. When he returned, posting new cowlicks from sweating, carrying the kettle full of sloshing rice wine, it was dark. His mother, the scrawny roofer's wife, waited outside the gate, angry at his delay. Holding a willow switch as a threat.

It was the roofer's wife who, one afternoon, to the rapt audience of women and children around her, proudly confessed how the night before she and her husband were in bed "stark naked" without even a thread on them. There, she paused for dramatic effect. As it happened, she resumed, a relative then strolled through the open gate for a chit chat with them. He coughed to announce his presence and started to open the sliding door to their room. She had to bolt out of the bed faster than a bean in a roasting pan. The roofer's wife was boasting: she imagined every woman on the street envied her her masculine husband.

But the women gaped, giggled and clucked their tongues, incredulous that the roofer, a notorious womanizer, still slept with his wife who looked like a dried chestnut. Since then, every evening when the roofer appeared on the street returning from work carrying his tool box, inexplicably sexy in his soiled work clothes, the women let out smiles of scorn and curiosity behind his broad sweat-stained back.

◆   ◆   ◆

One day, though, all the jockeying and gossiping came to a sudden halt. When we went out to the street, the very air we breathed in seemed to shiver with excitement and fear. Was it true that a pack of North Korean guerrillas were loose in our neighborhood? Nothing inspired more fear in us children than communist guerillas. We knew what they were capable of. In January that year, under the cover of a chilly, black night, thirty-one North Korean guerrillas had infiltrated Seoul. They came within several yards of the Blue House, the house where the president lived, before they were stopped. All of them were hunted down and killed. Except one. Every child in Korea could readily recite the name of the one lucky guerilla who had been captured alive. (We were very surprised to find that he looked just like any of us in the newspaper picture. He must have dispensed his horns and fangs before posing for the picture.) It wasn't just South Koreans the North Koreans hated, either. Not long after, they seized an American ship called *Pueblo* in the sea facing Wonsan. The swell of rumors and fear of war came and went as regularly as the summer monsoon season.

In school, we often wrote "comfort letters" and sent them off to soldier uncles who defended the frontiers day and night. Once, a soldier uncle sent me a reply. He said it was very, very cold up there in the DMZ. And very lonely too. My letter had given him so much joy. I wrote back. We became pen pals. Once a month, he also sent me the new issue of soldier's magazine, called *Freedom Road*. It arrived at school, rolled inside a white plastic tube and all the children were envious. Mother even borrowed a camera and took a black and white picture of me standing next to yellow and white chrysanthemums. Head cocked to the right as usual. Looking sad as usual. I mailed the picture with a letter. After that, he stopped writing. Mother said it could mean anything; he could have been accidentally and tragically killed by a mine as, there were plenty along the DMZ. Or he could have been discharged and gone back home. Or... I knew what that could be.

Every afternoon during the next several days of relentless late summer heat, a helicopter hovered in the white bleached sky like a summer dragonfly. From it, a fuzzy and static megaphone voice blared down. The voice — it was solemn and heroic — warned the invisible spies to surrender and find the "bright light" of freedom. We children cocked our heads, pricked up our ears and listened to the voice buzzing down from the sky. The rotating blades of the helicopter were hypnotizing. Even more so than the float-and-hop image of Mr. Armstrong on the moonwalk that we would see a year later on a silver-streaked TV screen. We watched and watched until our eyes were seared with tears.

We trembled at the very possibility of the spies lurking around us. Suddenly, the innocent shadows of castor bean plants and acacia trees began to look ominously suspicious. We went around peeping and checking the back of every gate and wall. We lifted open the lids of big glazed *kimchi* jars out on raised terraces and ran off screaming before we had the courage to look in. I could feel every strand of hair stand up. At any moment, I imagined, a hand, a communist hand, red as freshly-spilled blood, would grab me from behind.

Every night before going to bed, mother went out to the kitchen and made sure no extra cooked rice was lying around. It was always at night, in the cover of dark, that hungry spies ventured out from their hiding place to seek food. We prayed that the spies would not seek food in our kitchen. We couldn't fall asleep. Every little noise outside spiked unbearable fear.

Out on the street, children repeated to each other the story of a boy in a small mountain village on the east coast who had died at the hands of a North Korean spy. "Uncle, I don't like communists!" That was what the brave boy was supposed to have said just before he was murdered. And there were other gruesome stories: of a little girl and her family ruthlessly murdered by guerillas and of a postman who had the bad luck of running into them.

What would I do, I wondered, if I ever came to stand face to face with one of them! I would shrivel with fear. I would faint. In my dreams, North Korean spies multiplied. They hunted us children down the plunging street and up the slope. We ran and crawled. One night, I saw in my dream, mother crying and crying as I lay bleeding stricken by a spy's bullet! That was the saddest dream. I felt so sorry for mother. I cried too.

Whatever happened to the spies? One day, the voice that blared down from a hovering helicopter went silent. It took days though before the ghost image of the hovering helicopter completely disappeared from the sky and the sound of the rotating blades entirely faded away. The fear and excitement lingered like the heat.

Then one afternoon, a young woman appeared on the street and just like that, life slipped back to the same old routine. The young woman had never been seen before on the street. And it was the gate of the roofer's house she pushed and slipped in. To the great surprise of the roofer's scrawny wife. All the children and women gathered and lingered outside the gate to hear the woman of mystery, voluptuous under a bright sassy dress, talk and argue with the roofer's wife, much shriveled with shame. Soon, everyone knew that the woman was the roofer's new mistress who had been tricked into believing that the roofer was a lonely widower.

Emboldened by the presence of the neighbors outside, gathered thick like summer flies, the scrawny wife raised her voice and scolded her husband's mistress, making sure the two gold molars inside her mouth showed. After the mistress trod away in a feigned defeat, the scrawny wife triumphantly marched out to the gate and declared indignantly how the woman was nothing but a "sell spring" woman. A whore at a drinking house who served this and that man.

The roofer's wife was not the only woman on the street who had to swim through the tides of shame. There was mother, the only woman on the street with an absent husband. Mother's strange situation, not a widow, not a divorcee, was a subject of constant speculation. The women resented mother because mother somehow managed to elude them. But they also envied mother her smart children. They would borrow our school reports and wave them at their children's noses, turning us into reluctant role models for their children. The roofer's wife, without religion but with many superstitions, often said to mother, "The one in heaven is fair. Forget about your husband. I would give anything to have smart children like yours."

And then there was the fat woman, the pariah of the street. Because the man she called her husband — the tall bureaucrat at the Agriculture and Fisheries Department — had his real wife and children somewhere in the south. She was a "small wife," non-existent in her husband's family registration. Even her three children were not hers on any legal paper. She was a shadow, a ghost. Her bundle of fat and flesh, one hundred sixty pounds in all, pressed no weight on any official documents.

Once every month or so, the man's real wife, a regal figure with an unusual height, appeared at their doorway. As soon as she entered, the varnished, honey-colored gate closed shut behind her. The fat woman's three children were steered away into their rooms to remain quiet as mice. The window facing our yard — where every afternoon Bamboo Stick perched on top of their rice chest and begged us for easy answers to his math homework — was also shut tightly but through it we could glimpse the fat wife on tiptoe carrying tea and fruit into the "*anbang*" where the legal wife regally presided. The boisterous woman had become a shadow — no mouth to utter an opinion, no ears to hear, no eyes to see. But the next day when the real wife left regally, the street sighed with a clandestine relief and the women and children once again rushed through the gate, open wide.

The women gathered again and through laughter and giggles, ridiculed, dissected and defended their men and made fun of their lives with little luxury, small and big disasters and clinging children. The afternoon flew. The laughter and yelling of the children playing outside steadily grew sharper and more pronounced. It was time to start dinner. But they lingered until they heard the gate open outside with a squeak. They knew it was the bureaucrat — a diffident man who ran his double life as officially as his government job — returning home. The women hastily gathered their sewing things. Then out of the blue, the scrawny roofer's wife blurted out that at least he went to work in suit and tie. That counted a lot. The women greeted the man with sly side glances and slipped away, leaving the man perturbed. Life in the street never changed.

If anything changed, it was the stories women told when they gathered. As the weather turned colder, the stories they told grew grimmer and grimmer. So on a damp winter afternoon when snow poured silently from the soot-colored sky, the women rested their stiff, needle-pricked hands and told stories about the old days, the stories of hardship: the Japanese occupation and the war. Cliffhangers of death and survival. Stories about strange twists of fate. They told these grim stories to arm themselves with stoic resolution to get through the long and cold winter. Hoping with the return of the spring, life would somehow turn better. Sometimes, they paused and looked at their children tripping over the finished piles of gauze as they ran about, shrieking and pulling, and wondered aloud what they would become. Their hopes were all hinged on their children. They believed their children would do better. Better than their men. And that was good enough for them.

◆　◆　◆

Spring's arrival seemed sudden. Everywhere, forsythia bloomed all at once in great bursts and dappled the entire hilly plateau in hazy clouds of yellow. The thawed streets dried up and puffs of thick dust chased capricious spring winds. Walking home from school in the afternoon, we'd look up to find the whole hill disappearing behind the veil of ginger-colored dust.

One morning that early spring — it must have been Sunday because we weren't at school — the roofer climbed up to the roof of the fat woman's house to repair the snow damage of the winter. All morning, the roofer stood on the roof top and pitched down the old roof tiles to his assistant on the ground below. A pile of four tiles at a time. They were pitched down in exact intervals and speed. And each time, they landed in the hands of the assistant drawing a perfectly beautiful arc.

About noon when all the old tiles were pitched down and lay neatly stacked on the ground, the roofer was ready to come down for a lunch break. He had just reached the middle of the tall wooden ladder, when it wobbled and gave away from the bottom. For a second, the roofer seemed to be poised to fly. His arms spread out. In a gesture of celebration. Then with a loud thud, his big frame hit the ground. We could hear something crunch inside him.

It was tall and skinny Bamboo Stick, the fat woman's oldest child, who carried the roofer on his back to a clinic that spring afternoon. All the children in the street rushed down the steep road after Bamboo Stick carrying the big roofer. Behind the children, sniffling, followed the roofer's wife darting through the spring wind, hazy with pollen. Bamboo Stick rushed, huffing and puffing, down the steep road, struggling to defy gravity. His eyes bulged. Blood veins as thick as a twined rope mapped his pimpled forehead. The roofer's broken right leg dangled and a shoe-less foot dragged itself along, scraping the ground. Blood, syrupy and vermilion-colored, gushed out and ran down his collapsed cheekbone. The blood excited the children more. Yelling and screaming and whirling arms, the children followed, creating an air of carnival along the way.

After the roofer suffered the fall, something on the street

changed. The big roofer was crippled forever. He became the sad limping figure on the street. The scrawny wife went around, sour-faced and grumbling all the time. The women on the street became more wicked and more suspicious than ever. The children were growing fast. They were no longer simple and good and innocent.

I can see how life would have gone on and on had we stayed there. For better or for worse. But that spring, all the lives mother had observed with intense and irrepressible curiosity and endured with stoic calm became too much for her to bear. She was weary of the suffocating small world. Life on the street had become a constant and paranoid struggle for privacy. She could no longer welcome another woman ambling through the gate without being invited. So we were moving again.

One day, mother pulled out the bottom drawer of her chest and took out two small red velvet boxes. Inside the boxes were a large ruby, a cranberry-colored stone, set in double-gold rings and a matching ruby brooch. The ruby ring and the brooch she never wore but kept for the future of her children. They were from the days when father was a rich man with houses and buildings, when money seemed to grow on trees overnight, when he lavished it on relatives of his, buying them farm lands, building them houses and paying for their weddings, funerals and birthdays. It was the only part of the wealth mother had hoarded away on the advice of sly grandmother. (So innocent, grandmother never forgot to remind mother at every opportunity, she would have ended up without even that, had it not been for her.)

To the ruby ring and brooch, mother added her topaz ring. It was a gift her brother had brought for her from America. She found a pawn shop at the back street of a marketplace and pawned them at forty-five percent interest. She probably knew that she would not see her jewelry again.

One May day, we left the street and moved away to the northern outskirts of Seoul. Our rented house with a rusty steel gate stood at the end of a quiet street where women kept to themselves behind the gates. But it was the street up on the hill and the women and the children that I would long remember. And it was to that street I would return again and again in my dreams. To remember the year and the spring. The myriad of colors, sounds and smells.

CHAPTER 11

SOON-HEE

*E*very Monday morning, we children gathered on the school ground and sang aloud the Korean anthem: "Until the water of the East Sea dries up and Mountain Baekdoo wears away, may the King of Heaven protect our country..." It was a solemn song that had been sung in bitter tears by Koreans in exile during the long Japanese occupation. In history classes, we learned about the many tragedies that have struck Korea, "a small beautiful peninsula surrounded by breathtaking seacoasts and enveloped by lofty mountains." On the map of East Asia our teacher showed us, rabbit-shaped Korea was surrounded by Russia in the north, China in the west and Japan in the east. For much of her history, we also learned that Korea had been the pawn of these powerful neighbors who always lusted after her, "hanging like a golden fruit before their longing eyes," wrote Pearl S. Buck, the American writer.

It was during the Yi dynasty that Korea closed her door to the rest of the world and became a hermit kingdom. Her people's wish was to live in peace in the land they called "Morning Calm." In humble but joyful harmony with nature. Among the moon and the sun and the four seasons. On the folding screens that graced the backdrop to the king's throne in the royal palace for over five hundred years, the white sun and the red moon rise in perfect symmetrical brilliance over the landscape brocaded with silver rivers and jade mountains and red-branched pine trees. And in "Ideal Life" pictures on folding screens, a girl plays a harp under peony blossoms and a boy plays a lute on the back of a peacock in flight; happy births and peaceful deaths are desired; mountains and clouds and flowers and birds and trees accompany a happy daily life.

But the peace Korea wished for eluded her. It wouldn't be just the neighbors that came clamoring to her land. Later, there would come the French, the Americans and the British in their armed ships demanding an open door to the hermit kingdom. Weakened and threatened by various powers, the last kingdom of Korea disintegrated to fall under Japan's occupation. The Korea that Tagore, the Indian poet laureate, once called the "torchlight of the East," went dark.

The names and stories we found in history books that taught us about Korea's thousand tumultuous years were mostly those of men. The stories of Korean women — those who died anonymously, those who paid with their lives each time a disaster struck, a tragedy occurred, an invasion intruded upon the land — were not there. We heard their stories from women. They told us how women were violated and scarred repeatedly by the hostile outsiders and later even by men who came in friendly masks. As we listened, Korea seemed to become a bloodied Eden full of the voiceless souls of women.

Soon-hee moved onto our street on a snow-flurrying day of February with her mother. Soon-hee was fourteen although she looked more like a sixteen-year-old. Already a sweater-girl, she was tall and beautiful. She had movie-star eyes and the softest skin. She was that soft, pink cloud kind of girl my sister wasn't. I knew right away that she, like us, didn't belong to the street. She was beautiful and she was Catholic. I didn't know any Catholics.

Every afternoon when Soon-hee returned from school, looking terribly beautiful in her blue uniform with white sailor collars and bobby socks, I followed after her through the gate of the fat woman's house into the room she shared with her mother. There in the cramped room, I used to spend hours with Soon-hee.

The little room was like a sacred chapel. Everywhere, there were images of the Mother Mary, winged angels, saints and Jesus. These strange objects fascinated me. I'd linger in front of the lacquer table where a statue of the Virgin Mary stood, covered with fine dust, her cheeks rosy and her arms plump and porcelain-smooth. Surrounding the statue of the Virgin Mary were the half-melted candles, rosaries, crosses, plastic roses and a palm leaf, encased in a strange smell and fine dust. I'd sit there inhaling this scent I couldn't describe, feeling my head turn light.

A couple of times, Soon-hee carefully pulled out her white lace from the dresser and let me drape it over my head. The cascading white lace, so light and silky, instantly carried me to a land of miracles. Western miracles. I thought that was what Catholicism was about: Western miracles. If my grandmother's Protestant faith smelled to me of *kimchi*, Christmas card paper and the steam radiator in her church, Soon-hee's Catholic faith smelled of Western miracles of weeping saints, melting candle waxes and a bleeding Christ.

One cold March evening, Soon-hee took me along to the cathedral for a mass. I followed Soon-hee into the cavernous church, candle-lit dim and reverberating with almost inaudible metallic jangles of a pipe organ and felt very frightened. I stood seized with strange fear as Soon-hee, draped in her lace, purer and more beautiful than the Virgin Mary, repeatedly kneeled, prayed and recited from a book after an invisible father from behind a shining altar far, far away. The father's voice traveled through the long distance, solemn, echoing and vibrating as that of a sentencing judge. The tall columns shifted in the smoky light of the candles and the blue-eyed and blonde-haired angel ghosts in the stained glass window panes came to life and flapped their wings and darted about with a swishing sound. My head buzzed with a hum. The angel ghosts multiplied. These baby angel ghosts with their wings and round penetrating eyes were scarier than Korean ghosts. I felt faint and closed my eyes shut.

As soon as the mass was over, I raced out of the chapel and dashed to the bathroom in the basement of the church. Along the deep corridors and cold steps, the baby angels followed me, flapping their wings and whispering in their marble-clanking voices. I closed myself into the stall and peed and trembled. I knew it would be the first and the last time that I would ever step into Soon-hee's cathedral.

When I came out of the bathroom, Soon-hee was waiting. Soon-hee stood with a halo around her, smelling of the smoke inside the chapel. I was ashamed to show Soon-hee how frightened I was. I would never be able to become a Catholic! Soon-hee seemed disappointed but said nothing. Then Soon-hee led me through dark and dank corridors and back entrances to the Holy Mother Hospital next to the cathedral. We pushed through a steel door and entered the hospital kitchen where her mother worked as a cook. In the kitchen as large as a playground, sisters in gray robes and white hats moved around like shadows.

Soon-hee's mother sat us at a corner of a long wooden table, the kind I had seen in movies, inside a monastery. She scooped up thick soup from a giant steel kettle and gathered rice and vegetables on trays. While Soon-hee made the sign of the cross and prayed, I sat still shriveling with fear. Soon-hee's mother urged me to eat. I scooped up a spoonful of soup. It smelled of methyl alcohol and I couldn't swallow it down. The soup gurgled in my throat and I threw up all over. It took a special kind of person to become a Catholic.

◆   ◆   ◆

That spring, Soon-hee was like my own sister. She was a girl with a sunshine smile. Sweet and beautiful like the blonde-haired Barbie doll she had — a gift from an American family in Kansas City. I even thought that Soon-hee's sweetness was the reason she had an American family who sent her gifts, money and letters written in English on stiff scented paper. That all beautiful and sweet girls in Korea had kind American families like Soon-hee.

Afternoon after afternoon, we would sprawl on the floor of Soon-hee's room and read, talk, giggle and dream. Sometimes we painted pictures of Korea — hills with old, crooked pines and blazing azaleas — and rushed them to the post office to mail them to her American family. Soon-hee always said, "Via air mail, please," when she stood outside a clerk's window. It never failed to sound incredibly important and exotic to my ears. The clerk's expressionless face always puzzled me. I expected the expression "via air mail" would hit him with the same delight as well. After the envelope was weighed, we rushed to a corner with spanking new stamps of various sizes and numbers. We licked them and pounded them on the envelope dreaming of America. America I imagined or remembered from old magazines was where sunshine children drank hot chocolate and cream soda and went picnicking in shiny pink Cadillacs with chrome fins driven by their mothers in red checkered dresses and sunglasses pointed like bird wings. I didn't know then how strange it was that the fathers were missing in my picture of American families.

I remember the ink-smudged notebook that Soon-hee filled in with the English alphabet that spring. Soon-hee hoped one day she could write in English to her American family. Each day for half an hour, Soon-hee practiced the English alphabet on the cheap, blue-lined notebook which absorbed the ink instantly, turning each letter into a blurry mess. Soon-hee dipped her pen into the blue ink bottle and laboriously copied the capitals from A to Z and then repeated it all over again in small letters, blotting and blowing. The first time Soon-hee wrote her letter in English, it made her very proud.

◆　◆　◆

One quiet afternoon as I was reading a book, Soon-hee walked in through the gate of our house. She sat down next to me and asked what I was reading. I closed the book and told her the story of Cinderella I had just finished for the fifth or sixth time. Soon-hee just listened. The story didn't seem to impress her. Or I was a bad storyteller. We sat side by side, silent and pushing our faces out toward the sun. The March sun was feeble and every other minute we had to move up along the edge of the floor chasing the shifting sunlight. When we reached almost the other end of the floor, Soon-hee slouched forward. She cupped her beautiful face in her hands and stared at the space squinting her eyes. When the sunlight had shifted away completely sinking Soon-hee's face in the shadowy light, Soon-hee stirred and started chewing her thumb, nibbling at it like a lamb. Blood trickled down where she bit off a piece of skin, above the half moon of her thumb nail. It startled me to see Soon-hee, so perfect without a blemish anywhere, mangling her thumb.

Without turning her head, Soon-hee asked me dreamily if I knew that she had once lived in an orphanage. Her question shot up like a bamboo sprout from nowhere. I scrambled up from the floor.

"I was not an orphan but I lived in the orphanage," Soon-hee explained. "My father died during the war. When the war was over, my mother became very ill with consumption. She couldn't take care of me. So she took me to an orphanage. So I lived there until my mother came for me when she got better."

"Was it fun?" I asked. Often when I was bored, in my mind, I made up a world where only children lived. A world where everything was built in miniature. Like the world in *Gulliver's Travels*. I imagined marrying a little boy. And just because we were now husband and wife, I would soon become pregnant. I pictured myself tottering around pregnant with a baby. When I finally gave birth, from my belly button, a little baby girl popped out. Crying as all the babies came out crying. It was as small as the rag doll mother once had made me with her knitting yarn and discarded cloth. And it would of course stay small forever! It was so much fun, I could see it, taking care of the baby. I bathed her in a little stream. I fed her with honeysuckle. And I clothed her with dresses made of straw and leaves and flower petals.

"No," Soon-hee said. "I cried every night, hiding under the bed cover. I cried myself to sleep. I was afraid my mother would die and never come back for me."

Soon-hee said that she and the other children used to have the best time when American soldiers came to visit them on weekends. They always brought them gifts: toys, chocolates, candies and other gifts. As soon as the soldiers left, the children already looked forward to the next weekend. But, Soon-hee said, something happened to her one day.

"Is it a secret?" I asked. I always loved to hear secrets. Besides whenever someone told me secrets, I felt special. I raised my baby finger and looked at Soon-hee pleadingly. Soon-hee hooked hers to mine and shook halfheartedly.

One Sunday, Soon-hee said, an American soldier — Soon-hee remembered his eyes were as deep a blue as the bluest autumnal sky — came in an army jeep to pick Soon-hee up for an afternoon outing. When Soon-hee trotted after the American, ruffling her red-and-white dress and bobbing her bangs, envious children looked on, drooling and sucking their smudged fingers.

The American soldier took Soon-hee to a jeep parked outside the orphanage gate. The jeep seemed huge to her. Like a mountain. And cold. Like ice. The smiling American helped little Soon-hee climb into the jeep. Soon-hee remembered being scared when the jeep doors banged closed and she sat alone with the young soldier. The American soldier smiled at Soon-hee and let her play with the steering wheel and the clutch, gesturing, laughing and talking in words Soon-hee didn't understand.

Then the soldier started the jeep and drove it away. Soon the road ended and a dusty track began. Hanging curtains of brown powdery dust in the air, the jeep traveled farther and turned to an empty country of forlorn harvested fields and clumps of lonely pines. There the soldier stopped the jeep. Soon-hee sat in the metal-heavy quietness inside the jeep. Slowly the soldier pulled down the zipper of his pants and took out his penis. Soon-hee got scared at the sight of the strange thing, that pink and swollen and throbbing thing, and turned her head away. The smiling soldier pulled Soon-hee's little hand toward him. Soon-hee tried to pull her hand away but couldn't. Soon-hee started crying. The soldier covered her mouth with his hand. Soon-hee couldn't breathe. Soon-hee stopped crying. She couldn't remember what happened after that, Soon-hee said unsurely.

I didn't understand then what Soon-hee was telling me. I looked at Soon-hee and strangely she no longer looked like a sweet angel. She knew many, many things that I couldn't hope to know soon. Soon-hee's pink lips, soft flower petals, twitched for a second and it seemed as if she was going to cry. But she didn't.

Not long after, we moved away from the street. I would not see Soon-hee again until years later on a crowded street. In the blue light of the evening, she was walking down the street in a tight dress and high heels. Looking a little clownish. Like a child who played with mother's powder and lipstick for the first time. She was no longer the Soon-hee I had once known. Sweet and pious.

I still see her walking away in her silver lamé high-heeled shoes. On her way somewhere "to sell her laughter and looks." Spilling the perfume of cheap face powder. Touching her teased hair. Still beautiful in her iridescent polyester dress. A half woman. A half child.

When I saw Soon-hee on that street in the evening crowds, it was the story of the smiling American soldier I remembered. The story she had told me years back as we sat on the tip of the veranda floor chasing the scant sunlight. Of the soldier who had come to her in a friendly mask long ago. Carrying gifts and wearing a smile.

I walked by Soon-hee without saying hello. I somehow knew that was what Soon-hee would have wanted. To be left anonymous and alone on the crowded street. To go her way.

CHAPTER 12

SPRING LOVE

There was a certain section of a street I passed every afternoon returning home from school. It came at the trailing end of a commercial strip where the paving work stopped abruptly. It was a dry spring and rain that always left deep pot holes there rarely came. Instead, there hung a hazy film of dust in the air. All day long, fine dust rained and landed on the three shabby buildings standing there side by side in commiseration.

Although nobody ever noticed it, the building in the middle was an animal hospital. By now the carelessly painted sign — black calligraphy swirls — hanging on top of the building, "North Mountain Animal Hospital" had faded into the gray background. The interior was always as dark as a cave as the sun failed to penetrate the windows, caked with years of dust and grime.

Several times when there was no one around, I had pressed my face to the window, holding my hand to shield the sunlight and peered inside. Along a wall stood cages — rusting and skeletal — that held a few scrappy, dispirited puppies and a couple of sleepy cats. Against the other side of the wall, below colored and fading pictures of animals — dogs with bones and rabbits chewing on cabbages — stood an old dilapidated piano, its wood chipping. There sat the mystery man — the man sister was in love with — playing the piano and singing in his steely tenor voice. Korean arias and ariettas. Sometimes, I would also recognize a familiar aria from an Italian opera. Was it from *The Barber of Seville* or from *Rigoletto?* I don't remember.

At other times, I saw him carrying a dented tin bucket outside the hospital. He was a big imposing figure in blue denim overalls. He looked like an American farmer in Arkansas I had seen in a magazine. He had a tenor's paunch which he carried like a badge of honor, something I would see later in Luciano Pavarotti. I quickly hurried by him as if I had no business being there spying on him, stealing a look at his impressive bulldog face.

Sister was nineteen and in love with this bulldog-faced man. She looked up to him. She idolized him. He was the guru of her new faith. She believed what this man believed — that he was the best tenor Korea had ever produced. Wait and see. Time would prove that. In his dreams, often he stood with a flowing kerchief in his hand at the center of the stage at Carnegie Hall or Lincoln Center or La Scala. The cheers from the adulating crowd in front of him were deafening. Moved, he wept. But for now, this man, older than sister by more than a decade, honed the tool for his fame at a dusty animal hospital in a suburb of Seoul. And sister was in love with him.

Three evenings a week, sister raced to her church where he was a conductor and soloist for the church choir and sang in her soaring soprano under his approving eyes. Beaming like a morning star. Happier than ever. She was a chick dreaming of her first flight under his protective wing. Under his attention, she bloomed and bloomed each day as if there was no limit to how far a girl could go on blooming. She was beautiful in her love.

He urged sister to take up new piano lessons, to learn how to breathe properly and how to project her already beautiful voice. This man encouraged her, inspired her and cheered her on to sing better, better than anybody. This man blew his dreams into her soul. One day, he told her again and again like a man chanting a holy mantra, together they would build a flourishing career as a soprano and a tenor in Italy and in America. The world would be theirs to mold as if it were a ball of soft clay in the hand. Sister believed it. That was what she wanted, what she dreamed of and hoped for: a life of music with him.

On Christmas eve, mother went to the church to sneak a look at him. The man her daughter was so in love with. Mother took a seat in an inconspicuous corner and watched him conduct the church choir in a beautiful rendering of Handel's *Messiah*. In his flowing church robe, he looked like a spreading, soaring eagle. Built so big and solid and imposing as an oak tree. How impressed mother was with him! In contrast, her daughter, in the front row of the choir, looked like a child. Her mouth open wide in a big O, belching out her voice in such earnestness! She couldn't help but smile.

At midnight, the church choir showed up outside the gate of our house. We ran to the window and watched them stand in the snow drift and sing. How they cheerfully blasted away the calm of the snowy night with "Joy to the World!" They followed it with "The Holy City," our favorite. After the last song, "O Holy Night" was sung, mother invited them inside and treated them to scalding tea and red bean cakes.

That night, on the eve of Christmas, mother saw this man sister loved was not a shy man. He was a man as confident as a bull fighter. A man of conceit and self-assurance. He heartily consumed five red bean cakes and downed two cups of tea. When he spoke, his voice was as pleasing to the ear as a glazed candy on a tongue. He praised sister in glowing words and spoke of his ambitions with heroic charm. Mother easily saw that this man was a dreamer like her husband. A man who knew how to use words like her husband. A man who aimed at something big, bigger than life. A man whose ego was out of proportion. A man who was so much older than her daughter, as her husband had been for her. A man with a mountain-sized ambition and an empty pocket. A man who neglected his university training as a veterinarian for fame in an unknown world. A man who dreamed and dreamed.

◆　◆　◆

The night "Oratorio Company" held its debut concert in a downtown theater, in the middle of the front row, sister stood in a sleeveless silver lamé gown and matching pumps. With her teased up hair — the ends had been curled out and upward — and frosted pink lips, she looked like Diana Ross on the record jacket of the Supremes.

On the music bill mother saved was his picture: a bulldog with fiery eyes. He was the founder and artistic director of "Oratorio Company." Mother always said, "Titles don't make a man." We looked at the music bill with the same suspicion we did at father's new business cards where father's name was always accompanied by an impressive title: a president, a managing director or a chief executive. Those cards we later came upon in the corners of drawers spoke to us of broken dreams, dashed hopes and empty promises. Father's business cards were forged portraits. Futile attempts at an identity, a status. And was this man, we wondered, the other side of the same coin?

One brilliant, windy spring afternoon, I passed by the hospital and found the door locked and closed. I peeped into the dark. There was no one. No yapping dogs. No sleepy cats. The dilapidated piano, though, was still there, standing in the same corner, closed shut and covered thick with fine dust. I could almost hear his voice lilting in Italian. The impassioned plea he used to spit out like fire from his mouth! "I shall win! I shall win!" I had been his best audience. I still remembered the afternoon I had first heard him sing *Una furtiva lagrima*! I didn't have to know what those words meant. All the way home that day, the sad and lavish melodies had followed me like a long white satin scarf fluttering in the wind.

Another day, I noticed the rusting sign was missing. And inside there was nothing but empty cages and the fading pictures on the wall. The dilapidated piano was also gone and in its place an empty chair stood with a leg missing. So I knew that it was true: he was marrying that long-faced girl, a member of the church choir. She and sister had been "friends in faith." Grandmother had always preached to us: there are no friends like "friends in faith."

But did he love this girl? Did he share his dreams and soul with her as he had done with sister? He wasn't a fool. The girl's rich family was promising him a future in America. He must have said to himself, "Finally, a chance to have a go at my dream!" And must have felt that he was closer than ever before to the stages at Carnegie Hall and Lincoln Center and La Scala. Eagerly and zealously, he grabbed the chance. Why not? He lived to sing. He expected sister to understand that. He wouldn't have sacrificed his ambition and his ego for mere love. And he wasn't the first or the last man not to follow his heart.

On the way home from school, I still passed the animal hospital, now closed up and padlocked. Hoping and hoping to come across that monster of a man. I wanted to see him blush, stammer and crumble in shame. I wanted to stand in front of him face to face and spit and walk away although I had been taught never to spit at anyone. And I knew I would not be able to say a word even if I had come across him. I was a shy girl. A polite girl. Just like mother. Still, I couldn't help wanting to spit at this man. But I never came across him nor his shadow. I wondered if it were true, the words in a popular song: "Love could easily become the root of hatred."

Sister was inconsolable after that. Like a cactus flower that blooms just one night a year, she had bloomed briefly and gorgeously in her love and now stood in front of a world withered and wan. Another star of her life had fallen, crashed and burned to ashes. This man she had loved, idolized and hoped to build her life with had turned around and walked away. As if nothing had happened. That spring, sister stopped believing what she had always believed, "Ask, and it shall be given you; seek, and you shall find; knock, and it shall be opened unto you." Grandmother's favorite catch phrase from the Holy Bible.

CHAPTER 13

A HOLE IN THE HEART

Once there lived a mother bird. A nameless mother bird. One pristine night, under the indigo sky, she laid her eggs on a soft nest of dry twigs she had built in a ravine of solid rock. For many days and nights, the mother bird stayed put in the nest, covering the eggs with her feather-soft wings. The only time she left the nest was to fill her hunger.

One morning when the sunlight warmed her wings, the eggs' shells cracked open and baby chicks emerged pushing up their heads. They were little helpless things with gooey wings that were not ready to fly. They immediately opened their soft beaks and chirped noisily for food. Mother bird flew away and returned with worms and fed them to her little chicks. The baby chicks grew day by day — they never thanked the mother bird — and started to flap their wings.

One day, curious about the world where the mother bird ventured alone without them, the baby chicks flew out from the safe nest. First they twittered about, flying only a short distance, but each day, they flew higher and farther. Soon, they were flying in gliding motions, surveying the vast world. For the first time they saw there were many creatures other than themselves. The world they discovered was vast, dangerous, and exciting at the same time. Each day, they ventured farther away. They hopped from one branch to another, pecked a tree trunk and swooped down to a stream and alighted on a rock to catch a worm as a beast napped nearby. They grew cocky and never remembered their baby chick days.

I was told that one day when I reached a certain age, I would fly away from the nest of childhood just like these baby chicks. I would leave the round and soft world of childhood and enter one that was jagged and irregular. Then many familiar objects, shapes, sounds and colors would take on sudden transfigurations. I would be confused and lost for a while. A soft ripe peach that had been nothing but a peach to sink my teeth into to swallow its sweet pulp would be no longer just a peach. It would stir a feeling inside me. It would become the object of poetry. Its color I would desire for a dress. Its softness I would compare to that of an orange pink cloud in the sky. I would imagine riding the cloud to a land of romantic love with a handsome knight.

Suddenly a mere peach would carry my imagination to extremes. Like a pendulum in perpetual motion from left to right, my impression of a simple peach would vacillate back and forth. I would be like a mote caught in a shaft of afternoon light, floating around and around.

Every afternoon of that autumn, a man with a ripped straw hat used to come around with a cart full of *hong-ok*, red jade apples. They were sold by bamboo basketfuls and mother often bought a basketful from him. They were the size of a child's fist and crunchy and juicy. Their sweet juice spilled inside my mouth and the vinegary and fragrant scent lingered on my breath long after the last morsel.

That autumn — people refer to it as the season of high sky and fattened horses — fourteen-years-old, skinny and straight as a stick, my chest was forming hard little buds. Throbbing and throbbing as if baby chicks were caught inside. I was no longer a child running about the street after brother. Once inseparable — I still hear a woman's voice saying, "What a good boy he is, taking his sister with him everywhere!" — brother and I were now strangers. On streets we began to ignore each other, embarrassed about nothing and everything. Once with his friend perched behind him, brother furiously pedaled by in his bicycle. Desperately hoping that I wouldn't speak to him. It was unexplainable but somehow it made perfect sense.

Sometime that autumn the chicks inside my chest seemed to free themselves and flutter away with my childhood. My breasts started ballooning out. Faster than I could get used to. As if pushed by a hand from inside, my chest strutted out and my behind bulged, round and plump, pushing my blouse and skirt at their seams. Embarrassed, I stopped accompanying mother to the public bathhouse. But I hoped and hoped that mother would somehow notice that I was growing and growing into strange shapes. That she would open her eyes and see that I now needed a bra and a slip. But mother seemed to have gone blind. She never mentioned about my needing such things. And how does a shy child bring herself to ask for such things? I didn't know how. And mother went on ignoring these monstrous changes.

Several times in the afternoon after school, I rolled my savings inside the palm of my hand and walked to the market. I knew a lingerie shop where there were bras in every size heaped like mountains. Enough for many women to cover their breasts several times over. I passed by the shop, back and forth, being stricken with paralysis each time I came to the doorstep. Again and again, I came home without a bra, the money inside my palm clammy with sweat.

A lie is not a lie if it harms no one, I had read somewhere. So one day I concocted a story and told mother how earlier that day a teacher had reminded me that I now should start wearing a bra to school. Mother's mouth opened big into a smile; her baby girl was asking for a bra! She said I was still small. No bigger than hard green peaches. But mother immediately brought out a string, the kind for tying a package, and began measuring my chest; I giggled and thrashed about while she tugged the string around my chest. "Twenty-nine inches," mother declared when she measured the string on a ruler. Mother put the string into her snap-shut coin purse and took me to the same lingerie shop. There, I chose a couple of snow-white cotton bras with little pink satin ribbons and danced and skipped all the way back home, making mother laugh.

◆   ◆   ◆

One ordinary afternoon that autumn, walking home from school in the ripples of sunlight that spread like sharp electric currents, I passed a house that had persimmon trees in its garden. The sight of the deep brown trees holding a dozen persimmons, vermilion-colored against a cloudless blue sky, gave me a feverish jolt. I stood in the middle of a lane, gazing at the persimmon trees against the electric blue and felt an emptiness inside me where the birds had dwelled before flying away batting their wings. Into this emptiness, sadness seeped. Sad, sad, sad, a voice inside me whispered.

Since that afternoon, this emptiness grew, hungering and demanding, a storm raging inside. The emptiness was a hunger clamoring to be filled. And it was often filled with sadness. This sadness was also shame. And this shame seeped in. This sadness was also unhappiness. And this unhappiness seeped in.

It was then, every afternoon, I began to climb into the attic above the kitchen and devour words off the pages of book after book. I remember how faint afternoon light slashed in through the hinged window and the cooking smell floated up from the kitchen as I read and read munching on an apple.

There in the attic, its walls pasted over with yellowing news-papers, books opened to me a world in chaotic disarray, stranger than my dreams. There, my head was filled with strange streets and peoples and sounds and smells. With my head swirling and buzzing with all these images and sounds, I plodded around like a girl who had sold her mind to the devil. I'd pass through a market street and smell a back street of Paris. When I'd see a blank sky, against it, I'd build the towers of an English castle. And in the winds passing outside on a rainy night, I'd hear the name "Heathcliff!" Then one day, after reading about a book — "*Gray Notebook*" was its translated title — by Martin du Gard, a French writer, a girl and I bought two gray-covered identical notebooks and exchanged our diaries every morning in school. We pasted pages with dried petals, filled them with drawings and wrote sad little poems.

It seemed then that books were flying off the bookshelves by themselves and landing in my hands at random. One afternoon, I would be doubled over, pecking over the confessions of anony-mous women in a monthly women's magazine — a short-lived summer affair at a moonlit beach, a secret life with a married boss, betrayals of every kind, adultery with all the sordid details and tips on the first honeymoon night. On another, I would be struggling through Nietzsche — *Thus Spake Zarathustra* — or speeding through Bertrand Russell's autobiography. Words danced, twisted and transformed into vague conceptions.

At the start of each month, I eagerly waited for the arrival of the new issue of the monthly woman's magazine sister subscribed to. It came with a bonus world classic series, translated into Korean and printed on yellow flimsy paper. While cold, blustery winter nights hurried and raced to the still frosty dawns, my frozen fingers turned page after page of *Jane Eyre*, *Madame Bovary* and *Of Human Bondage*. Always sorry at the end of a book that a journey had ended.

Afterwards, the devoured novels by Thomas Mann, Stendal, Balzac, the Bronte sisters, Maugham and Flaubert were deposited in the attic, piled together with old magazines and newspapers to be sold by weight. In between the series, I turned to the bookshelves filled with hardcover books sister amassed with a fervent zeal as if inside her there was also emptiness, demanding to be filled. The colorfully clothed series of spiritual essays, of Greek mythologies and of world philosophy were cold dripping rain drops and dead fossils and shifting shadows of clouds, unequal to the dramas full of smoldering passion and dark secrets and unbridled desires on those flimsy pages of the discarded series.

Then I began to find the words I read in books fanciful and elusive — sunlight streaming through my fingers. They could pass right through me and leave me still hungry and empty. Words tumbled down like a waterfall and flew away like a stream of water to join the rivers and the seas of words, leaving only the trail of a journey; a dry pebble bottom.

The house that stood on top of a green hill, the cobblestone street trod by men and women, the garden with roses and tulips all disappeared with the words down the stream. Leaving me with impressions but without the possession of any word. A word was a tricky thing. It could change meaning from one sentence to another. A word could betray me, fail me and confuse me.

But I discovered if words are put to music and a voice sings them, they become permanent. In this way, the words form a link from one day to another. Like a spring dress put away in a chest for the winter, words in a song can be forgotten for a while. But passing a street alone on a quiet afternoon, at the sight of a red rose behind an iron gate, I would suddenly remember the song again. Its words and snatches of melody rolled out of my mouth. The words returned as mine again, evoking a memory of such and such a day. I saw the face and heard the voice of so-and-so who, on a long-ago afternoon, sang along with the song by the window with a view of a rose garden. I saw again a record turning smoothly on the record player, spilling out words that had once meant so much to me. The words reminded me of the smell of a certain cloudy day or a foolish thought that I once had. The words evoked all kinds of memories. They made the days, past and gone, tangible again.

◆　◆　◆

The year I turned sixteen, I would suddenly find everything funny — all the sadness and hunger suddenly evaporated — and hopelessly giggle through the days. A rolling leaf in the wind, a boy slipping in the snow, a pimple on a girl's nose and a cowlick on a boy's head — all these would pull out giggles from my mouth.

I giggled through the whole chaotic spring. Brother, then a first year student at the prestigious Seoul National University, dated and meditated and chanted and took to the streets for antigovernment demonstrations. He'd often come home scraped, bruised and bleary-eyed from tear gas and missing a shoe or shirt. He could have died or gotten hurt but the sight of him limping in without a shoe sent me rolling. When his overly-serious short story was published in his school paper, giggling, I read it out loud to the girls in school. Afterwards, a gaggle of admiring girls appeared at the gate of ours. It was my job to persuade them to go home.

That spring, songs entered into my world when one afternoon brother walked into the house carrying a portable record player with him. It looked like one of the many junk machines he often brought home to tinker with. With his tool box spilling out tiny screw drivers and with wires littered about, brother worked on the machine all afternoon. Then he summoned mother, sister and me around him and plugged the blue-and-cream colored machine into the outlet. He carefully placed a record on the turntable and put the needle on. The black round disk turned slowly and a wonderful voice flew out.

I remember the precise moment when the voice of Julie Andrews, that of a skylark, opened up a new horizon for me. Wonderful English words played magic in her voice. (I who had once sworn that no song more beautiful than *Una furtiva lagrima* existed in the world!) Words tumbled out in clear diction unlike the dramatic wail of indecipherable Italian arias sister shot up from her belly. I could almost see Julie Andrews dancing through the alpine meadows in *The Sound of Music* which our entire school had gone to see in a musky theater. I knew then the words in her songs were mine forever; no longer elusive rays of sunlight or flowing streams of water.

After that afternoon, every day, we listened to songs in English that tumbled out from the portable record player. Songs from spaghetti Westerns, James Bond movies, *Doctor Zhivago* and *Romeo and Juliet*. I was in love with English. The English words formulated in the voices of singers were simply delicious. Cool, velvety, heroic and touchingly dramatic.

One day, brother brought home a new record, a second-hand one, with a scratch here and there. It was played right away. One particular song, a song of many words with delightful "oops," "pops," and "kerplops," captured our imagination. Later I found out the song, "High Hopes," was from an American movie *A Hole in the Head* and the owner of the twenty-four-carat diamond voice was Frank Sinatra. But then, it mattered little who the singer was.

We played the song hundreds of times, over and over. Sister who had no taste for anything except classical music would often complain; she couldn't stand hearing that "silly song" being played again and again with its lollypop childishness. But we continued playing the song all through the winter. Every time we played the song, its words never failed to perk up our spirits. An ant who thinks he can move a rubber tree plant, an old ram who keeps butting his head thinking he'd punch a hole in a dam made us think we could reach for the sky with sheer will, cockiness and daring.

Now whenever I look back to those days, days once filled with confusion, terror and the pain of growing up, the song that dared me to hope comes back word for word with the smile that used to appear on mother's face when the song reached the part of the silly old ram.

CHAPTER 14

VALLEY OF CLOVER

*W*e go up the hill to bury father. The men of father's clan carry the coffin – varnished in red brown, the coffin bleeds in the heat – up the path shaded by magnolias and maples. Sister and I follow at the heels of brother carrying father's portrait draped with black ribbons. I imagine the silent clucking of the tongues from the wailing women down the hill following me, and I stumble on the tall weeds. What a pity those high-nosed, smart and well-educated children can't even wail properly! That is what they are saying.

I step onto the mounds of fresh soil dug up from the ground. Under the flammable sun, the soil cracks and gives way under the feet and a musty smell floats up. Slowly, father's coffin, secured at each end with ropes, is lowered into the cool and dark ground. Brother kicks a shiny shovel into the soil and spills the flying dust onto the top of the coffin.

His eyes well up with tears. Brother swallows all that musty wet air and looks away. A short spastic cry escapes from sister's mouth as the soil spatters on the lid.

I can see, as if in a dream, the soil seep through the cracks of the coffin and blind father's eyes and gag father's mouth. I can almost hear father gasp as if he were shut in alive. Then comes the fitful cry of a bird from the top of the mountain. The earth begins to move in a gentle undulating motion, like the bottom of the sea in an earthquake. Suddenly the coffin squeaks open and a black bird flaps out and soars straight up. I jerk my head and follow it up into the sky. The sun tumbles down from the sky in a ball of flame and blinds my eyes. I cannot see anything. No bird. When I finally pull my head back and look at the ground, the coffin is all but buried by the soil poured down from the shovels of the grave diggers.

The same night, the bird that escaped from father's coffin appears in my dream. I follow the bird over nine peaks of mountains covering thousands of li. The bird alights on a lonely path in lofty mountains. There, the bird sheds its wings and becomes father, in a man's traditional white gown. Father, the sole traveler on the long path, begins walking toward the twilight of the Never Never Land.

The path leads him through the mountains of old pines — their branches and trunks are bright red — past cascading waterfalls and golden deer. Father walks swiftly without effort, his white gown flying in the wind, his feet young and strong.

I try to catch up with father but I fall farther and farther behind. Soon, father becomes a moving dot far ahead in the folds of mountains, emerald green and sapphire blue in mist. Over the peaks of two lofty mountains, the sun and the moon rise in bright symmetry — the sun bright red and the moon metallic white. They are so huge and so bright, the mountains shimmer and deer jump and sparkles from waterfalls break into diamonds.

I run as fast as I can and when I think I have gained some distance,

*the mountains shift away to remain as a shimmering mirage. Finally, I
arrive at a tall red wooden gate guarded by two gigantic soldiers of the
netherworld. They have bulging eyes, bawdy red lips and long beards.
They forbid me to enter. Their thunderous voices shake the ground. They
say no living soul has ever set foot beyond the gate. I bow and beg them,
full of tears, to let me in as I am the daughter of a man who has just
entered the gate. They hiss and brandish their swords. I wake up as they
are about to snap my body in two with their swords.*

*This dream was never repeated. Later I began to think that it wasn't
just a dream but had really happened. I had really accompanied father in
the last journey of his spirit. In that fantastically out-of-the-ordinary
journey.*

I still see father walking through the folds of the fluttering laundry
and passing through the white wooden arch where luscious clusters
of dark purple grapes hung from tangled vines. Just like yesterday.
That was how he had last returned home. His eyes proclaiming
nothing. His hands empty. His glib tongue mostly dry. His fifty-eight
years scattered along the roads. Father returned that unceremoniously.

What had finally guided his feet back home? He didn't offer
any explanation. Words alone couldn't explain anything any
longer. Just as he had done so many times, he walked in as if he
were returning after a day's work. And stayed.

We tried to bury the questions and to forget all the memories of
pain. But they remained, pain unhealed. We wondered if father
knew how so often we had wanted to run away from the questions:
Where is your father? What does your father do? But now we had
grown up and were no longer hurt by them. We saw and understood that father had no more control of his fate than he did of
ours. But it didn't make it easier to untangle all those emotions

that had heaped up all those years.

For two years, we lived together in the same house, separated by a wide gulf that never closed. Evening after evening, he came home, still a stranger. Just as he had been that evening so long before when he had come home in his double breasted suit and fedora hat. He was a dreamer then. An inspired and incorrigible dreamer. And he had made us dreamers too, in that brief autumn when he showered us with blissful happiness.

Till the end, father remained a shadow on the dark side of the gulf that separated us. So many things foregone, so many moments lost, so many memories unshared. His words no longer painted a bright future. His dreams were dead, no longer realizable. He was not bitter though, only silent, like a stone. Like a dry river that had run its course, father, once a harbor of youthful promises and high hopes and limitless dreams, was a silent bed of broken pebbles. And mother and father, they rarely spoke to each other. The silence between them always reminded us that it was all too late to change anything. We had to accept whatever had happened and move on.

Two summers later, father lay unconscious on a hospital bed. His once handsome head had been shaved and cut in a circular flap to remove the blood clot and then sewed back. The scar remained ugly, like a soiled knee cap, slow to heal. Through the long hot months of July and August, we kept a vigil at his bedside as he fought and struggled for his life, lingering in that foggy state of consciousness and unconsciousness. The sound of his perforated throat gurgling filled the heat-throbbing, sunny hospital room, sometimes the only sign of life. Slowly, he was perishing. His bedsores festered. His purplish hands were always cold and stiff. Each day, hope inexorably diminished.

That summer, often I rode a bus with sister to her friend's house to get sunflowers. With fervor and stubbornness, sister turned the sunflowers — they followed the sun — into a symbol of hope. Many hot afternoons, we sat in an empty bus rattling along the baked road, sister and I, silent and sad. Our hair blowing in the hot sticky winds. On the way back, the sunflowers sister clutched in her hand always seemed to wither too fast.

With the sunflowers, we returned to the hospital. Hot and tired. It was always then, late in the afternoon, when the sunlight streamed in melting the window panes and drenching his room, that father seemed to be coming out of the dark tunnel. He would attempt a word only to give up. The hose attached to his throat, the needles attached to his arms and hands seemed to infuriate him. Furiously, he would whirl his arms, trying to pull off all the things that kept him alive. Then he would fall into a deep exhausted sleep. Afterwards, in that room, time seemed to dissolve into an eternity. The electric fan roared up and down and the fruit in the basket rotted and the petals of the sunflower drifted down. Outside, the summer sun blazed on.

During his last week, father lay incarcerated but calm, like a monk who had been on a long and agonizing path to Nirvana. His head started growing fuzzy hair like weeds on a barren soil. Then one night, father breathed his last breath and expired, having never regained consciousness.

◆ ◆ ◆

I must have felt no sadness as I didn't cry or wail. Someone had said death is the other side of life, like a turned overcoat. Death is followed by rebirth. Death does not exclude life. Life is a continuous circle. Unending and infinite.

The death was so personal and so close, but I couldn't

understand it. I remained dumb and numb in the face of father's death. Without understanding, there is no possibility of feeling. Death puzzles people. People mourn and cry and wail when a death comes to the door. But I didn't even understand that. The only thing I understood was that I would never see him again. At the end of such long years of uncertainty, one thing had become sure. Although it was not what I would have chosen.

While women of father's clan wailed in front of the mourning table, I stood in a corner, eyes dry and throat shut, voiceless and unfeeling like a bird that had cried to death, bleeding in its throat. Just like mother who seemed dazed, puzzled and devastated by this strange end of her life with father. Mother had poured out years of her torment in her tearless wailing and stood dissipated, finally accepting her fate.

Grandmother came and sat in the corner with a Bible on her lap, mumbling a rosary of words and singing hymns. Father's clan would not allow her to bring in her minister to offer, according to her, "just a simple prayer of comfort." Father's clan, they were Confucians who stuck to the old ways. I could smell all those hundreds of years preserved in them. Unfazed and indignant, grandmother in her ample skirt perched like a big bird and kept her post. And clucked her tongue disapprovingly each time another female relative came in and started to wail.

This went on all day long. The haunting melody of the women's wailing was exasperating: death was a wailing contest for the women — the worshipers of mountain spirits, totem poles, shamanistic ghosts and Confucius' rules. And then the women would wipe their dry eyes and talk and laugh. They could barely hide the pride of performers who had an unexpected chance to show off their artistry. Afterwards, they descended over us one by one to offer condolences. "I had one son-in-law and he smoked, drank and lied," grandmother said to them. "He did everything the Bible forbade you to do. If only he had been saved by the love of Jesus while he was alive... He will go to hell now and it's my fault." Grandmother sniffled.

◆   ◆   ◆

One night, a week after we buried father, our doorbell rang. Sister went out and rushed back in. She had the look of someone who had just seen a ghost. We all hurried out to the gate to find a small young man standing in an ill-fitting maroon suit. One look at him and we all knew. For we heard the murmurs of the shared blood. He was our ghost mother's son. Father's other son. He had father's slight beaked nose and deep-set eyes as mother had once said. Unmistakable. He took after father more closely than the three of us did but in a strange way, the good looks and the gracefulness father had were missing from him.

When we all entered the room, he insisted on paying his respects to mother. Mother tried to stop him but he was already prostrating himself. Mother sat stiffly. Her face was flushed red. Afterward, mother introduced us to him. Each time, he bowed his head, eagerly searching out our faces with his eyes. In the bright light, though, we found him rather ordinary and weathered. All the mystery we had built upon him was not there. Mother asked him how old he was. He scratched his head and said he was twenty-five. On his chin though, pimples still flowered in tiny, red angry bursts. Then we all fell into an awkward silence. It was all so strange and yet so natural. It was as if we had expected all along that one day we would meet him, father's secret son. But all the questions we would have liked to ask somehow simply vanished. We felt like we knew what it would have been like for him all

204 • HOUSE OF THE WINDS

these years. It was touching and sad. The box of oranges he had brought with him remained in the middle of the room all forgotten to be offered and accepted.

Then finally, mother told him that father had passed away. He nodded his head quietly. He knew already. The day father passed away, he received a telegram from Small Father, father's brother, he said. He had wished very much to come to the funeral but had finally decided not to. He would have been out of place. His presence would have been disruptive. Two big drops of tears rolled down his sun-seared face. Then he finally looked up at mother. His lips were trembling. Mother took his hand and led him to the altar. For a long time, he stared at father's portrait before he prostrated slowly and dropped his head to the floor. He wept. Quietly first. And then all his defenses crumbled. His sob erupted into a wail. His shoulders jerked. I could feel in his sobbing all the pain he must have had growing up in the shadow as a secret child. His pain of growing up having but not having a father. He went on sobbing, his body prostrated on the floor.

Before he left to catch the last bus for his town, mother held his hands in hers and told him to take good care of himself and stay in touch. And then in silence, we watched his small figure disappear into the night. It seemed strange that he should return to his old life at his chicken farm and to his aging grandmother who had brought him up. That nothing should change. The night turned chilly as we stood puzzled, baffled and a little sad.

◆   ◆   ◆

On father's one-hundredth-day memorial, we traveled to the mountain. The October hills were turning deep red, bright yellow and burnt brown. As we strutted up the path, father's grave, a round mound, came into view behind the pines and maples. It reminded me of father's shaved head that had started growing fuzzy hair when he died.

Mother, sister, brother and I moved up the lane in single file, silent and holding our breath. Then we stood in front of his grave, covered with grass, grown tall over the summer. Brother planted the incense sticks in the ground and lit them. The smoke floated up, like a ghostly wind. Each of us, taking turns, poured *soju*, father's favorite drink, into a cup and offered it to the grave. Then, all together, we placed our hands and knees to the ground, repeating the bow three times.

I wondered if father was happy that we had come. If he knew at all that we were here. If his soul was away where he had gone in my dream and under the mound only his body was turning into a handful of dust. I was still puzzled with the cessation of a life. I almost understood but then I didn't.

I thought of the young man who had come to us after the funeral, his son. All his life, father had never mentioned him to us children. Not even once. Why, I wondered. I thought of the four lined *sijo*s, Korean poems, we had found in his notebook pages after he died. I could imagine a man stopping on a lonely country road to compose a poem but somehow that man was not my father. I could imagine a man searching for his ancestral mountain lost during the Japanese rule but I could not believe that was how father spent the last several years of his life. I could picture a dab of cloud in a blue sky, a whip of wind on the tip of wild reeds and the shriek of a bird perching on a tree branch in his poem but I could not imagine it was father who wrote them. And that he was ever as lonely as his poem said. He had his family. A wife and children. And that must not have been enough for him. What was he chasing after?

If father ever felt pride in his search for the lost ancestral land, he kept it a secret. If father ever felt pain for his life gone astray, he never expressed it. If he was ever lonely, he kept his loneliness to himself. How strange we had to find out all this from someone else, from sources other than himself. And that, only after he died. It was also to Small Father, to his brother, not to his children, father left all of his notebooks and papers and instructions. Perhaps he saw that his only life's mission for us children was to inspire us. So when he finally left us, he left as a stranger.

Sister went down to the stream with an empty bottle to get water for the flowers she had brought. Brother and mother were busy tending the grave, pulling out the weeds and cutting grass. I bent to pull off a wild flower behind father's tombstone and hesitated. That small lavender flower might be father's spirit, I thought. As a child, I used to believe a flower on a grave was a soul of the dead.

I turned around and looked down the valley where sister had gone off. There were mounds of uncut stones lying about blocking the view of the stream. The stones were waiting to be cut, chiseled and engraved with another name and another date. The stone cutters' hammering sound bounced back from the hill across and returned as peals of echoes. Sister came up from behind the bank of the stream. She was humming a song. I wondered if father's death was still hurting her. If she was still hurt by the promises father had made but never fulfilled. We never talked about it, afraid to dig deep into the curious black well of emotions inside. Afraid that we might end up so deep and lost.

Mother took bunches of weeds and heaped them to one side. She climbed up to the grass bank and said as if to herself, "There are baby maples growing everywhere." I looked down. She was right. Everywhere tiny maple saplings, with a leaf or two were pushing through the grass. Like people, the maples spread their life. Life went on even in the mountain where the dead were buried. Mother said she was going to take some saplings home and plant them in pots. Suddenly, the idea seemed to delight her.

Mother straightened her back and gazed down at the valley stretching below all the way to the misty horizon. From up there, it looked like the earth had been turned upside down. We were standing on earth looking down at the sky. I knew what mother was thinking: one day she would be buried here next to father. Half of father's tombstone was left empty, to be engraved with her name and dates of birth and death. She would be again bound to father, the husband she didn't choose. I could just imagine mother lying in the grave and turning her back on him. Still unhappy, still puzzled and still reluctant to accept the inscrutable ways of fate.

Before we left, we looked around father's grave one more time. Rid of weeds, grass cut, the green mound seemed less forlorn. The tall maple tree was cascading a long branch of sienna leaves — waving baby hands — over the grave.

Following the stream, we walked down to the lower ground. There were Mandarin ducks gliding in the pond where caretakers raised fish. It was strange to see the ducks, symbols of marriage affinity, there. Less than three decades had passed since that day mother and father had made marriage vows that they would stay together until their black hair turned as white as scallion roots. But they were already separated by the shadow-line of life and death before their hair turned even gray. Father's hair was still jet-black when he died.

"*Umma*, do you remember the story of the stupid couple you used to tell us when we were little?" sister asked, turning to mother. Mother nodded and smiled. I remembered the story well. Long long ago, during the days when Korean tigers smoked pipes, mother used to begin the story: there in a village lived a stupid couple. One day the husband went to a marketplace to look for a way to make money. He was passing a street when a delicious smell tickled his nose. He followed the smell and entered a store. He asked the owner what was the delicious smell. The owner told him it was the smell of roasting sesame seeds. He thought that would make him a lot of money. The delicious smell of roasting sesame seeds would bring in lots of customers. He emptied his pocket and bought a big sack of sesame seeds. He brought them home and immediately sent his wife into the kitchen to roast the sesame seeds. As the sesame seeds were roasted, another brilliant idea hit the stupid husband. He went to the kitchen and gathered all the roasted sesame seeds and went out to the field and planted them. Then the stupid couple waited and waited for the sesame seeds to sprout and bring them ten folds of what they had planted. But nothing happened. The roasted sesame seeds just rotted in the soil. They ended up even poorer.

"I don't know why but the story reminds me of you and father," sister said laughing.

"But I ended up rich with three smart children," mother replied proudly. We all laughed. In a rush of love, mother drew our hands into hers. Her hand was warm and tiny. It was a hand I knew so well. I could close my eyes at any time and draw each freckle, line and contour of her hand. And also those of her face. With lightly drooping eyes, small nose and tentatively drawn lips. I squeezed mother's arm into mine. Mother looked at me and smiled.

"Look at sister," brother said, shaking his head. Sister had stopped again. She was squatting in the middle of the green patch by the stream. She was looking for four-leaf clovers, her symbol of good luck. She was again the thirteen-year-old with her shiny straight black hair who always looked for four-leaf clovers in the craggy hills we used to climb in summer. Mother stood and watched sister. She was going to wait for her no matter how long.

Sister ran toward us, waving a four-leaf clover in her hand. We all clucked our tongues and teased her. "Look, what I've found!" sister exclaimed, catching her breath. Her face was flushed pink with excitement. Surrounding mother, we walked down to the clearing where the shuttle bus was waiting. Soon the bus jolted down the uneven road through the valley. Through the dusty window, we kept looking back at the receding hill where father lay. Alone. As he had been. Always.

CHAPTER 15

THE CARP

As children, we always looked forward to the future. Each today was for tomorrow. Tomorrow for the next year. That was how we coped with our shabby present. In our innocence, we never doubted that the future would bring only good, savory things.

Then one day, walking down the street, I found that I was no longer thinking of the future or even of the present. My mind raced only toward the past. But the past was suddenly retrievable only through my own dim memories. Mother was no longer in this world.

◆   ◆   ◆

It was so out of the blue. Mother's illness. It jumped out of nowhere and gripped her tightly. She was easily tired. Her legs swelled into tree trunks. Her shoes didn't fit. Grandmother, who always imagined that her body harbored myriads of illnesses, thus giving her the motive of prayer, came and took charge of mother's illness.

She had just experienced faith-healing; she had retreated into a prayer center, one of those that proliferated in the folds of hills around the outskirts of the city. At the end of ten day's fasting — I drank only water, grandmother proudly said — and fervent praying, she stood in front of a minister. The very moment the minister laid his trembling hand on her, she insisted, she felt a big swirl erupt inside and churn. She graphically described what happened next: She rushed to the bathroom to relieve herself. She sat sweating and trembling as all the poison she had been carrying for years gushed out. In an endless, foul, stinking stream! And with that, every little ailment seeped out of her body. Remember that big, solid lump that has been pressing down her low belly for years? It was gone too, melted away, like candle wax! Her stomach used to be as big as Mount Nam. But it collapsed like a sink hole, leaving folds of loose flaps around it. She felt like a newborn. So clean. So light. We should have seen her walking out of the prayer center. With a new life! Her feet had never been so light. Like they had been padded by goose feathers!

In between the sessions of Bible reading and preaching and tuneless singing, grandmother accompanied mother to herb doctors. No Western medicine would cure mother's illness, she insisted. Day and night, the concoction of herbs was boiled in the glazed medicine pot. She made sure mother drank that bitter stew to the last drop. "Drink it up and pray. There's nothing faith cannot cure!"

But mother didn't get better. Her belly started to swell. It was maddening. It was no wonder to grandmother that mother didn't get better. She lacked faith. "Beg God to make you better! Move him with your hot tears of faith!" On mother's swelled belly, grandmother applied moxa and smoldering mugwort pads which left ugly reddish burned marks on her. So single-minded grandmother was and so fervent she was in her belief, to our regrets later, we let her be in charge. We could hardly slip in a word of our opinions. Wistful, maybe we were afraid that our doubts might just kill mother.

Soon, desperate and searching for someone to blame, grandmother convinced herself that her spiteful husband ghost was again at work. She reminded us of the old story. When her husband died, his belly was the size of a big pumpkin. Remember? He must be lonely for a companion. He couldn't get her to come to him so he now wanted his favorite daughter by his side. While grandmother prayed and cursed her husband ghost, mother's liver was dying, poisoned by her expensive concoction.

One afternoon, I came home from school and found a huge, live carp swimming in a large plastic jar filled with water. The carp was really beautiful. Almost unworldly. Grandmother was proud that she had paid an enormous sum for it. Later, the live carp disappeared into a pot of boiling water. I still remember the strangely unpleasant smell that seeped out of the pot and permeated the house. In the old Korean stories, I remembered, carps talked and cried just like people. They were sacred fish. And grandmother put it in boiling water alive!

After mother drank that carp soup, overnight her belly stretched and expanded and swelled up into a fantastically huge mound. Mother could hardly sit up or breathe. As mother moaned lying on her side, grandmother sang and prayed and cursed her husband's ghost. We had to literally wrench mother away from her grip to rush mother to the hospital. Grandmother plummeted to the floor. She cried.

◆　◆　◆

The day he was leaving for France, on the way to Kimpo Airport, brother stopped to see mother at the hospital. He looked so young. He had a new haircut. I don't know why but I suddenly remembered the day he graduated from high school. How he had seemed embarrassed about the presence of mother and me outside his classroom. When he saw us smiling and waving through the window, he quickly ducked his head. I wondered if it was mother's old-fashioned dress that shamed him. Or the humble chrysanthemums we had brought for him instead of a fancy bouquet of red and pink carnations with a willow branch of velvety buds. Or the lack of a camera in our hands.

Just like that day when brother graduated at the top of his class, mother was proud of him. He was going to France on a scholarship for a year of research. I don't remember what words brother and mother exchanged. It was the unspoken words I remember. The fear.

Mother always loved brother in a different way. If her love for us daughters was a jubilant and demonstrative one, her love for him, for her only son, was a stoic one. It was a constant and quiet vigil. An absolute devotion. That is the way perhaps mothers love their sons in Korea.

Mother tried so hard that afternoon not to show tears to him. Not to weigh him down with her tears. It was wrong to show tears to someone embarking on a long journey. No matter how slim, there was always a chance that her tears might pull his plane down to the ground. Unthinkable. Then as soon as brother left, mother turned her face away. In her hands, she buried her feverish eyes and cried.

I don't think brother saw that fear that erupted in mother's eyes like black waves the moment he turned away to leave. It was the fear that she might not see him again. That she might die before he returned home. She experienced that fear again and again.

Mother was there to welcome him home one year later. We shared some good happy days. Mother cooked special dishes for him. We played cards, talked and laughed. On weekends when brother came up to Seoul, we went out to see movies. (We didn't forget how mother used to love movies.) Then he left again, this time for England. In fear and wistfulness, we went through another year. Letters and a couple of phone calls — they were expensive — kept us reassured.

A few years later, selfish in our pursuit of dreams, six months apart, brother and I left for America to study. Mother's incurable illness was stabilized for now but we weren't sure what that would mean in the days and weeks and months to come. The fear was still there. If only digging deeper. Unspoken but always present.

I still have the wristwatch, called Marianne, mother bought me just before I left for America. It stopped working long ago and its strap is missing. Why a watch? Mother didn't want me to forget the passage of time. She wanted me to remember to come back home. In the taxi on the way to the airport, mother was already crying. By the time I tore myself away from her at the airport, our eyes had puffed up like bread dough. Just as the door closed, through the fog of tears, I saw mother standing with brother and sister, crying. She had always cherished her baby daughter. There in a special corner in her heart, she kept a place reserved only for her baby child. I knew that. We all knew that. Less than six months later, she took another trip to the airport to send brother away.

That's the irony of life. Mother ended up with sister, the tormenting child, the child she used to say in moments of anger, she didn't wish even on an enemy. It was on that child that later she relied, from whom she sought comfort and for whom her heart broke — her daughter was reaching thirty and unmarried. It was that child who took her to doctors, shopping and tended to her needs while her two other children pursued their dreams in a far away country.

Two years later, at the Kimpo airport where I landed in the early winter morning, there was no sight of sister or mother waiting. I had flown all the way across the sea, dreaming of their smiling faces. The phone at home rang and rang. An hour late, sister came running in through the revolving door. When we got into a taxi, sister said we were going straight to the hospital. With the luggage and all. It was a complete surprise. That mother was in the hospital. Had been for over two weeks. Why had she chosen not to tell me until that moment? She was just like father! All his life, father ran away whenever he had bad news. Because he abhorred confronting us with it. He ran off, leaving us to deal with the wreckage. If he came back, it was only because he had money to buy us things, because he had titles to show us, because he had new projects brewing. For that we suffered. I wanted to but didn't ask sister why she hadn't called and told me that mother had gone into the hospital. I knew the answer. It was she who took care of mother while we were away. It was she who dealt with the problems while we were away. I had no right to ask her why. I had relinquished that right when I left.

Mother lay in a near coma when I arrived at the hospital. It was a shock. A jolt. I despaired. Mother looked so small. She looked like a child. And her face was a colorless carving. I bent over her and cried. I couldn't help it. Mother must have sensed I was there.

From the corner of her closed eyes, tears gushed out and tumbled down. They were from joy and relief.

That afternoon, mother miraculously opened her eyes. When she looked at me, there was such gladness. Then with sheer will, mother clung to life. Day and night, I sat by her side, wrapping her small hands with mine. I hoped and wished that somehow she would live. For nine days, she lingered. She could barely talk. The only time she talked was to tell me that she had so much to tell me. I told her just to get better. She and I would then talk and talk. But those became her last words. The chance to talk was lost forever.

One morning, going out for breakfast, I told mother that I would be back very soon. Mother looked at me and smiled that warm smile only she possessed. She must have known there was very little time left and must have wanted me to stay next to her. But she didn't ask me to and would never have asked me to. She wanted me to eat, to satisfy my hunger even as she was dying. When I came back, mother was slipping into the foggy tunnel that connects life and death.

When mother finally closed her eyes, brother was still in America. We gave him the news by phone. I don't remember how we told him. The exact words are lost in my memory. What I remember was the deafening silence that followed. Long heart-wrenching silence. He couldn't utter a word. Not even a moan. All the light inside him simply went out. It was too much to bear. Sister and I clutched the silent receiver together and wept.

Unable to be there when mother was buried, brother must have suffered even more than us. Later, we would learn that brother, alone with his grief in Texas, shut himself inside his room for days. It devastated him. As mother's only son, he felt he had relinquished all his duties for his selfish pursuits.

Grandmother didn't come to the mountain when we went up

to bury mother on that frigid January day. It is a sin for a mother to send her child to the other world ahead of her. Maybe in that sense, mother was lucky.

After we buried mother, sister and I, two motherless daughters, rarely spent time together. Each of us was an unanchored leaf boat, drifting away. Lost. We had to deal with the grief alone and apart from each other. Together, it was unbearable. And then there was the blame, resentment and regret we had to sort out and swim through. It was lonely. Lonelier than anything.

◆ ◆ ◆

How few things mother left behind. There were her clothes (including the immaculate Korean dresses of long ago), a sewing box, a few pieces of jewelry, a Bible, some books and little notebooks where she had jotted down, with a pencil, recipes from the radio. Inside her black velvet coin purse, I found a roughly hewn bronze cross wrapped with a yellow nylon cord. It connoted a shamanistic belief. Where had she gotten it from? Who had given it to her? She must have carried it with her all the time. It was her talisman. Her fervent wish to live until we children returned.

Inside a drawer, I also found new pictures of mother. She had them taken to send to us in America. I remembered a letter mother had written promising to send new pictures of her. The promised pictures had never come. Now I knew why. She didn't look well in them. Her face was puffy. The puffiness buried her small features. I could hardly recognize the face in the picture. There were other snapshots. Strays. Among them was the one taken on a Mother's Day. It was the year I had entered middle school. Mother and I stood in front of cannas and gladioluses. I had pinned a red carnation on her light pink *geogori*. In her *hanbok*, neat and modest, mother looks untouched by the passage of time. Mother leans toward me, smiling. And I stand straight, a little sullen. Why? Was the sun in my eyes? Life was now made up only of memories, not all of them clear.

A long month after mother died, I found a lonely blue aerogram in the mail box. Dizzily stamped in Korean and English. It was the last letter mother had written to me in America. It had traveled all the way to America and back. "Return to Sender," the stamp read. But the sender, mother, was no longer here. I had not the courage to open it. I put it away in between the pages of a book. For years, the letter would remain there, unopened. As long as I kept it unopened, there seemed to exist possibility and hope. Of and for what? I didn't know.

The sense of loss and the pain from the loss never lessened with the passage of time. Weeks after, months after, they were the same. I missed her. I pined for her. I clung to the memories that I excavated, one by one, searching them out from the foggy folds where all memories go and wait to be resurrected. I clung to them even though they were only so many fragments of stone, hoping that some day, one by one, I might piece them back together as one brilliant stone.

◆　◆　◆

In my memories, mother will always remain that vibrant, young woman, perfectly happy with her children behind the blue gate of hers. She forever stands in the sunny cabbage patch. She was like one of those white cabbage flowers. Like them and like all flowers, one day it was time for her to go. That was all.

Some day, I will no longer be sad and lost. Only lonely for her. Life is a river. It flows incessantly.

A PENGUIN READERS GUIDE TO

HOUSE OF THE WINDS

Mia Yun

AN INTRODUCTION
TO *HOUSE OF THE WINDS*

"I had become [mother's] sorcerer. I had seen mother's history. Her
very own history, a legacy of a river full of hopes and dreams and
despair of women before her. I tell her it is her turn now to
continue the journey on her own. I will stand by her until there is
no more time to write it and I will be the next carrier of her hopes
and dreams when I become a woman one day."

In *House of the Winds*, first-time novelist Mia Yun weaves a
spellbinding story from her memories of growing up in a Korea
torn apart both by war and by long years of Japanese rule.
Kyung-A—a young girl whose greatest strength is drawn from the
dreams and magical stories of her mother, Young Wife—is our
guide through the ethereal world created by Yun. Kyung-A
resurrects women who have "voiceless souls," giving them at last the
opportunity to speak of their struggles, of their war-ravaged pasts,
of male domination, and of timeless Korean customs and beliefs.
As the young narrator's mother said to her, "everything's in front of
you and it is up to you how you see and remember."

As Kyung-A's family is forced to move from one house to
another, closer and closer to the outskirts of Seoul, she introduces
readers to an array of characters whose stories will not be forgotten.
There is the manic Pumpkin Wife, who repeatedly tells the tale of
her lost son, each time with a different ending; there is Young-ok,
who is married off to a limping older man in order to save face for
the family; Soon-hee, a young girl who was raped by an American
soldier and becomes a prostitute; and Big Sister, who runs away
hoping to find the life her father promised her. And through it all,
there is Young Wife, a mother who grew up pampered as her

2

father's favorite child until Japanese soldiers took away their family lands. Married to a dreaming, useless, mostly absent husband, she must search for ways to support her children. Along the way, she deals with the criticism of her mother, who constantly invokes the wrath of Christianity upon her; the anger of her oldest daughter; the prying eyes and ears of the neighborhood women, who find her and her children stuck-up; and the knowledge that she will forever be tied to a man she did not choose. The burdens she must carry are many, yet she never loses hope in her dreams for her children, even as she fingers the rich cloth she cannot afford and chooses instead to buy her son and daughter a rice cake treat.

The hardships visited upon these Korean women, and the sacrifices they've made, are starkly apparent in *House of the Winds*. Through Yun's vivid imagery and exquisite storytelling, the realities of their lives come soaring, like the words of the Pumpkin Wife, from its pages.

ABOUT MIA YUN

Mia Yun was born and grew up in Korea. She graduated from Hankuk University of Foreign Studies in Seoul and received her MFA in creative writing from City College of New York. She has worked as a reporter, translator, and freelance writer, and is currently the Korea correspondent for the *Evergreen Review*. Yun now makes her home in New York City. *House of the Winds* is her first novel.

A CONVERSATION WITH
MIA YUN

*The line between myth and reality is almost seamless in your novel.
Is there one scene in particular which speaks directly to an experience
from your childhood in Korea?*

A lot of my childhood experiences made their way into the
novel, and one of them appears in the the very beginning of the
book: a little girl standing in the middle of a sunny cabbage patch
with her mother.

Writing a novel is a mysterious process. A book's life often
begins long before a single sentence gets to be written. It often
begins with an idea or an image that flashes through your mind.
And unlike the others, this particular image or idea somehow takes
root and sprouts a leaf or two. And it grows into a leafy tree!

House of the Winds began like that for me. With this very vivid
particular image of a girl standing in the middle of a sunny cabbage
field with her mother. It is the image that always came to me
whenever I thought of my childhood in Korea. I am not sure, but it
has to be the earliest memory of mine, as it seems to precede all
other bits of memory I have. And yet, it is the clearest memory I
have. In fact, it is so clear, I often feel like I am right there,
standing with my mother in the middle of the sunny cabbage patch
behind the little house of ours in Seoul. It is a sunny spring
afternoon. The sunlight is so phosphorescent it is like fine gold
powder let loose from a bottle—I can almost grab it. And the white
butterflies are still there, hovering over the cabbages in white bloom.

It was the one perfect, blissfully happy moment every child has,
although too fleetingly. I made it the beginning of the book. A little
girl standing in a sparkling, sun-soaked world her mother created
behind their small, wooden, baby blue gate. It was a bright and

dreamy world of flowers, starched clothes, waxed floors, and made-up stories. Before the girl began to discover the stories of women and Korea.

Why did you choose to use such strong and vivid dream imagery throughout the novel?

The fact that *House of the Winds* is written from a child's point of view has a lot to do with it. A child sees things but does not necessarily understand what he or she sees. There's a mystery and a dreamlike quality to everything. It is really like seeing things through a soap bubble. Time and place do not play out logically when we are children. The reality does not play out as strongly as it does to us grown-ups. A child merely tries to make sense of what is in front of him or her. To quote Barbara Grizzuti Harrison: "Do you remember any room so well as you remember the room of your childhood? Has any kitchen ever been so sunny as the remembered kitchen of your childhood? . . . Our memory knows that childhood is the cause, and everything else . . . is the effect." Here, the word "remembered" explains much of what I try to say.

You write, "Korea seemed . . . a bloodied Eden full of the voiceless souls of women. . . ." How do you feel the power of words can rescue the souls of the women of Korea from their silences?

By simply telling the stories of the women, I hope I am giving them voices.

How is the role of Korean women changing within the present society?

It has seen a lot of changes. Nowadays, many Korean women work outside the home and continue to work after marriage.

They have more legal protections than ever before from sexual discrimination and sexual harassment. And they have more opportunities to pursue educational and career advancement. What is more important though is the acceptance of the changing role of women by Korean society in general.

What has been the response of women, both in America and in Korea, to House of the Winds?

As the Korean translation is yet to come out there, I cannot say what the response has been in Korea. In America, it depends on who the reader is. To American women, it is more like a learning experience, as they often tell me that they had no idea what it is or was like for Korean women. And to Korean-American or Asian-American women, the response is more like a recognition and understanding. Although the book describes Korean women's experience, it should have more or less the same resonance with women everywhere, as any book telling women's experience, regardless of where they are and where they come from. At least, I hope so.

What is the meaning of the title?

The title of the book comes from a passage in Henry Miller's *Black Spring,* one of my favorite books. "House" refers to the family in the novel and also to Korea. "Wind" implies change and instability by its very nature. So you can say the title, *House of the Winds,* has a double meaning: it implies the unstable life of the family or also the tumultuous history of Korea.

Author Cynthia Ozick wrote that your "moving and surprising— and unique—Korean stories merit attention on their own account, and cannot be stereotypically lumped under 'Asian.' Surely it is time for

*Mia Yun's distinctive and enriching talent, rooted in a vision utterly new to our marveling eyes, to find the wider recognition it deserves."
Have you encountered much resistance in being recognized as a Korean writer?*

I do not know if it is accurate to say that I have encountered resistance in being recognized as a Korean writer. I think the right word to define my experience as a Korean writer would be "frustration." The fact is that Americans in general know so little about Korea. They are much more familiar with things Chinese or Japanese and tend to assume that Korea falls somewhere in between. Another problem is that we are often lumped together simply as "Asians," which implies that we are a homogeneous group. But Asia is so vast: there are more differences than similarities among the many Asian countries and peoples. Each of us comes with different and unique experiences and backgrounds, whether they are cultural, economic, political, or geographical. But these differences are not always recognized here.

The wonder that the young girl discovers in books transports her from the realities of her poverty. Were these the same stories that encouraged your love of writing? Who are your great literary influences? What are you reading now?

In seventh grade, when I really started reading a lot and writing by keeping diaries and composing poems, I had a wonderful teacher who encouraged me to read and write. It was to him that I first declared my desire to become a writer. In a letter to me during the summer break, he wrote that in order to become a great writer, one must do three things a lot: read a lot, write a lot, and think a lot. I think he was trying to tell me that one does not become a writer so much out of desire as out of hard work. And I cannot imagine a writer who is not a reader. I am always reading. Cynthia

Ozick once said, "I don't read to be entertained." I mostly read to be inspired and educated.

The Sound and the Fury by William Faulkner, *The Great Gatsby* by F. Scott Fitzgerald, *Of Human Bondage* by Somerset Maugham, *A Portrait of the Artist as a Young Man* by James Joyce, *Remembrance of Things Past* by Marcel Proust, *Jane Eyre* by Charlotte Brontë, and *Emma* by Jane Austen are some of the books I read early and loved absolutely. I also loved *The Woman Warrior* by Maxine Hong Kingston.

Nowadays, I tend to read books set in the so-called third world. I have just finished reading *A Bend in the River* by V. S. Naipaul, which is set in Africa. I am also rereading Graham Greene's *The Quiet American*, a prophetic novel set in Vietnam during the period when the French presence in Indochina was declining. I will probably reread *Burmese Days* by George Orwell soon. I often read several books at the same time.

What was your family's response to your novel?

Completely supportive. I am lucky to have a family who loves and greatly values literature and understands what we call a writer's "artistic interpretations."

You speak about the common bond that all humans, no matter their geography or culture, must share. What exactly is this bond, and how do you think it came across in your novel?

The human emotions are the same wherever you go. And I believe the strongest human bond is a familial bond. Obviously, we do not get to choose our parents and siblings and other family members, and yet we are bound to them whether we like it or not, in both good and bad ways. I do not know a more intense source or cause of happiness, sorrow, love, and pain than one's own family.

We struggle; embracing, rejecting, rebelling against our families. Sometimes one's family is a burden, and even a curse, but never avoidable and always inevitable. And I hope that came across in my novel.

There are many stories and dreams throughout House of the Winds. *Which one is your favorite?*

I like the story toward the end of the book, the story about the foolish farmer who plants roasted sesame seeds and waits for them to grow. It reminds me of Aesop's Fables I used to read as a child. The story always brings a smile to my face. There's nothing so tragic and yet so funny as human folly.

What are you working on now?

I am working on another novel. I am rather superstitious and hesitant to talk about it. All I can say at this point is that the novel is quite different from *House of the Winds*, is mostly set in New York, and it is again about a family—a subject that never stops intriguing me—that continues to struggle in a new country to deal with the aftermath of an old misfortune.

QUESTIONS FOR DISCUSSION

1. As Young Wife comes upon harder times, she moves her family out of the safe house with the blue gate and toward the periphery of the city. How does this affect the children and their dreams? Do any of the children ever stop believing in their mother's dreams for them?

2. What do you think is the author's view of men in Korean society? Has the little girl learned to recognize her father by the end of the novel? How does she see him?

3. All of the women suffer from the loss of a man in their lives, be it a husband, son, father, or boyfriend. Many, like the Pumpkin Wife and Young Wife, must create stories in order to deal with their loss. Why is it so important for them to be able to share these stories with each other?

4. The *Korean Quarterly* wrote, "Although never clearly stated, the story contains an underlying theme and purpose, that this account, unlike many others, will describe and authenticate women's experiences and define women's reality in Korea. In this intent, the narrator is faithful and unique." Do you agree with this?

5. Why do you think Yun chose to tell her story through the eyes of a young girl?

6. What common family values does Yun portray in *House of the Winds*? What is she saying about the hardships—and joys—of being a single mother?

7. The voices of many women are distinctly heard throughout the novel. Did you identify with any of these women? Would you have liked to hear more about one of these characters in particular? Which one and why?

8. The young girl and her mother have many dreams. The little girl says that she will be the "next carrier of [mother's] hopes and dreams when I become a woman one day." Does she accomplish this?

9. What role does religion play in the lives of the characters? Is it a positive or negative force?

For more information about other Penguin Readers Guides, please call the Penguin Marketing Department at (800) 778-6425, e-mail at reading@penguinputnam.com, or write to us at:

Penguin Books Marketing, Dept. CC
Readers Guides
375 Hudson Street
New York, NY 10014-3657

FOR THE BEST IN PAPERBACKS, LOOK FOR THE Ⓟ

In every corner of the world, on every subject under the sun, Penguin represents quality and variety—the very best in publishing today.

For complete information about books available from Penguin—including Puffins, Penguin Classics, and Arkana—and how to order them, write to us at the appropriate address below. Please note that for copyright reasons the selection of books varies from country to country.

In the United Kingdom: Please write to *Dept. EP, Penguin Books Ltd, Bath Road, Harmondsworth, West Drayton, Middlesex UB7 0DA.*

In the United States: Please write to *Penguin Putnam Inc., P.O. Box 12289 Dept. B, Newark, New Jersey 07101-5289* or call 1-800-788-6262.

In Canada: Please write to *Penguin Books Canada Ltd, 10 Alcorn Avenue, Suite 300, Toronto, Ontario M4V 3B2.*

In Australia: Please write to *Penguin Books Australia Ltd, P.O. Box 257, Ringwood, Victoria 3134.*

In New Zealand: Please write to *Penguin Books (NZ) Ltd, Private Bag 102902, North Shore Mail Centre, Auckland 10.*

In India: Please write to *Penguin Books India Pvt Ltd, 11 Panchsheel Shopping Centre, Panchsheel Park, New Delhi 110 017.*

In the Netherlands: Please write to *Penguin Books Netherlands bv, Postbus 3507, NL-1001 AH Amsterdam.*

In Germany: Please write to *Penguin Books Deutschland GmbH, Metzlerstrasse 26, 60594 Frankfurt am Main.*

In Spain: Please write to *Penguin Books S. A., Bravo Murillo 19, 1° B, 28015 Madrid.*

In Italy: Please write to *Penguin Italia s.r.l., Via Benedetto Croce 2, 20094 Corsico, Milano.*

In France: Please write to *Penguin France, Le Carré Wilson, 62 rue Benjamin Baillaud, 31500 Toulouse.*

In Japan: Please write to *Penguin Books Japan Ltd, Kaneko Building, 2-3-25 Koraku, Bunkyo-Ku, Tokyo 112.*

In South Africa: Please write to *Penguin Books South Africa (Pty) Ltd, Private Bag X14, Parkview, 2122 Johannesburg.*